A WILD CAT B
STARTLING
STORIES
FALL 2010

Vol. 2, No.5 A WILD CAT BOOKS PUBLICATION

Classic Reprints

Novella

Short Stories

Features

A WILD CAT BOOKS PUBLICATION Fall 2010

Departments

• • • • • • • • • • • • • • • • • • •

WILLIAM L. CARNEY, JR., Editor • RON HANNA, Editor-In-Chief

Cover Art by Gary McCluskey—Illustrating 'Dawn of Flame'

Back Cover by Hubert Rogers—'Temple Trouble' (from Astounding Science Fiction, April 1951)

Interior Illustrations by Hubert Rogers, Lawrence Sterne Stevens and William L. Carney, Jr.

ISBN: 978-0-9844765-6-5

Ron Hanna, Editor and Publisher

www.wildcatbooks.net

This issue we're proud to feature two of the most influential authors in the history of sci-fi literature; Stanley G. Weinbaum and E. E. 'Doc' Smith. Stanley Weinbaum, in a tragically short, but meteoric career changed the face of SF with his classic tale *A Martian Odyssey*. One of the most enduring tales in the genre's history, *Odyssey* introduced the first truly alien, intelligent character. Tweel, the strange bird-like creature of the tale was the first alien that was as intelligent as the human protagonist but utterly different in thought and motivation. After this seminal story, simple anthropomorphized, human-motivated ETs just couldn't stack up. Weinbaum's thoughtful, carefully plotted fiction epitomized the "thought variant" concept of SF espoused by *Astounding Stories'* editor Orlin F. Tremaine. Stories such as *Parasite Planet, Valley of Dreams,* and *The Red Peri* took readers 'where no man had gone before.' *Dawn of Flame* (and its sequel, *The Black Flame*), published after Weinbaum's untimely death from cancer at the age of 33, is a classic of post-apocalyptic SF.

And then there's Doc Smith. Although not the first author to launch mankind out into the galaxy, no one before had ever conceived of space opera on such a vast scale! His tales of mind-blowing adventure spanned billions of years of galactic history, inconceivably vast distances, planet-sized weapons of super-science, and the blackest, universe-spanning evil truly earned him the title "The Father of Modern Space Opera." Beginning with *The Skylark of Space* in 1928 and reaching its height in the massive *Lensman* series, Doc Smith's boundless imagination and fast-paced adventure forever changed the face of SF and has inspired all succeeding generations of SF authors.

That spirit of imagination continues here at *Startling Stories* with two modern tales of thrilling SF action from Wm. Michael Mott, Gerald W. Page and Carleton Grindle. Mott and Page's Cthulhu Mythos-inspired *Cask of Ages* takes readers on a terrifying trip into the very bowels of evil while Grindle's light-hearted *Star Guard* recalls the glory days of Henry Kuttner, Leigh Brackett, Ray Bradbury and a host of Golden Age tale-spinners.

Also in this issue we're proud to present a heart warming tale from our own humble publisher, Ron 'The Wild Cat' Hanna and the debut story of two "wild and crazy guys," John Casey and Jack Nemo. John and Jack's *I Saved Tokyo... With The Honorable Assistance of The Army, Navy, and Air Force of Japan* presents a novel (and strangely logical) solution of what to do when you're attacked by a giant, prehistoric monster while Ron's sequel to the great Fritz Leiber's tribute to everyone's favorite feline friend *Space-Time for Springers* will bring a tear to your eye. Unless, of course, *you* are a strange bird-like creature with bizarre thought processes!

In addition, we have another *Paratime* tale by one of your editor's favorite authors, H. Beam Piper along with our regular features Golden Age Comic Reprint—featuring the great Wally Wood—and Ron Wilber's next installment of *Saucy Blaine*, and new Retro-Reviews by Chris Carney and Rob Morganbesser.

And, finally, we have a special *Startling Portfolio* of one of pulp fandom's all-time great artists, the award-winning Ron Wilber. For over thirty years, Ron's beautifully rendered drawings have graced the pages of the genre's best publications and entertained all fans of the classic pulp heroes. So we hope you all enjoy this latest issue of *Startling Stories* and wish everyone Happy Holidays from Wild Cat Books!

William Carney, *Editor*

WILD CAT BOOKS
Where Pulp Lives!
PULPS • FANTASY
HORROR • SCI-FI
STARTLING STORIES
THE GIRL IN THE GOLDEN ATOM
TO BITE THE WORM
THE CURSED STELE
THE ART OF VER CURTISS
TIM JONES
UNDER THE SUNS OF ANTARES
TALES OF THE NORSE GODS
WILD CAT BOOKS
KI-GOR
Barry Reese
A WILDCAT BOOKS PUBLICATION
www.wildcatbooks.net

DAWN OF FLAME

Lovely but cruel, young but immortal, the Black Princess rode into Ormiston... ...with death like a gift in her hand!

a Novelette by

Stanley G. Weinbaum

CHAPTER ONE

The World

HULL TARVISH looked backward but once, and that only as he reached the elbow of the road. The sprawling little stone cottage that had been home was visible as he had seen it a thousand times, framed under the cedars. His mother still watched him, and two of his younger brothers stood staring down the Mountainside at him. He raised his hand in farewell, then dropped it as he realized that none of them saw him now; his mother had turned indifferently to the door, and the two youngsters had spied a rabbit. He faced about and strode away, down the slope out of Ozarky.

He passed the place where the great steel road of the Ancients had been, now only two rusty streaks and a row of decayed logs. Beside it was the mossy heap of stones that had been an ancient structure in the days before the Dark Centuries, when Ozarky had been a part of the old state of M'souri. The mountain people still sought out the place for squared stones to use in building, but the tough metal of the steel road itself was too stubborn for their use, and the rails had rusted quietly these three hundred years.

That much Hull Tarvish knew, for they were things still spoken of at night around the fireplace. They had been mighty sorcerers, those Ancients; their steel roads went everywhere, and everywhere were the ruins of their towns, built, it was said, by a magic that lifted weights. Down in the valley, he knew, men were still seeking that magic; once a rider had stayed by night at the Tarvish home, a little man who said that in the far south the secret had been found, but nobody ever heard any more of it.

So Hull whistled to himself, shifted the rag bag on his shoulder, set his bow more comfortably on his mighty back, and trudged on. That was why he himself was seeking the valley; he wanted to see what the world was like. He had been always a restless sort, not at all like the other six Tarvish sons, nor like the three Tarvish daughters. They were true mountainies, the sons great hunters, and the daughters stolid and industrious.

Originally published in
Dawn of Flame - The Weinbaum Memorial Volume, 1936

Not Hull, however; he was neither lazy like his brothers nor stolid like his sisters, but restless, curious, dreamy. So he whistled his way into the world, and was happy.

At evening he stopped at the Hobel cottage on the edge of the mountains. Away before him stretched the plain, and in the darkening distance was visible the church spire of Norse. That was a village; Hull had never seen a village, or no more of it than this same distant steeple, shaped like a straight white pine. But he had heard all about Norse, because the mountainies occasionally went down there to buy powder and ball for their rifles, those of them who had rifles.

Hull had only a bow. He didn't see the use of guns; powder and ball cost money, but an arrow did the same work for nothing, and that without scaring all the game a mile away.

Morning he bade goodbye to the Hobels, who thought him, as they always had, a little crazy, and set off. His powerful, brown bare legs flashed under his ragged trousers, his bare feet made a pleasant *soosh* in the dust of the road, the June sun beat warm on his right cheek. He was happy; there never was a pleasanter world than this, so he grinned and whistled, and spat carefully into the dust, remembering that it was bad luck to spit toward the sun. He was bound for adventure.

Adventure came. Hull had come down to the plain now, where the trees were taller than the scrub of the hill country, and where the occasional farms were broader, well tilled, more prosperous. The trail had become a wagon road, and here it cut and angled between two lines of forest. And unexpectedly a man—no, two men—rose from a log at the roadside and approached Hull. He watched them; one was tall and light-haired as himself, but without his mighty frame, and the other was a head shorter, and dark. Valley people, surely, for the dark one had a stubby pistol at his belt, wooden-stocked like those of the Ancients, and the tall man's bow was of glittering spring steel.

"Ho, mountainy!" said the dark one. "Where going?"

"Norse," answered Hull shortly,

"What's in the bag?"

"My tongue,"* snapped the youth.

"Easy, there," grunted the light man. "No offense, mountainy. We're just curious. That's a good knife you got. I'll trade it."

"For what?"

"For lead in your craw," growled the dark one. Suddenly the blunt pistol was in his hand. "Pass it over, and the bag too."

Hull scowled from one to the other. At last he shrugged, and moved as if to lift his bag from his shoulders. And then, swift as the thrust of a striking diamondback, his left foot shot forward, catching the dark one squarely in the pit of his stomach, with the might of Hull's muscles and weight behind it.

The man had breath for a low grunt; he doubled and fell, while his weapon spun a dozen feet away into the dust. The light one sprang for it, but Hull caught him with a great arm about his throat, wrenched twice, and the brief fight was over. He swung placidly on toward Norse with a blunt revolver primed and capped at his hip, a glistening spring-steel bow on his shoulder, and twenty-two bright tubular steel arrows in his quiver.

He topped a little rise and the town lay before him. He stared. A hundred houses at least. Must be five hundred people in the town, more people than he'd ever seen in his life all together. He strode eagerly on, goggling at the church that towered high as a tall tree, at the windows of bits of glass salvaged from ancient ruins and carefully pieced together, at the tavern with its swinging emblem of an unbelievably fat man holding a mammoth mug. He stared at the houses, some of them with shops before them, and at the people, most of them shod in leather.

He himself attracted little attention. Norse was used to the mountainies, and only a girl or two turned appraising eyes toward his mighty figure. That made him uncomfortable, however; the girls of the mountains giggled and blushed, but never at that age did they stare at a man. So he gazed defiantly back, letting his eyes wander from their bonnets to the billowing skirts above their leather strap-sandals, and they laughed and passed on.

Hull didn't care for Norse, he decided. As the sun set, the houses loomed too close, as if

*Idiom of the second century of the Enlightenment. To have 'one's tongue in the bag' was to refuse to answer questions.

they'd stifle him, so he set out into the countryside to sleep. The remains of an ancient town bordered the village, with its spectral walls crumbling against the west. There were ghosts there, of course, so he walked farther, found a wooded spot, and lay down, putting his bow and the steel arrows into his bag against the rusting effect of night-dew. Then he tied the bag about his bare feet and legs, sprawled comfortably, and slept with his hand on the pistol grip. Of course there were no animals to fear in these woods save wolves, and they never attacked humans during the warm parts of the year, but there were men, and *they* bound themselves by no such seasonal laws.

He awoke dewy wet. The sun shot golden lances through the trees, and he was ravenously hungry. He ate the last of his mother's brown bread from his bag, now crumbled by his feet, and then strode out to the road. There was a wagon creaking there, plodding northward; the bearded, kindly man in it was glad enough to have him ride for company.

"Mountainy?" he asked.

"Yes."

"Bound where?"

"The world," said Hull.

"Well," observed the other, "it's a big place, and all I've seen of it much like this. All except Selui. That's a city. Yes, that's a city. Been there?"

"No."

"It's got," said the farmer impressively, "twenty thousand people in it. Maybe more. And they got ruins there the biggest you ever saw. Bridges. Buildings. Four—five times as high as the Norse church, and at that they're fallen down. The Devil knows how high they used to be in the old days."

"Who lived in 'em?" asked Hull.

"Don't know. Who'd want to live so high up it'd take a full morning to climb there? Unless it was magic. I don't hold much with magic, but they do say the Old People knew how to fly."

Hull tried to imagine this. For a while there was silence save for the slow clump of the horses' hooves. "I don't believe it," he said at last.

"Nor I. But did you hear what they're saying in Norse?"

"I didn't hear anything."

"They say," said the farmer, "that Joaquin Smith is going to march again."

"Joaquin Smith!"

"Yeah. Even the mountainies know about him, eh?"

"Who doesn't?" returned Hull. "Then there'll be fighting in the south, I guess. I have a notion to go south."

"Why?"

"I like fighting," said Hull simply.

"Fair answer," said the farmer, "but from what folks say, there's not much fighting when the Master marches. He has a spell; there's great sorcery in N'Orleans, from the merest warlock up to Martin Sair, who's blood-son of the Devil himself, or so they say."

"I'd like to see his sorcery against the mountainy's arrow and ball," said Hull grimly. "There's none of us can't spot either eye at a thousand paces, using rifle. Or two hundred with arrow."

"No doubt; but what if powder flames, and guns fire themselves before he's even across the horizon? They say he has a spell for that, he or Black Margot."

"Black Margot?"

"The Princess, his half-sister. The dark witch who rides beside him, the Princess Margaret."

"Oh... but why Black Margot?"

The farmer shrugged. "Who knows? It's what her enemies call her."

"Then so I call her," said Hull.

"Well, I don't know," said the other. "It makes small difference to me whether I pay taxes to N'Orleans or to gruff old Marcus

---

Stanley G. Weinbaum (1902 - 1935), in a career that lasted but a scant eighteen months, was quite likely (with the possible exception of E.E. Smith) the most influential SF author of the 1930s. He is best remembered as author of the seminal short story *A Martian Odyssey*, which introduced the first sympathetic non-human alien and changed the manner in which all subsequent SF was written. It is one of the most enduring tales in SF history and the oldest short story (and one of the top vote-getters) selected by the SFWA for inclusion in *The Science Fiction Hall of Fame, Volume One, 1929–1964*. Weinbaum's fiction was much more thoughtful and carefully plotted than the standard outer space shoot-em-ups of the day. His nine tale Planetary series, including *Parasite Planet, Valley of Dreams, The Red Peri, Flight On Titan,* and *The Mad Moon* were set in a scientifically consistent solar system considered accurate by 1930s standards. *The Black Flame*, the sequel to *Dawn of Flame* (itself published posthumously) was published in the first issue of *Startling Stories* (January 1939) after his untimely death at age 33 of lung cancer.

Ormiston, who's eldarch of Ormiston village there." He flicked his whip toward the distance ahead, where Hull now descried houses and the flash of a little river. "I've sold produce in towns within the Empire, and the people of them seemed as happy as ourselves, no more, no less."

"There is a difference, though. It's freedom."

"Merely a word, my friend. They plow, they sow, they reap, just as we do. They hunt, they fish, they fight. And as for freedom, are they less free with a warlock to rule them than I with a wizened fool?"

"The mountainies pay taxes to no one."

"And no one builds them roads, nor digs them public wells. Where you pay little you get less, and I *will* say that the roads within the Empire are better than ours."

"Better than this?" asked Hull, staring at the dusty width of the highway.

"Far better. Near Memphis town is a road of solid rock, which they spread soft through some magic, and let harden, so there is neither mud nor dust."

Hull mused over this. "The Master," he burst out suddenly, "is he really immortal?"

The other shrugged. "How can I say? There are great sorcerers in the southlands, and the greatest of them is Martin Sair. But I do know this, that I have seen sixty-two years, and as far back as memory goes here was always Joaquin Smith in the south, and always an Empire gobbling cities as a hare gobbles carrots. When I was young it was far away, now it reaches close at hand; that is all the difference. Men talked of the beauty of Black Margot then as they do now, and of the wizardry of Martin Sair."

Hull made no answer, for Ormiston was at hand. The village was much like Norse save that it huddled among low hills, on the crest of some of which loomed ancient ruins. At the near side his companion halted, and Hull thanked him as he leaped to the ground.

"Where to?" asked the farmer.

Hull thought a moment. "Selui," he said.

"Well, it's a hundred miles, but there'll be many to ride you."

"I have my own feet," said the youth. He spun suddenly about at a voice across the road: "Hi! Mountainy!"

It was a girl. A very pretty girl, slim waisted, copper haired, blue eyed, standing at the gate before a large stone house. "Hi!" she called. "Will you work for your dinner?"

Hull was ravenous again. "Gladly!" he cried.

The voice of the farmer sounded behind him. "It's Vail Ormiston, the dotard eldarch's daughter. Hold her for a full meal, mountainy. My taxes are paying for it."

But Vail Ormiston was above much converse with a wandering mountain-man. She surveyed his mighty form approvingly, showed him the logs he was to quarter, and then disappeared into the house. If, perchance, she peeped out through the clearest of the ancient glass fragments that formed the window, and if she watched the flexing muscles of his great bare arms as he swung the axe—well, he was unaware of it.

So it happened that afternoon found him trudging toward Selui with a hearty meal inside him and three silver dimes in his pocket, ancient money, with the striding figure of the woman all but worn away. He was richer than when he had set out by those coins, by the blunt pistol at his hip, by the shiny steel bow and arrows, and by the memory of the copper hair and blue eyes of Vail Ormiston.

CHAPTER TWO

Old Einar

THREE WEEKS in Selui had served to give Hull Tarvish a sort of speaking acquaintancy with the place. He no longer gaped at the sky-piercing ruins of the ancient city, or the vast fallen bridges, and he was quite at home in the town that lay beside it. He had found work easily enough in a baker's establishment, where his great muscles served well; the hours were long, but his pay was munificent—five silver quarters a week. He paid two for lodging, and food—what he needed beyond the burnt loaves at hand from his employment—cost him another quarter, but that left two to put by. He never gambled other than a wager now and then on his own marksmanship, and that was more profitable than otherwise.

Ordinarily Hull was quick to make friends, but his long hours hindered him. He had but one, an incredibly old man who sat at evening on the step beyond his lodging, Old Einar. So this evening Hull wandered out as usual to join him, staring at the crumbling towers of the Ancients glowing in the sunset. Trees sprung on many, and all were green with vine and tussock and the growth of wind-carried seeds. No one dared build among the ruins, for none could guess when a great tower might come crashing down.

"I wonder," he said to Old Einar, "what the Ancients were like. Were they men like us? Then how could they fly?"

"They were men like us, Hull. As for flying… well, it's my belief that flying is a legend. See here; there was a man supposed to have flown over the cold lands to the north and those to the south, and also across the great sea. But this flying man is called in some accounts Lindbird and in others Bird and surely one can see the origin of such a legend. The migrations of birds, who cross land and seas each year, that is all."

"Or perhaps magic," suggested Hull.

"There *is* no magic. The Ancients themselves denied it and I have struggled through many a moldy book in a curious, archaic tongue."

Old Einar was the first scholar Hull had ever encountered. Though there were many during the dawn of that brilliant age called the Second Enlightenment, most of them were still within the Empire. John Holland was dead, but Olin was yet alive in the world, and Kohlmar, and Jorgensen, and Teran, and Martin Sair, and Joaquin Smith the Master. Great names—the names of demigods.

But Hull knew little of them. "You can read!" he exclaimed. "That in itself is a sort of magic. And you have been within the Empire, even in N'Orleans. Tell me, what is the Great City like? Have they really learned the secrets of the Ancients? Are the Immortals truly immortal? How did they gain their knowledge?"

Old Einar settled himself on the step and puffed blue smoke from his pipe filled with the harsh tobacco of the region. "Too many questions breed answers to none," he observed. "Shall I tell you the true story of the world, Hull… the story called History?"

"Yes. In Ozarky we spoke little of such things."

"Well," said the old man comfortably, "I will begin then, at what to us is the beginning, but to the Ancients was the end. I do not know what factors, what wars, what struggles, led up to the mighty world that died during the Dark Centuries, but I do know that three hundred years ago the world reached its climax. You cannot imagine such a place, Hull. It was a time of vast cities, too… fifty times as large as N'Orleans with its hundred thousand people."

He puffed slowly. "Great steel wagons roared over the iron roads of the Ancients. Men crossed the oceans to east and west. The cities were full of whirring wheels, and instead of the many little city-states of our time, there were giant nations with thousands of cities and a hundred million—a hundred and fifty million people."

Hull stared. "I do not believe there are so many people in the world," he said.

Old Einar shrugged. "Who knows?" he returned. "The ancient books—all too few—tell us that the world is round, and that beyond the seas lie one, or several continents, but what races are there today not even Joaquin Smith can say." He puffed smoke again. "Well, such was the ancient world. These were warlike nations, so fond of battle that they had to write many books about the horrors of war to keep themselves at peace, but they always failed. During the time they called their twentieth century there was a whole series of wars, not such little quarrels as we have so often between our city-states, nor even such as that between the Memphis League and the Empire, five years ago. *Their* wars spread like storm clouds around the world, and were fought between millions of men with unimaginable weapons that flung destruction a hundred miles, and with ships on the seas, and with gases."

"What's gases?" asked Hull.

Old Einar waved his hand so that the wind of it brushed the youth's brown cheek. "Air is a gas," he said. "They knew how to poison the air so that all who breathed it died. And they fought with diseases, and legend says that they fought also in the air with wings, but that is only legend."

"Diseases!" said Hull. "Diseases are the breath of Devils, and if they controlled Devils they used sorcery, and therefore they knew magic."

"There *is* no magic," reiterated the old man. "*I* do not know how they fought each other with diseases, but Martin Sair of N'Orleans knows. That was *his* study, not mine, but I know there was no magic in it." He resumed his tale. "So these great fierce nations flung themselves against each other, for war meant more to them than to us. With us it is something of a rough, joyous, dangerous game, but to them it was a passion. They fought for any reason, or for none at all save the love of fighting."

"*I* love fighting," said Hull.

"Yes, but would you love it if it meant simply the destroying of thousands of men beyond the horizon? Men you were never to see?"

"No. War should be man to man, or at least no farther than the carry of a rifle ball."

"True. Well, some time near the end of their twentieth century, the ancient world exploded into war like a powder horn in a fire. They say every nation fought, and battles surged back and forth across seas and continents. It was not only nation against nation, but race against race, black and white and yellow and red, all embroiled in a titanic struggle."

"Yellow and red?" echoed Hull. "There are a few black men called Nigs in Ozarky, but I never heard of yellow or red men."

"I have seen yellow men," said Old Einar. "There are some towns of yellow men on the edge of the western ocean, in the region called Friscia. The red race, they say, is gone, wiped out by the plague called the Grey Death, to which they yielded more readily than the other races."

"I have heard of the Grey Death," said Hull. "When I was very young, there was an old, old man who used to say that his grandfather had lived in the days of the Death."

Old Einar smiled. "I doubt it, Hull. It was something over two and a half centuries ago. However," he resumed, "the great ancient nations were at war, and as I say, they fought with diseases. Whether some nation learned the secret of the Grey Death, or whether it grew up as a sort of cross between two or more other diseases, I do not know. Martin Sair says that diseases are living things, so it may be so. At any rate, the Grey Death leaped suddenly across the world, striking alike at all people. Everywhere it blasted the armies, the cities, the countryside, and of those it struck, six out of every ten died. There must have been chaos in the world; we have not a single book printed during that time, and only legend tells the story.

"But the war collapsed. Armies suddenly found themselves unopposed, and then were blasted before they could move. Ships in mid-ocean were stricken, and drifted unmanned to pile in wreckage, or to destroy others. In the cities the dead were piled in the streets, and after a while, were simply left where they fell, while those who survived fled away into the country. What remained of the armies became little better than roving robber bands, and by the third year of the plague there were few if any stable governments in the world."

"What stopped it?" asked Hull.

"I do not know. They end, these pestilences. Those who take it and live cannot take it a second time, and those who are somehow immune do not take it at all, and the rest… die. The Grey Death swept the world for three years; when it ended, according to Martin Sair, one person in four had died. But the plague came back in lessening waves for many years; only a pestilence in the Ancient's fourteenth century, called the Black Death, seems ever to have equaled it.

"Yet its effects were only beginning. The ancient transport system had simply collapsed, and the cities were starving. Hungry gangs began raiding the countryside, and instead of one vast war there were now a million little battles. The weapons of the Ancients were everywhere, and these battles were fierce enough, in all truth, though nothing like the colossal encounters of the great war. Year by year the cities decayed until by the fiftieth year after the Grey Death, the world's population had fallen by three-fourths, and civilization was ended. It was barbarism now that ruled the world, but only barbarism, not savagery. People still remembered the mighty ancient civilization, and everywhere there were attempts to combine into the old nations, but these failed for lack of great leaders."

"As they should fail," said Hull. "We have freedom now."

"Perhaps. By the first century after the Plague, there was little left of the Ancients save their ruined cities where lurked robber bands that scoured the country by night. They had little interest in anything save food or the coined money of the old nations, and they did incalculable damage. Few could read, and on cold nights was usual to raid the ancient libraries for books to burn and to make things worse, fire gutted the ruins of all cities, and there was no organized resistance to it. The flames simply burned themselves out, and priceless books vanished."

"Yet in N'Orleans they study, don't they?" asked Hull.

"Yes, I'm coming to that. About two centuries after the Plague—a hundred years ago, that is—the world had stabilized itself. It was much as it is here today, with little farming towns and vast stretches of deserted country. Gunpowder had been rediscovered, rifles were used, and most of the robber bands had been destroyed. And then, into the town of N'Orleans, built beside the ancient city, came young John Holland.

"Holland was a rare specimen, anxious for learning. He found the remains of an ancient library and began slowly to decipher the archaic words in the few books that had survived. Little by little others joined him, and as the word spread slowly, men from other sections wandered in with books, and the Academy was born. No one taught, of course; it was just a group of studious men living a sort of communistic, monastic life. There was no attempt at practical use of the ancient knowledge until a youth named Teran had a dream—no less a dream than to recondition the centuries-old power machines of N'Orleans, to give the city the power that travels on wires!"

"What's that?" asked Hull. "What's that, Old Einar?"

"You wouldn't understand, Hull. Teran was an enthusiast; it didn't stop him to realize that there was no coal or oil to run his machines. He believed that when power was needed, it would be there, so he and his followers scrubbed and filed and welded away, and Teran was right. When he needed power, it was there.

"This was the gift of a man named Olin, who had unearthed the last, the crowning secret of the Ancients, the power called atomic energy. He gave it to Teran, and N'Orleans became a miracle city where lights glowed and wheels turned. Men came from every part of the continent to see, and among these were two called Martin Sair and Joaquin Smith, come out of Mexico with the half-sister of Joaquin, the Satanically beautiful being sometimes called Black Margot.

"Martin Sair was a genius. He found his field in the study of medicine, and it was less than ten years before he had uncovered the secret of the hard rays. He was studying sterility but he found—immortality!"

"Then the Immortals *are* immortal!" murmured Hull.

"It may be, Hull. At least they do not seem to age, but… Well, Joaquin Smith was also a genius, but of a different sort. He dreamed of the re-uniting of the peoples of the country. I think he dreams of even more, Hull; people say he will stop when he rules a hundred cities, but I think he dreams of an American Empire, or…" Old Einar's voice dropped "…a world Empire. At least, he took Martin Sair's immortality and traded it for power. The Second Enlightenment was dawning and there was genius in N'Orleans. He traded immortality to Kohlmar for a weapon, he offered it to Olin for atomic power, but Olin was already past youth, and refused, partly because he didn't want it, and partly because he was not entirely in sympathy with Joaquin Smith. So the Master seized the secret of the atom despite Olin, and the Conquest began.

"N'Orleans, directly under the influence of the Master's magnetic personality, was ready to yield, and yielded to him cheering. He raised his army and marched north, and everywhere cities fell or yielded willingly. Joaquin Smith is magnificent, and men flock to him, cities cheer him, even the wives and children of the slain swear allegiance when he forgives them in that noble manner of his. Only here and there men hate him bitterly, and speak such words as tyrant, and talk of freedom."

"Such are the mountainies," said Hull.

"Not even the mountainies can stand the ionic beams that Kohlmar dug out of ancient books, nor the Erden resonator that explodes gunpowder miles away. I think that Joaquin Smith will succeed, Hull. Moreover, I do not think it entirely bad that he should, for he is a great ruler, and a bringer of civilization."

"What are they like, the Immortals?"

"Well, Martin Sair is as cold as mountain rock, and the Princess Margaret is like black fire. Even my old bones feel younger only to look at her, and it is wise for young men not to look at her at all, because she is quite heartless, ruthless, and pitiless. As for Joaquin Smith, the Master… I do not know the words to describe so complex a character, and I know him well. He is mild, perhaps, but enormously strong, kind or cruel as suits his purpose, glitteringly intelligent, and dangerously charming."

"You *know* him!" echoed Hull, and added curiously, "What is your other name, Old Einar, you who know the Immortals?"

The old man smiled. "When I was born," he said, "my parents called me Einar *Olin*."

CHAPTER THREE

The Master Marches

JOAQUIN SMITH was marching.

Hull Tarvish leaned against the door of File Ormson's iron worker's shop in Ormiston, and stared across the fields and across the woodlands, and across to the blue mountains of Ozarky in the south. There is where he should have been, there with the mountainy men, but by the time the tired rider had brought the news to Selui, and by the time Hull had reached Ormiston, it was already too late, and Ozarky was but an outlying province of the expanding Empire, while the Master camped there above Norse, and sent representations to Selui.

Selui wasn't going to yield. Already the towns of the three months old Selui Confederation were sending in their men, from Bloom'ton, from Cairo, even from distant Ch'cago on the shores of the saltless sea Mitchin. The men of the Confederation hated the little, slender, dark Ch'cagoans, for they had not yet forgotten the disastrous battle at Starved Rock, but any allies were welcome against Joaquin Smith. The Ch'cagoans were good enough fighters, too, and heart and soul in the cause, for if the Master took Selui, his Empire would reach dangerously close to the saltless seas, spreading from the ocean on the east to the mountains on the west, and north as far as the great confluence of the M'sippi and M'souri.

Hull knew there was fighting ahead, and he relished it. It was too bad that he couldn't have fought in Ozarky for his own people, but Ormiston would do. That was his home for the present, since he'd found work here with File Ormson, the squat iron-worker, broad-shouldered as Hull himself and a head shorter. Pleasant work for his mighty muscles, though at the moment there was nothing to do.

He stared at the peaceful countryside. Joaquin Smith was marching, and beyond the village, the farmers were still working in their fields. Hull listened to the slow Sowing Song:

This is what the ground needs:
First the plow and then the seeds,

Then the harrow and then the hoe,
And rain to make the harvest grow.

This is what the man needs:
First the promises, then the deeds,
Then the arrow and then the blade,
And last the digger with his black spade.

This is what his wife needs:
First a garden free of weeds,
Then the daughter, and their the son,
And a fireplace warm when the work is done.

This is what his son needs...

Hull ceased to listen. They were singing, but Joaquin Smith was marching, marching with the men of a hundred cities, with his black banner and its golden serpent fluttering. That serpent, Old Einar had said, was the Midgard Serpent, which ancient legend related had encircled the earth. It was the symbol of the Master's dream, and for a moment Hull had a stirring of sympathy for that dream.

"No!" he growled to himself. "Freedom's better, and it's for us to blow the head from the Midgard Serpent."

A voice sounded at his side. "Hull! Big Hull Tarvish! Are you too proud to notice humble folk?"

It was Vail Ormiston, her violet eyes whimsical below her smooth copper hair. He flushed; he was not used to the ways of these valley girls, who flirted frankly and openly in a manner impossible to the shy girls of the mountains. Yet he—well, in a way, he liked it, and he liked Vail Ormiston, and he remembered pleasantly an evening two days ago when he had sat and talked a full three hours with her on the bench by the tree that shaded Ormiston well. And he remembered the walk through the fields when she had shown him the mouth of the great ancient storm sewer that had run under the dead city, and that still stretched crumbling for miles underground toward the hills, and he recalled her story of how, when a child, she had lost herself in it, so that her father had planted the tangle of blackberry bushes that still concealed the opening.

He grinned, "Is it the eldarch's daughter speaking of humble folk? Your father will be taxing me double if he hears of this."

She tossed her helmet of metallic hair. "He will if he sees you in that Selui finery of yours." Her eyes twinkled. "For whose eyes was it bought, Hull? For you'd be better saving your money."

"Save silver, lose luck," he retorted. After all, it wasn't so difficult a task to talk to her. "Anyway, better a smile from you than the glitter of money."

She laughed. "But how quickly you learn, mountainy! Still, what if I say I liked you better in tatters, with your powerful brown muscles quivering through the rips?"

"Do you say it, Vail?"

"Yes, then!"

He chuckled, raising his great hands to his shoulders. There was the rasp of tearing cloth, and a long rent gleamed in the back of his Selui shirt. "There, Vail!"

"Oh!" she gasped. "Hull, you wastrel! But it's only a seam." She fumbled in the bag at her belt. "Let me stitch it back for you."

She bent behind him, and he could feel her breath on his skin, warm as spring sunshine. He set his jaw, scowled, and then plunged determinedly into what he had to say. "I'd like to talk to you again this evening, Vail."

He sensed her smile at his back. "Would you?" she murmured demurely.

"Yes, if Enoch Ormiston hasn't spoken first for your time."

"But he has, Hull."

He knew she was teasing him deliberately. "I'm sorry," he said shortly.

"But... I told him I was busy," she finished.

"And are you?"

Her voice was a whisper behind him. "No. Not unless you tell me I am."

His great roar of a laugh sounded. "Then I tell you so, Vail."

He felt her tug at the seam, then she leaned very close to his neck, but it was only to bite the thread with her white teeth. "So!" she said gaily. "Once mended, twice new."

Before Hull could answer there came the clang of File Ormson's sledge, and the measured bellow of his Forge Song. They listened as his resounding strokes beat time to the song.

Then it's ho—oh—ho—oh—ho! While
I'm singing to the ringing Of each blow—
blow—blow! Till the metal's soft as butter
Let my forge and bellows sputter Like the

revels of the devils down below—low—LOW! Like the revels of the devils down below!

"I must go," said Hull, smiling reluctantly. "There's work for me now."

"What does File make?" asked Vail.

Instantly Hull's smile faded. "He forges… a sword!"

Vail too was no longer the joyous one of a moment ago. Over both of them had come a shadow, the shadow of the Empire. Out in the blue hills of Ozarky Joaquin Smith was marching.

EVENING. HULL watched the glint of a copper moon on Vail's copper hair, and leaned back on the bench. Not the one near the pump this time; that had been already occupied by two laughing couples, and though they had been welcomed eagerly enough, Hull had preferred to be alone. It wasn't mountain shyness any more, for his great, good-natured presence had found ready friendship in Ormiston village; it was merely the projection of that moodiness that had settled over both of them at parting, and so they sat now on the bench near Vail Ormiston's gate at the edge of town. Behind them the stone house loomed dark, for her father was scurrying about in town on Confederation business, and the help had availed themselves of the evening of freedom to join the crowd in the village square. But the yellow daylight of the oil lamp showed across the road in the house of Hue Helm, the farmer who had brought Hull from Norse to Ormiston.

It was at this light that Hull stared thoughtfully. "I like fighting," he repeated, "but somehow the joy has gone out of this. It's as if one waited an approaching thunder cloud."

"How," asked Vail in a timid, small voice, "can one fight magic?"

"There is no magic," said the youth, echoing Old Einar's words. "There is no such thing—"

"Hull! How can you say such stupid words?"

"I say what was told me by one who knows."

"No magic!" echoed Vail. "Then tell me what gives the wizards of the south their power. Why is it that Joaquin Smith has never lost a battle? What stole away the courage of the men of the Memphis League, who are good fighting men? And what—for this I have seen with my own eyes—pushes the horseless wagons of N'Orleans through the streets, and what lights that city by night? If not magic, then what?"

"Knowledge," said Hull. "The knowledge of the Ancients."

"The knowledge of the Ancients was magic," said the girl. "Everyone knows that the Ancients were wizards, warlocks, and sorcerers. If Holland, Olin, and Martin Sair are not sorcerers, then what are they? If Black Margot is no witch, then my eyes never looked on one."

"Have you seen them?" queried Hull.

"Of course, all but Holland, who is dead. Three years ago during the Peace of Memphis my father and I traveled into the Empire. I saw all of them about the city of N'Orleans."

"And is she… what they say she is?"

"The Princess?" Vail's eyes dropped. "Men say she is beautiful."

"But you think not?"

"What if she *is*?" snapped the girl almost defiantly. "Her beauty is like her youth, like her very life—artificial, preserved after its allotted time, frozen. That's it—frozen by sorcery. And as for the rest of her…" Vail's voice lowered, hesitated, for not even the plain-spoken valley girls discussed such things with men. "They say she has outworn a dozen lovers," she whispered.

Hull was startled, shocked. "Vail!" he muttered.

She swung the subject back to safer ground, but he saw her flush red. "Don't tell *me* there's no magic!" she said sharply.

"At least," he returned, "there's no magic will stop a bullet save flesh and bone. Yes, and the wizard who stops one with his skull lies just as dead as an honest man."

"I hope you're right," she breathed timidly. "Hull, he must be stopped! He *must!*"

"But why feel so strongly, Vail? I like a fight… but men say that life in the Empire is much like life without, and who cares to whom he pays his taxes if only—" He broke off suddenly, remembering. "Your father!" he exclaimed. "The eldarch!"

"Yes, my father, Hull. If Joaquin Smith takes Ormison, my father is the one to suffer. His taxes will be gone, his lands parceled out, and he's old, Hull... old. What will become of him then? I know many people feel the way you... the way you said, and so they fight halfheartedly, and the Master takes town after town without killing a single man. And then they think there is magic in the very name of Joaquin Smith, and he marches through armies that outnumber him ten to one." She paused. "But not Ormiston!" she cried fiercely. "Not if the women have to bear arms!"

"Not Ormiston," he agreed gently.

"You'll fight, Hull, won't you? Even though you're not Ormiston born?"

"Of course. I have bow and sword, and a good pistol. I'll fight."

"But no rifle? Wait, Hull." She rose and slipped away in the darkness.

In a moment she was back again. "Here. Here is rifle and horn and ball. Do you know its use?"

He smiled proudly. "What I can see I can hit," he said, "like any mountain man."

"Then," she whispered with fire in her voice, "send me a bullet through the Master's skull. And one besides between the eyes of Black Margot... for me!"

"I do not fight women," he said.

"Not woman but witch!"

"None the less, Vail, it must be two bullets for the Master and only the captive's chains for Princess Margaret, at least so far as Hull Tarvish is concerned. But wouldn't it please you fully as well to watch her draw water from your pump, or shine pots in your kitchen?" He was jollying her, trying to paint fanciful pictures to lift her spirit from the somber depths.

But she read it otherwise. "Yes!" she blazed. "Oh, yes, Hull, that's better. If I could ever hope to see that..." She rose suddenly, and he followed her to the gate. "You must go," she murmured, "but before you leave, you can—if you wish it, Hull—kiss me."

Of a sudden he was all shy mountainy again. He set the rifle against the fence with its horn swinging from the trigger guard. He faced her flushing a furious red, but only half from embarrassment, for the rest was happiness. He circled her with his great arms and very hastily, fire touched his lips to her soft ones.

"Now," he said exultantly, "now I will fight if I have to charge the men of the Empire alone."

CHAPTER FOUR

The Battle of Ealgefoot Flow

THE MEN of the Confederation were pouring into Ormiston all night long, the little dark men of Ch'cago and Selui, the tall blond ones from the regions of Iowa, where Dutch blood still survived, mingled now with a Scandinavian infusion from the upper rivers. All night there was a rumble of wagons, bringing powder and ball from Selui, and food as well for Ormiston couldn't even attempt to feed so many ravenous mouths. A magnificent army, ten thousand strong, and all of them seasoned fighting men, trained in a dozen little wars and in the bloody War of the Lakes and Rivers, when Ch'cago had bitten so large a piece from Selui territories.

The stand was to be at Ormiston, and Norse, the only settlement now between Joaquin Smith and the Confederation, was left to its fate. Experienced leaders had examined the territory, and had agreed on a plan. Three miles south of the town, the road followed an ancient railroad cut, with fifty-foot embankments on either side, heavily wooded for a mile north and south of the bridge across Eaglefoot Flow.

Along this course they were to distribute their men, a single line where the bluffs were high and steep, massed forces where the terrain permitted. Joaquin Smith *must* follow the road; there was no other. An ideal situation for ambush, and a magnificently simple plan. So magnificent and so simple that it could not fail, they said, and forgot completely that they were facing the supreme military genius of the entire Age of the Enlightenment.

It was mid-morning when the woodsrunners that had been sent into Ozarky returned with breath-taking news. Joaquin Smith had received the Selui defiance of his representations, and was marching. The Master was marching, and though they had come swiftly and had ridden horseback from Norse, he could not now be far distant. His forces? The runners estimated them at four thousand men, all mounted, with perhaps another thousand auxiliaries. Outnumbered two to one! But Hull Tarvish remembered tales of other encounters where Joaquin Smith had overcome greater odds than these.

The time was at hand. In the little room beside File Ormson's workshop, Hull was going over his weapons while Vail Ormiston, pale and nervous and very lovely, watched him. He drew a bit of oiled rag through the bore of the rifle she had given him, rubbed a spot of rust from the hammer, blew a speck of dust from the pan. Beside him on the table lay powder horn and ball, and his steel bow leaned against his chair.

"A sweet weapon!" he said admiringly, sighting down the long barrel.

"I… I hope it serves you well," murmured Vail tremulously. "Hull, he must be stopped. He *must!*"

"We'll try, Vail." He rose. "It's time I started."

She was facing him. "Then, before you go, will you… kiss me, Hull?"

He strode toward her, then recoiled in sudden alarm, for it was at that instant that the thing happened. There was a series of the faintest possible clicks, and Hull fancied that he saw for an instant a glistening of tiny blue sparks on candle-sticks and metal objects about the room, and that he felt for a brief moment a curious tingling. Then he forgot all of these strange trifles as the powder horn on the table roared into terrific flame, and flaming wads of powder shot meteor-like around him.

For an instant he froze rigid. Vail was screaming; her dress was burning. He moved into sudden action, sweeping her from her feet, crashing her sideways to the floor, where his great hands beat out the fire. Then he slapped table and floor; he brought his ample sandals down on flaming spots, and finally there were no more flames.

He turned coughing and choking in the black smoke, and bent over Vail, who gasped half overcome. Her skirt had burned to her knees, and for the moment she was too distraught to cover them, though there was no modesty in the world in those days like that of the women of the middle river regions. But as Hull leaned above her she huddled back.

"Are you hurt?" he cried. "Vail, are you burned?"

"No… no!" she panted.

"Then outside!" he snapped, reaching down to lift her.

"Not… not like this!"

He understood. He snatched his leather smith's apron from the wall, whipped it around her, and bore her into the clearer air of the street.

Outside there was chaos. He set Vail gently on the step and surveyed a scene of turmoil. Men ran shouting, and from windows along the street black smoke poured. A dozen yards away a powder wagon had blasted itself into a vast mushroom of smoke, incinerating horses and driver alike. On the porch across the way lay a writhing man, torn by the rifle that had burst in his hands.

He comprehended suddenly. "The sparkers!"* he roared. "Joaquin Smith's sparkers! Old Einar told me about them." He groaned. "There goes our ammunition."

The girl made a great effort to control herself. "Joaquin Smith's sorcery," she said dully. "And there goes hope as well."

He started. "Hope? No! Wait, Vail."

He rushed toward the milling group that surrounded bearded old Marcus Ormiston and the Confederation leaders. He plowed his way fiercely through, and seized the panic-stricken greybeard. "What now?" he roared. "What are you going to do?"

"Do? Do?" The old man was beyond comprehending.

"Yes, do! I'll tell you." He glared at the five leaders. "You'll carry through. Do you see? For powder and ball there's bow and sword, and just as good for the range we need. Gather your men! Gather your men and march!"

And such, within the hour, was the decision. Hull marched first with the Ormiston men, and he carried with him the memory of Vail's farewell. It embarrassed him cruelly to be kissed thus in public, but there was great pleasure in the glimpse of Enoch Ormiston's sour face as he had watched her.

*The Erden resonators. A device, now obsolete, that projected an inductive field sufficient to induce tiny electrical discharges in metal objects up to a distance of many miles. Thus it ignited inflammables like gunpowder.

The Ormiston men were first on the line of the Master's approach, and they filtered to their forest-hidden places as silently as foxes. Hull let his eyes wander back along the cut and what he saw pleased him, for no eye could have detected that along the deserted road lay ten thousand fighting men. They were good woodsmen too, these fellows from the upper rivers and the saltless seas.

Down the way from Norse a single horseman came galloping. Old Marcus Ormiston recognized him, stood erect, and hailed him. They talked; Hull could hear the words. The Master had passed through Norse, pausing only long enough to notify the eldarch that henceforth his taxes must be transmitted to N'Orleans, and then had moved leisurely onward. No, there had been no sign of sorcery, nor had he even seen any trace of the witch Black Margot, but then, he had ridden away before the Master had well arrived.

Their informant rode on toward Ormiston, and the men fell to their quiet waiting. A half hour passed, and then, faintly drifting on the silent air, came the sound of music. Singing; men's voices in song. Hull listened intently, and his skin crept and his hair prickled as he made out the words of the Battle Song of N'Orleans:

"Queen of cities, reigning
Empress, starry pearled
See our arms sustaining
Battle flags unfurled!
Hear our song rise higher,
Fierce as battle fire,
Death our one desire
Or
the Empire of the World!"

Hull gripped his bow and set feather to cord. He knew well enough that the plan was to permit the enemy to pass unmolested until his whole line was within the span of the ambush, but the rumble of that distant song was like spark to powder. And now, far down the way beyond the cut, he saw the dust rising. Joaquin Smith was at hand.

Then—the unexpected! Ever afterward Hull told himself that it should have been the expected, that the Master's reputation should have warned them that so simple a plan as theirs must fail. There was no time now for such vain thoughts, for suddenly, through the trees to his right, brown-clothed, lithe little men were slipping like charging shadows, horns sounding, whistles shrilling. The woods runners of the Master! Joaquin Smith had anticipated just such an ambush.

Instantly Hull saw their own weakness. They were ten thousand, true enough, but here they were strung thinly over a distance of two miles, and now the woods runners were at a vast advantage in numbers, with the main body approaching. One chance! Fight it out, drive off the scouts, and retire into the woods. While the army existed, even though Ormiston fell, there was hope.

He shouted, strung his arrow, and sent it flashing through the leaves. A bad place for arrows; their arching flight was always deflected by the tangled branches. He slung bow on shoulder and gripped his sword; close quarters was the solution, the sort of fight that made blood tingle and life seem joyous.

Then—the second surprise! The woods runners had flashed their own weapons, little blunt revolvers.* But they sent no bullets; only pale beams darted through leaves and branches, faint blue streaks of light. Sorcery? And to what avail?

He learned instantly. His sword grew suddenly scorching hot in his hands, and a moment later the queerest pain he had ever encountered racked his body. A violent, stinging, inward tingle that twitched his muscles and paralyzed his movements. A brief second and the shock ceased, but his sword lay smoking in the leaves, and his steel bow had seared his shoulders. Around him men were yelling in pain, writhing on the ground, running back into the forest depths. He cursed the beams; they flicked like sunlight through branched and leafy tangles where an honest arrow could find no passage.

Yet apparently no man had been killed. Hands were seared and blistered by weapons that grew hot under the blue beams, bodies were racked by the torture that Hull could not know was electric shock, but none was slain. Hope flared again, and he ran to head off a retreating group.

*Koblmar's ionic beams. Two parallel beams of highly actinic light ionize a path of air, and along these conductive lanes of gas an electric current can he passed, powerful enough to kill or merely intense enough to punish.

"To the road!" he roared. "Out where our arrows can fly free! Charge the column!"

For a moment the group halted. Hull seized a yet unheated sword from someone, and turned back. "Come on!" he bellowed. "Come on! We'll have a fight of this yet!"

Behind him he heard the trample of feet. The beams flicked out again, but he held his sword in the shadow of his own body, gritted his teeth, and bore the pain that twisted him. He rushed on; he heard his own name bellowed in the booming voice of File Ormson, but he only shouted encouragement and burst out into the full sunlight of the road.

Below in the cut was the head of the column, advancing placidly. He glimpsed a silver helmeted, black haired man on a great white mare at its head, and beside him a slighter figure on a black stallion. Joaquin Smith! Hull roared down the embankment toward him.

Four men spurred instantly between him and the figure with the silver helmet. A beam flicked; his sword scorched his skin and he flung it away. "Come on!" he bellowed. "Here's a fight!"

Strangely, in curious clarity, he saw the eyes of the Empire men, a smile in them, mysteriously amused. No anger, no fear—just amusement. Hull felt a sudden surge of trepidation, glanced quickly behind him, and knew finally the cause of that amusement. No one had followed him; he had charged the Master's army alone!

Now the fiercest anger he had ever known gripped Hull. Deserted! Abandoned by those for whom he fought. He roared his rage to the echoing bluffs, and sprang at the horseman nearest him.

The horse reared, pawing the air. Hull thrust his mighty arms below its belly and heaved with a convulsion of his great muscles. Backward toppled steed and rider, and all about the Master was a milling turmoil where a man scrambled desperately to escape the clashing hooves. But Hull glimpsed Joaquin Smith sitting statuelike and smiling on his great white mare.

He tore another rider from his saddle, and then caught from the corner of his eye, he saw the slim youth at the Master's side raise a weapon, coolly, methodically. For the barest instant Hull faced icy green eyes where cold, passionless death threatened. He flung himself aside as a beam spat smoking against the dust of the road.

"Don't!" snapped Joaquin Smith, his low voice clear through the turmoil. "The youth is splendid!"

But Hull had no mind to die uselessly. He bent, flung himself halfway up the bluff in a mighty leap, caught a dragging branch, and swung into the forest. A startled woods runner faced him; he flung the fellow behind him down the slope, and slipped into the shelter of leaves. "The wise warrior fights pride," he muttered to himself. "It's no disgrace for one man to run from an army."

He was mountain bred. He circled silently through the forest, avoiding the woods runners who were herding the Confederation army back towards Ormiston. He smiled grimly as he recalled the words he had spoken to Vail. He had justified them; he *had* charged the army of the Master alone.

CHAPTER FIVE

Black Margot

HULL CIRCLED wide through the forest, and it took all his mountain craft to slip free through the files of woods runners. He came at last to the fields east of Ormiston, and there made the road, entering from the direction of Selui.

Everywhere were evidences of rout. Wagons lay overturned, their teams doubtless used to further the escape of their drivers. Guns and rifles, many of them burst, littered the roadside, and now and again he passed black smoking piles and charred areas that marked the resting place of an ammunition cart.

Yet Ormiston was little damaged. He saw the firegutted remains of a shed or two where powder had been stored, and down the street a house roof still smoked. But there was no sign of battle carnage, and only the crowded street gave evidence of the unusual.

He found File Ormson in the group that stared across town to where the road from Norse elbowed east to enter. Hull had outsped the leisurely march of the Master, for there at the bend was the glittering army, now halted. Not even the woods runners had come into Ormiston town, for there they were too, lined in a brown-clad rank along the edge of the wood-lots beyond the nearer fields. They had made no effort, apparently, to take prisoners but had simply herded the terrified defenders into the village. Joaquin Smith had done it again; he had taken a town without a single death, or at least no casualties other than whatever injuries had come from bursting rifles and blazing powder.

Suddenly Hull noticed something. "Where are the Confederation men?" he asked sharply.

File Ormson turned gloomy eyes on him. "Gone. Flying back to Selui like scared gophers to their holes." He scowled, then smiled. "That was a fool's gesture of yours at Eaglefoot Flow, Hull. A fool's gesture, but brave."

The youth grimaced wryly. "I thought I was followed."

"And so you should have been, but that those fiendish ticklers tickled away our courage. But they can kill as well as tickle; when there was need of it before Memphis they killed quickly enough."

Hull thought of the green-eyed youth. "I think I nearly learned that," he said smiling.

Down the way there was some sort of stir. Hull narrowed his eyes to watch, and descried the silver helmet of the Master. He dismounted and faced someone; it was—yes, old Marcus Ormiston. He left File Ormson and shouldered his way to the edge of the crowd that circled the two.

Joaquin Smith was speaking. "And," he said, "all taxes are to be forwarded to N'Orleans, including those on your own lands. Half of them I shall use to maintain my government, but half will revert to your own district, which will be under a governor I shall appoint in Selui when that city is taken. You are no longer eldarch, but for the present you may collect the taxes at the rate I prescribe."

Old Marcus was bitterly afraid; Hull could see his beard waggling like an oriole's nest in a breeze. Yet there was a shrewd, bargaining streak in him. "You are very hard," he whined. "You left Pace Helm as eldarch undisturbed in Norse. Why do you punish me because I fought to hold what was mine? Why should that anger you so?"

"I am not angry," said the Master passively. "I never blame any for fighting against me, but it is my policy to favor those eldarchs who yield peacefully." He paused. "Those are my terms, and generous enough."

They were generous, thought Hull, especially to the people of Ormiston, who received back much less than half their taxes from the eldarch as roads, bridges, or wells.

"My… my lands?" faltered the old man.

"Keep what you till," said Joaquin Smith indifferently. "The rest of them go to their tenants." He turned away, placed foot to stirrup, and swung upon his great white mare.

Hull caught his first fair glimpse of the conqueror. Black hair cropped below his ears, cool greenish grey eyes, a mouth with something faintly humorous about it. He was tall as Hull himself, more slender, but with powerful shoulders, and he seemed no older than the late twenties, or no more than thirty at most, though that was only the magic of Martin Sair, since more than eighty years had passed since his birth in the mountains of Mexico. He wore the warrior's garb of the southlands, a shirt of metallic silver scales, short thigh-length trousers of some shiny, silken material, cothurns on his feet. His bronzed body was like the ancient statues Hull had seen in Selui, and he looked hardly the fiend that most people thought him. A pleasant seeming man, save for something faintly arrogant in his face—no, not arrogant, exactly, but proud or confident, as if he felt himself a being driven by fate, as perhaps he was.

He spoke again, now to his men. "Camp there," he ordered, waving at Ormiston square, "and there," pointing at a fallow field. "Do not damage the crops." He rode forward, and a dozen officers followed. "The Church," he said.

A voice, a tense, shrieking voice behind Hull. "You! It is, Hull! It's you!" It was Vail, teary eyed and pale. "They said you were—" She broke off sobbing, clinging to him, while Enoch Ormiston watched sourly.

He held her. "It seems I failed you," he said ruefully. "But I did do my best, Vail."

"Failed? I don't care." She calmed. "I don't care, Hull, since you're here."

"And it isn't as bad as it might be," he consoled. "He wasn't as severe as I feared."

"Severe!" she echoed. "Do you believe those mild words of his, Hull? First our taxes then our lands, and next it will be our lives... or at least my father's life. Don't you understand? That was no eldarch from some enemy town, Hull—that was Joaquin Smith. Joaquin Smith! Do you trust *him?*"

"Vail, do you believe that?"

"Of course I believe it!" She began to sob again. "See how he has already won over half the town with... with that about the taxes. Don't *you* be won over, Hull. I... couldn't stand it!"

"I will not," he promised.

"He and Black Margot and their craft! I hate them, Hull. I—Look there! *Look there!*"

He spun around. For a moment he saw nothing save the green-eyed youth who had turned death-laden eyes on him at Eagle-foot Flow, mounted on the mighty black stallion. Youth! He saw suddenly that it was a woman—a girl rather. Eighteen—twenty-five? He couldn't tell. Her face was averted as she scanned the crowd that lined the opposite side of the street, but the sunset fell on a flaming black mop of hair, so black that it glinted blue—an intense, unbelievable black. Like Joaquin Smith she wore only a shirt and very abbreviated shorts, but a caparison protected the slim daintiness of her legs from any contact with the mount's ribs. There was a curious grace in the way she sat the idling steed, one hand on its haunches, the other on withers, the bridle dangling loose. Her Spanish mother's blood showed only in the clear, transparent olive of her skin, and of course, in the startling ebony of her hair.

"Black Margot!" Hull whispered, "Brazen! Half naked! What's so beautiful about *her?*"

As if she heard his whisper, she turned suddenly, her emerald eyes sweeping the crowd about him, and he felt his question answered. Her beauty was starkly incredible—audacious, outrageous. It was more than a mere lack of flaws; it was a sultry, flaming positive beauty with a hint of sullenness in it. The humor of the Master's mouth lurked about hers as mockery; her perfect lips seemed always about to smile, but to smile cruelly and sardonically. Hers was a ruthless and pitiless perfection, but it was nevertheless perfection, even to the faintly Oriental cast given by her black hair and sea-green eyes.

Those eyes met Hull's and it was almost as if he heard an audible click. He saw recognition in her face, and she passed her glance casually over his mighty figure. He stiffened, stared defiantly back, and swept his own gaze insolently over her body from the midnight hair to the diminutive cothurns on her feet. If she acknowledged his gaze at all, it was by the faintest of all possible smiles of mockery as she rode coolly away toward Joaquin Smith.

Vail was trembling against him, and it was a great relief to look into her deep but not at all mysterious blue eyes, and to see the quite understandable loveliness of her pale features. What if she hadn't the insolent brilliance of the Princess, he thought fiercely. She was sweet and honest and loyal to her beliefs, and he loved her. Yet he could not keep his eyes from straying once more to the figure on the black stallion.

"She... she smiled at you, Hull!" gasped Vail. "I'm frightened. I'm terribly frightened."

His fascination was yielding now to a surge of hatred for Joaquin Smith, for the Princess, for the whole Empire. It was Vail he loved, and she was being crushed by these. An idea formed slowly as he stared down the street to where Joaquin Smith had dismounted and was now striding into the little church. He heard an approving murmur sweep the crowd, already half won over by the distribution of land. That was simply policy, the Master's worshipping in Ormiston church, a gesture to the crowd.

He lifted the steel bow from his back and bent it. The spring was still in it; it had been heated enough to scorch his skin but not enough to untemper it. "Wait here!" he snapped to Vail, and strode up the street toward the church.

Outside stood a dozen Empire men, and the Princess idled on her great black horse. He slipped across the churchyard, around behind where a tangle of vines stretched toward the roof. Would they support his weight? They did, and he pulled himself hand over hand to the eaves, and thence to the peak. The spire hid him from the Master's men, and not one of the Ormiston folk glanced his way.

He crept forward to the base of the steeple. Now he must leave the peak and creep precariously along the steep slope around it. He reached the street edge and peered cautiously over.

The Master was still within. Against his will he glanced at Black Margot, and even put cord to feather and sighted at her ivory throat. But he could not. He could not loose the shaft.

Below him there was a stir. Joaquin Smith came out and swung to his white horse. Now was the moment. Hull rose to his knees, hoping that he could remain steady on the sharp pitch of the roof. Carefully, carefully, he drew the steel arrow back.

There was a shout. He had been seen, and a blue beam sent racking pain through his body. For an instant he bore it, then loosed his arrow and went sliding down the roof edge and over.

He fell on soft loam. A dozen hands seized him, dragged him upright, thrust him out into the street. He saw Joaquin Smith still on his horse, but the glistening arrow stood upright like a plume in his silver helmet, and a trickle of blood was red on his cheek.

But he wasn't killed. He raised the helmet from his head, waved aside the cluster of officers, and with his own hands bound a white cloth about his forehead. Then he turned cool grey eyes on Hull.

"You drive a strong shaft," he said, and then recognition flickered in his eyes. "I spared your life some hours ago, did I not?"

Hull said nothing.

"Why," resumed the Master, "do you seek to kill me after your eldarch has made peace with me? You are part of the Empire now, and this is treason."

"I made no peace!" growled Hull.

"But your leader did, thereby binding you."

Hull could not keep his gaze from the emerald eyes of the Princess, who was watching him without expression save faint mockery.

"Have you nothing to say," asked Joaquin Smith.

"Nothing."

The Master's eyes slid over him. "Are you Ormiston born?" he asked. "What is your name?"

No need to bring troubles on his friends. "No," said Hull. "I am called Hull Tarvish."

The conqueror turned away. "Lock him up," he ordered coolly. "Let him make whatever preparations his religion requires, and then... execute him."

Above the murmur of the crowd Hull heard Vail Ormiston's cry of anguish. He turned to smile at her, watched her held by two Empire men as she struggled to reach him. "I'm sorry," he called gently. "I love you, Vail." Then he was being thrust away down the street.

He was pushed into Hue Helm's stone-walled tool shed. It had been cleared of everything, doubtless for some officer's quarters. Hull drew himself up and stood passively in the gathering darkness where a single shaft of sunset light angled through the door, before which stood two grim Empire men.

One of them spoke. "Keep peaceful, Weed,"* he said in his N'Orleans drawl. "Go ahead with your praying, or whatever it is you do."

"I do nothing," said Hull. "The mountainies believe that a right life is better than a right ending, and right or wrong a ghost's but a ghost anyway."

The guard laughed. "And a ghost you'll be."

"If a ghost I'll be," retorted Hull, turning slowly toward him, "I'd sooner turn one... fighting!"

He sprang suddenly, crashed a mighty fist against the arm that bore the weapon, thrust one guard upon the other, and overleaped the tangle into the dusk. As he spun to circle the house, something very hard smashed viciously against the back of his skull, sending him sprawling half dazed against the wall.

CHAPTER SIX
The Harriers

AFTER A brief moment Hull sprawled half stunned, then his muscles lost their paralysis and he thrust himself to his feet, whirling to face whatever assault threatened. In the doorway the guards still scrambled, but directly before him towered a rider on a black mount, and two men on foot flanked him. The rider, of course, was the Princess,

*Weed: The term applied by Dominists [the Master's partisans] to their opposers. It originated in Joaquin Smith's remark before the Battle of Memphis: "Even the weeds of the fields have taken arms against me."

her glorious green eyes luminous as a cat's in the dusk as she slapped a short sword into its scabbard. It was a blow from the flat of its blade that had felled him.

She held now the blunt weapon of the blue beam. It came to him that he had never heard her speak, but she spoke now in a voice low and liquid, yet cold, cold as the flow of an ice-crusted winter stream. "Stand quiet, Hull Tarvish," she said. "One flash will burst that stubborn heart of yours forever."

Perforce he stood quiet, his back to the wall of the shed. He had no doubt at all that the Princess would kill him if he moved; he couldn't doubt it with her icy eyes upon him. He stared sullenly back, and a phrase of Old Einar's came strangely to his memory. "Satanically beautiful," the old man had called her, and so she was. Hell or the art of Martin Sair had so fashioned her that no man could gaze unmoved on the false purity of her face, no man at least in whom flowed red blood.

She spoke again, letting her glance flicker disdainfully over the two appalled guards. "The Master will be pleased," she said contemptuously, "to learn that one unarmed Weed outmatches two men of his own cohort."

The nearer man faltered, "But your Highness, he rushed us unexpect—"

"No matter," she cut in, and turned back to Hull. For the first time now he really felt the presence of death as she said coolly, "I am minded to kill you."

"Then do it!" he snapped.

"I came here to watch you die," she observed calmly. "It interests me to see men die, boldly or cowardly or resignedly. I think you would die boldly."

It seemed to Hull that she was deliberately torturing him by this procrastination. "Try me!" he growled.

"But I think also," she resumed, "that your living might amuse me more than your death, and..." for the first time there was a breath of feeling in her voice "...God knows I need amusement!" Her tones chilled again. "I give you your life."

"Your Highness," muttered the cowed guard, "the Master has ordered—"

"I countermand the orders," she said shortly. And then to Hull. "You are a fighter. Are you also a man of honor?"

"If I'm not," he retorted, "the lie that says I am would mean nothing to me."

She smiled coldly. "Well, I think you are, Hull Tarvish. You go free on your word to carry no weapons, and your promise to visit me this evening in my quarters at the eldarch's home." She paused. "Well?"

"I give my word."

"And I take it." She crashed her heels against the ribs of the great stallion, and the beast reared and whirled. "Away, all of you!" she ordered. "You two, carry tub and water for my bath." She rode off toward the street.

Hull let himself relax against the wall with a low "whew!" Sweat started on his cold forehead, and his mighty muscles felt almost weak. It wasn't that he had feared death, he told himself, but the strain of facing those glorious, devilish emerald eyes, and the cold torment of the voice of Black Margot, and the sense of her taunting him, mocking him, even her last careless gesture of freeing him. He drew himself erect. After all, fear of death or none, he loved life, and let that be enough.

He walked slowly toward the street. Across the way lights glowed in Marcus Orison's home, and he wondered if Vail were there, perhaps serving the Princess Margaret as he had so lately suggested the contrary. He wanted to find Vail; he wanted to use her cool loveliness as an antidote for the dark poison of the beauty he had been facing. And then, at the gate, he drew back suddenly. A group of men in Empire garb came striding by, and among them, helmetless and with his head bound, moved the Master.

His eyes fell on Hull. He paused suddenly and frowned. "You again!" he said. "How is it that you still live, Hull Tarvish?"

"The Princess ordered it."

The frown faded. "So," said Joaquin Smith slowly, "Margaret takes it upon herself to interfere somewhat too frequently. I suppose she also freed you?"

"Yes, on my promise not to bear arms."

There was a curious expression in the face of the conqueror. "Well," he said almost gently, "it was not my intention to torture you, but merely to have you killed for your treason. It may be that you will soon wish that my orders had been left unaltered." He strode on into the eldarch's dooryard, with his silent men following.

Hull turned his steps toward the center of the village. Everywhere he passed Empire men scurrying about the tasks of encampment, and supply wagons rumbled and jolted in the streets. He saw files of the soldiers passing slowly before cook-wagons and the smell of food floated on the air, reminding him that he was ravenously hungry. He hurried toward his room beside File Ormson's shop, and there, tragic-eyed and mist-pale, he found Vail Ormiston.

She was huddled on the doorstep with sour Enoch holding her against him. It was Enoch who first perceived Hull, and his jaw dropped and his eyes bulged, and a gurgling sound issued from his throat. And Vail looked up with uncomprehending eyes, stared for a moment without expression, and then, with a little moan, crumpled and fainted.

She was unconscious only a few moments, scarcely long enough for Hull to bear her into his room. There she lay now on his couch, clinging to his great hand, convinced at last of his living presence.

"I think," she murmured, "that you're as deathless as Joaquin Smith, Hull. I'll never believe you dead again. Tell me... tell me how it happened."

He told her. "Black Margot's to thank for it," he finished.

But the very name frightened Vail. "She means evil, Hull. She terrifies me with her witch's eyes and her hellstained hair. I haven't even dared go home for fear of her."

He laughed. "Don't worry about me, Vail. I'm safe enough."

Enoch cut in. "Here's one for the Harriers, then," he said sourly. "The pack needs him."

"The Harriers?" Hull looked up puzzled.

"Oh, Hull, yes!" said Vail. "File Ormson's been busy. The Harriers are what's left of the army... the better citizens of Ormiston. The Master's magic didn't reach beyond the ridge, and over the hills there's still powder and rifles. And the spell is no longer in the valley, either. One of the men carried a cup of powder across the ridge, and it didn't burn."

The better citizens, Hull thought smiling. She meant, of course, those who owned land and feared a division of it such as Marcus Ormiston had suffered. But aloud he said only, "How many men have you?"

"Oh, there'll be several hundred with the farmers across the hills." She looked into his eyes, "I know it's a forlorn hope, Hull, but... we've got to try. You'll help, won't you?"

"Of course. But all your Harriers can attempt is raids. They can't fight the Master's army."

"I know. I know it, Hull. It's a desperate hope."

"Desperate?" said Enoch suddenly. "Hull, didn't you say you were ordered to Black Margot's quarters this evening?"

"Yes."

"Then... see here! You'll carry a knife in your armpit. Sooner or later she'll want you alone with her, and when *that* happens, you'll slide the knife quietly into her ruthless heart! There's a hope for you—*if* you've courage!"

"Courage!" he growled. "To murder a woman?"

"Black Margot's a devil!"

"Devil or not, what's the good of it? It's Joaquin Smith that's building the Empire, not the Princess."

"Yes," said Enoch, "but half his power is the art of the witch. Once she's gone the Confederation could blast his army like ducks in a frog pond."

"It's true!" gasped Vail. "What Enoch says is true!"

Hull scowled. "I swore not to bear weapons!"

"Swore to *her!*" snapped Enoch. "That needn't bind you."

"My word's given," said Hull firmly. "I do not lie."

Vail smiled. "You're right," she whispered, and as Enoch's face darkened, "I love you for it, Hull."

"Then," grunted Enoch, "if it's not lack of courage, do this. Lure her somehow across the west windows. We can slip two or three Harriers to the edge of the woodlot, and if she passes a window with the light behind her... well, they won't miss."

"Oh, I won't," said Hull wearily. "I won't fight women, nor betray even Black Margot to death."

But Vail's blue eyes pleaded. "That won't be breaking your word, Hull. Please. It isn't betraying a woman. She's a sorceress. She's evil. Please, Hull."

Bitterly he yielded. "I'll try, then." He frowned gloomily. "She saved my life, and… Well, which room is hers?"

"My father's. Mine is the western chamber, which she took for her… her maid," Vail's eyes misted at the indignity of it. "We," she said, "are left to sleep in the kitchen."

An hour later, having eaten, he walked somberly home with Vail while Enoch slipped away toward the hills. There were tents in the dooryard, and lights glowed in every window, and before the door stood two dark Empire men who passed the girl readily enough, but halted Hull with small ceremony. Vail cast him a wistful backward glance as she disappeared toward the rear, and he submitted grimly to the questioning of the guards.

"On what business?"

"To see the Princess Margaret."

"Are you Hull Tarvish?"

"Yes."

One of the men stepped to his side and ran exploratory hands about his body. "Orders of Her Highness," he explained gruffly.

Hull smiled. The Princess had not trusted his word too implicitly. In a moment the fellow had finished his search and swung the door open.

Hull entered. He had never seen the interior of the house, and for a moment its splendor dazzled him. Carved ancient furniture, woven carpets, intricately worked standards for the oil lamps, and even—for an instant he failed to comprehend it—a full-length mirror of ancient workmanship wherein his own image faced him. Until now he had seen only bits and fragments of mirrors.

To his left a guard blocked an open door whence voices issued. Old Marcus Ormiston's voice. "But I'll pay for it. I'll buy it with all I have." His tones were wheedling.

"No." Cool finality in the voice of Joaquin Smith. "Long ago I swore to Martin Sair never to grant immortality to any who have not proved themselves worthy." A note of sarcasm edged his voice. "Go prove yourself deserving of it, old man, in the few years left to you."

Hull sniffed contemptuously. There seemed something debased in the old man's whining before his conqueror. "The Princess Margaret?" he asked, and followed the guard's gesture.

Upstairs was a dimly lit hall where another guard stood silently. Hull repeated his query, but in place of an answer came the liquid tones of Margaret herself. "Let him come in, Corlin."

A screen within the door blocked sight of the room. Hull circled it, steeling himself against the memory of that soul-burning loveliness he remembered. But his defense was shattered by the shock that awaited him.

The screen, indeed, shielded the Princess from the sight of the guard in the hall, but not from Hull's eyes. He stared utterly appalled at the sight of her lying in complete indifference in a great tub of water, while a fat woman scrubbed assiduously at her bare body. He could not avoid a single glimpse of her exquisite form, then he turned and stared deliberately from the east windows, knowing that he was furiously crimson even to his shoulders.

"Oh, sit down!" she said contemptuously. "This will be over in a moment."

He kept his eyes averted while water splashed and a towel whisked sibilantly. When he heard her footsteps beside him he glanced up tentatively, still fearful of what he might see, but she was covered now in a full robe of shiny black and gold that made her seem taller, though its filmy delicacy by no means concealed what was beneath. Instead of the cothurns she wore when on the march, she had slipped her feet into tiny high-heeled sandals that were reminiscent of the footgear he had seen in ancient pictures. The black robe and her demure coif of short ebony hair gave her an appearance of almost nunlike purity, save for the green hell-fires that danced in her eyes.

In his heart Hull cursed that false aura of innocence, for he felt again the fascination against which he had steeled himself.

"So," she said. "You may sit down again. I do not demand court etiquette in the field." She sat opposite, and produced a black cigarette, lighting it at the chimney of the lamp on the table. Hull stared; not that he was unaccustomed to seeing women smoke, for every mountainy woman had her pipe, and every cottage its tobacco patch, but cigarettes were new to him.

"Now," she said with a faintly ironic smile, "tell me what they say of me here."

"They call you witch."

"And do they hate me?"

"Hate you?" he echoed thoughtfully. "At least they will fight you and the Master to the last feather on the last arrow."

"Of course. The young men will fight—except those that Joaquin has bought with the eldarch's lands—because they know that once within the Empire, fighting is no more to be had. No more joyous, thrilling little wars between the cities, no more boasting and parading before the pretty provincial girls." She paused. "And you, Hull Tarvish… what do you think of me?"

"I call you witch for other reasons."

"Other reasons?"

"There is no magic," said Hull, echoing the words of Old Einar in Selui. "There is only knowledge."

The Princess looked narrowly at him. "A wise thought for one of you," she murmured, and then, "You came weaponless."

"I keep my word."

"You owe me that. I spared your life."

"And I," declared Hull defiantly, "spared yours. I could have sped an arrow through that white throat of yours, there on the church roof. I aimed one."

She smiled. "What held you?"

"I do not fight women." He winced as he thought of what mission he was on, for it belied his words.

"Tell me," she said, "was that the eldarch's pretty daughter who cried so piteously after you there before the church?"

"Yes."

"And do you love her?"

"Yes." This was the opening he had sought, but it came bitterly now, facing her. He took the opportunity grimly. "I should like to ask one favor."

"Ask it."

"I should like to see…" lies were not in him but this was no lie "…the chamber that was to have been our bridal room. The west chamber." That might be—should be—truth.

The Princess laughed disdainfully. "Go see it then."

For a moment he feared, or hoped, perhaps, that she was going to let him go alone. Then she rose and followed him to the hall, and to the door of the west chamber.

CHAPTER SEVEN

Betrayal

HULL PAUSED at the door of the west chamber to permit the Princess to enter. For the merest fraction of a second her glorious green eyes flashed speculatively to his face, then she stepped back. "You first, Weed," she commanded.

He did not hesitate. He turned and strode into the room, hoping that the Harrier riflemen, if indeed they lurked in the copse, might recognize his mighty figure in time to stay their eager trigger fingers. His scalp prickled as he moved steadily across the window, but nothing happened.

Behind him the Princess laughed softly. "I have lived too long in the aura of plot and counterplot in N'Orleans," she said. "I mistrust you without cause, honest Hull Tarvish."

Her words tortured him. He turned to see her black robe mold itself to her body as she moved, and, as sometimes happens in moments of stress, he caught an instantaneous picture of her with his senses so quickened that it seemed as if she, himself, and the world were frozen into immobility. He remembered her forever as she was then, with her limbs in the act of striding, her green eyes soft in the lamplight, and her perfect lips in a smile that had a coloring of wistfulness. Witch and devil she might be, but she looked like a dark-haired angel, and in that moment his spirit revolted.

"No!" he bellowed, and sprang toward her, striking her slim shoulders with both hands in a thrust that sent her staggering back into the hallway, there to sit hard and suddenly on the floor beside the amazed guard.

She sprang up instantly, and there was nothing angelic now in her face. "You… hurt me!" she hissed. "Me! Now, I'll—" She snatched the guard's weapon from his belt, thrust it full at Hull's chest, and sent the blue beam humming upon him.

It was pain far worse than that at Eaglefoot Flow. He bore it stolidly, grinding into silence the groan that rose in his throat, and in a moment she flicked it off and slapped it angrily into the guard's holster. "Treachery again!" she said. "I won't kill you, Hull Tarvish. I know a better way." She whirled toward the stair-well. "Lebeau!" she called. "Lebeau! There's..." She glanced sharply at Hull, and continued, *"Il y a des tirailleurs dans le bois. Je vais les tireer en avant!"** It was the French of N'Orleans, as incomprehensible to Hull as Aramaic.

She spun back. "Sora!" she snapped, and then, as the fat woman appeared, "Never mind. You're far too heavy." Then back to Hull. "I've a mind," she blazed, "to strip the Weed clothes from the eldarch's daughter and send her marching across the window!"

He was utterly appalled. "She... she was in town!" he gasped, then fell silent at the sound of feet below.

"Well, there's no time," she retorted. "So, if I must..." She strode steadily into the west chamber, paused a moment, and then stepped deliberately in front of the window!

Hull was aghast. He watched her stand so that the lamplight must have cast her perfect silhouette full on the pane, stand tense and motionless for the fraction of a breath, and then leap back so sharply that her robe billowed away from her body.

She had timed it to perfection. Two shots crashed almost together, and the glass shattered. And then, out in the night, a dozen beams crisscrossed, and, thin and clear in the silence after the shots, a yell of mortal anguish drifted up, and another, and a third.

The Princess Margaret smiled in malice, and licked a crimson drop from a finger gashed by flying glass. "Your treachery reacts," she said in the tones of a sneer. "Instead of my betrayal, you have betrayed your own men."

"I need no accusation from you," he said gloomily. "I am my own accuser, and my own judge. Yes, and my own executioner as well. I will not live a traitor."

She raised her dainty eyebrows, and blew a puff of grey smoke from the cigarette still in her hand. "So strong Hull Tarvish will die a suicide," she remarked indifferently. "I had intended to kill you now. Should I leave you to be your own victim?"

He shrugged. "What matter to me?"

"Well," she said musingly, "you're rather more entertaining than I had expected. You're strong, you're stubborn, and you're dangerous. I give you the right to do what you wish with your own life, but..." her green eyes flickered mockingly "...if I were Hull Tarvish, I should live on the chance of justifying myself. You can wipe out the disgrace of your weakness by an equal courage. You can sell your life in your own cause, and who knows?—perhaps for Joaquin's—or mine!"

He chose to ignore the mockery in her voice. "Perhaps," he said grimly, "I will."

"Why, then, did you weaken, Hull Tarvish? You might have had my life."

"I do not fight women," he said despondently. "I looked at you—and turned weak." A question formed in his mind. "But why did you risk your life before the window? You could have had fifty woods runners scour the copse. That was brave, but unnecessary."

She smiled, but there was a shrewd narrowness in her eyes. "Because so many of these villages are built above the underground ways of the Ancients—the subways, the sewers. How did I know but that your assassins might slip into some burrow and escape? It was necessary to lure them into disclosure."

Hull shadowed the gleam that shot into his own eyes. He remembered suddenly the ancient sewer in which the child Vail had wandered, whose entrance was hidden by blackberry bushes. Then the Empire men were unaware of it! He visioned the Harriers creeping through it with bow and sword—yes, and rifle, now that the spell was off the valley—springing suddenly into the center of the camp, finding the Master's army, sleeping, disorganized, unwary. What a plan for a surprise attack!

"Your Highness," he said grimly, "I think of suicide no more, and unless you kill me now, I will be a bitter enemy to your Empire army."

"Perhaps less bitter than you think," she said softly. "See, Hull, the only three that know of your weakness are dead. No one can name you traitor or weakling."

"But *I* can," he returned somberly. "And you."

"Not *I*, Hull," she murmured. "I never blame a man who weakens because of me—there have been many. Men as strong as you, Hull, and some that the world still calls

*"There are snipers in the copse. I'll draw them out!"

great." She turned toward her own chamber. "Come in here," she said in altered tones. "I will have some wine. Sora!" As the fat woman padded off, she took another cigarette and lit it above the lamp, wrinkling her dainty nose distastefully at the night-flying insects that circled it.

"What a place!" she snapped impatiently.

"It is the finest house I have ever seen," said Hull stolidly.

She laughed. "It's a hovel. I sigh for the day we return to N'Orleans, where windows are screened, where water flows hot at will, where lights do not flicker as yellow oil lamps nor send heat to stifle one. Would you like to see the Great City, Hull?"

"You know I would."

"What if I say you may?"

"What could keep me from it if I go in peace?"

She shrugged. "Oh, you can visit N'Orleans, of course, but suppose I offered you the chance to go as the... the *guest*, we'll say, of the Princess Margaret. What would you give for that privilege?"

Was she mocking him again? "What would you ask for it?" he rejoined guardedly.

"Oh, your allegiance, perhaps. Or perhaps the betrayal of your little band of Harriers, who will be the devil's own nuisance to stamp out of these hills."

He looked up startled that she knew the name. "The Harriers? How?"

She smiled. "We have friends among the Ormiston men. Friends bought with land," she added contemptuously. "But what of my offer, Hull?"

He scowled. "You say as your *guest*. What am I to understand by that?"

She leaned across the table, her exquisite green eyes on his, her hair flaming blue-black, her perfect lips in a faint smile. "What you please, Hull. Whatever you please."

Anger was rising. "Do you mean," he asked huskily, "that you'd do that for so small a thing as the destruction of a little enemy band? You, with the whole Empire at your back?"

She nodded. "It saves trouble, doesn't it?"

"And honesty, virtue, honor, mean as little to you as that? Is this one of your usual means of conquest? Do you ordinarily sell your... your favors for...?"

"Not ordinarily," she interrupted coolly. "First I must like my co-partner in the trade. You, Hull... I like those vast muscles of yours, and your stubborn courage, and your slow, clear mind. You are not a great man, Hull, for your mind has not the cold fire of genius, but you are a strong one, and I like you for it."

"Like me!" he roared, starting up in his chair. "Yet you think I'll trade what honor's left me for... that! You think I'll betray my cause! You think... Well, you're wrong, that's all. You're wrong!"

She shook her head, smiling. "No. I wasn't wrong, for I thought you wouldn't."

"Oh, you did!" he snarled. "Then what if I'd accepted? What would you have done then?"

"What I promised." She laughed at his angry, incredulous face. "Don't look so shocked, Hull. I'm not little Vail Ormiston. I'm the Princess Margaret of N'Orleans, called Margaret the Divine by those who love me, and by those who hate me called... Well, you must know what my enemies call me."

"I do!" he blazed. "Black Margot, I do!"

"Black Margot!" she echoed smiling. "Yes, so called because a poet once amused me, and because there was once a very ancient, very great French poet named François Villon, who loved a harlot called Black Margot." She sighed. "But my poet was no Villon; already his works are nearly forgotten."

"A good name!" he rasped. "A good name for you!"

"Doubtless. But you fail to understand, Hull. I'm an Immortal. My years are three times yours. Would you have me follow the standards of death-bound Vail Ormiston?"

"Yes! By what right are you superior to all standards?"

Her lips had ceased to smile, and her deep green eyes turned wistful. "By the right that I can act in no other way, Hull," she said softly. A tinge of emotion quavered in her voice. "Immortality!" she whispered. "Year after year after year of sameness, tramping up and down the world on conquest! What do I care for conquest? I have no sense of destiny like Joaquin, who sees before him Empire... Empire... Empire, ever larger, ever growing. What's Empire to me? And year by year I grow bored until fighting, killing, danger, and love are all that keep me breathing!"

His anger had drained away. He was staring at her aghast, appalled.

"And then *they* fail me!" she murmured. "When killing palls and love grows stale, what's left? Did I say love? How can there be love for me when I know that if I love a man, it will be only to watch him age and turn wrinkled, weak, and flabby? And when I beg Joaquin for immortality for him, he flaunts before me that promise of his to Martin Sair, to grant it only to those already proved worthy. By the time a man's worthy he's old." She went on tensely, "I tell you, Hull, that I'm so friendless and alone that I envy you death-bound ones! Yes, and one of these days I'll join you!"

He gulped. "My God!" he muttered. "Better for you if you'd stayed in your native mountains with friends, home, husband, and children."

"Children!" she echoed, her eyes misting with tears. "Immortals can't have children. They're sterile; they should be nothing but brains like Joaquin and Martin Sair, not beings with feelings… like me. Sometimes I curse Martin Sair and his hard rays. I don't want immortality; I want *life!*"

Hull found his mind in a whirl. The impossible beauty of the girl he faced, her green eyes now soft and moist and unhappy, her lips quivering, the glisten of a tear on her cheek—these things tore at him so powerfully that he scarcely knew his own allegiance. "God!" he whispered. "I'm sorry!"

"And you, Hull… will you help me… a little?"

"But we're enemies—enemies!"

"Can't we be… something else?" A sob shook her.

"How can we be?" he groaned.

Suddenly some quirk to her dainty lips caught his attention. He stared incredulously into the green depths of her eyes. It was true. There was laughter there. She had been mocking him! And as she perceived his realization, her soft laughter rippled like rain on water.

"You… devil!" he choked. "You black witch! I wish I'd let you be killed!"

"Oh, no," she said demurely. "Look at me, Hull."

The command was needless. He couldn't take his fascinated gaze from her exquisite face.

"Do you love me, Hull?"

"I love Vail Ormiston," he rasped.

"But do you love *me?*"

"I hate you!"

"But do you love me as well?"

He groaned. "This is bitterly unfair," he muttered.

She knew what he meant. He was crying out against the circumstances that had brought the Princess Margaret—the most brilliant woman of all that brilliant age, and one of the most brilliant of any age—to flash all her fascination on a simple mountainy from Ozarky. It wasn't fair; her smile admitted it, but there was triumph there, too.

"May I go?" he asked stonily.

She nodded. "But you will be a little less my enemy, won't you, Hull?"

He rose. "Whatever harm I can do your cause," he said, "that harm will I do. I will not be twice a traitor." But he fancied a puzzling gleam of satisfaction in her green eyes at his words.

CHAPTER EIGHT

Torment

HULL LOOKED down at noon over Ormiston valley, where Joaquin Smith was marching. At his side Vail paused, and together they gazed silently over Selui road, now black with riding men and rumbling wagons on their way to attack the remnant of the Confederation army in Selui. But Ormiston was not entirely abandoned, for three hundred soldiers and two hundred horsemen remained to deal with the Harriers, under Black Margot herself. It was not the policy of the Master to permit so large a rebel band to gather unopposed in conquered territory; within the Empire, despite the mutual hatred among rival cities, there existed a sort of enforced peace.

"Our moment comes tonight," Hull said soberly. "We'll never have a better chance than now, with our numbers all but equal to theirs, and surprise on our side."

Vail nodded. "The ancient tunnel was a bold thought, Hull. The Harriers are shoring up the crumbled places. Father is with them."

"He shouldn't be. The aged have no place in the field."

"But this is his hope, Hull. He lives for this."

"Small enough hope! Suppose we're successful, Vail. What will it mean save the return of Joaquin Smith and his army? Common sense tells me this is a fool's hunt, and if it were not for you and the chance of fairer fighting than we've had until now... well, I'd be tempted to concede the Master his victory."

"Oh, no!" cried Vail. "If our success means the end of Black Margot, isn't that enough? Besides, you know that half the Master's powers are the work of the witch. Enoch... poor Enoch... said so."

Hull winced. Enoch had been one of the three marksmen slain outside the west windows, and the girl's words brought memory of his own part in that. But her words pricked painfully in yet another direction, for the vision of the Princess that had plagued him all night long still rose powerfully in his mind, nor could he face the mention of her death unmoved.

But Vail read only distress for Enoch in his face. "Enoch," she repeated softly. "He loved me in his sour way, Hull, but once I had known you, I had no thoughts for him."

Hull slipped his arm about her, cursing himself that he could not steal his thought away from Margaret of N'Orleans, because it was Vail he loved, and Vail he wanted to love. Whatever spell the Princess had cast about him, he knew her to be evil, ruthless, and inhumanly cold—a sorceress, a devil. But he could not blot her Satanic loveliness from his inward gaze.

"Well," he sighed, "let it be tonight, then. Was it four hours past sunset? Good. The Empire men should be sleeping or gaming in Tigh's tavern by that time. It's for us to pray for our gunpowder."

"Gunpowder? Oh, but didn't you hear what I told File Ormson and the Harriers, back there on the ridge? The casters of the spell are gone; Joaquin Smith has taken them to Selui. I watched and listened from the kitchen this morning."

"The sparkers? They're gone?"

"Yes. They called them reson... resators..."

"Resonators," said Hull, recalling Old Einar's words.

"Something like that. There were two of them, great iron barrels on swivels, full of some humming and clicking magic, and they swept the valley north and south, and east and west, and over toward Norse there was the sound of shots and the smoke of a burning building. They loaded them on wagons and dragged them away toward Selui."

"They didn't cross the ridge with their spell,"* said Hull. "The Harriers still have powder."

"Yes," murmured Vail, drawing his arm closer about her. "Tell me," she said suddenly, "what did she want of you last night?"

Hull grimaced. He had told Vail little enough of that discreditable evening, and he had been fearing her question. "Treason," he said finally. "She wanted me to betray the Harriers."

"You? She asked that of you?"

"Do you think I would?" countered Hull.

"I know you never would. But what did she offer you for betrayal?"

Again he hesitated. "A great reward," he answered at last. "A reward out of all proportion to the task."

"Tell me, Hull, what is she like face to face?"

"A demon. She isn't exactly human."

"But in what way? Men say so much of her beauty, of her deadly charm. Hull... did you feel it?"

"I love *you*, Vail."

She sighed, and drew yet closer. "I think you're the strongest man in the world, Hull. The very strongest."

"I'll need to be," he muttered, staring gloomily over the valley. Then he smiled faintly as he saw men plowing, for it was late in the season for such occupation. Old Marcus Ormiston was playing safe; remembering the Master's words, he was tilling every acre across which a horse could drag a blade.

Vail left him in Ormiston village and took her way hesitantly homeward. Hull did what he could about the idle shop, and when the sun slanted low, bought himself a square loaf of brown bread, a great slice of cheese, and a bottle of the still, clear wine of the re-

*The field of the Erden resonator passes readily through structures and walls, but it is blocked by any considerable natural obstructions, hills, and for some reason fog-banks or low clouds.

gion. It was just as he finished his meal in his room that a pounding on the door of the shop summoned him.

It was an Empire man. "Hull Tarvish?" he asked shortly. At Hull's nod he continued, "From Her Highness," and handed him a folded slip of black paper.

The mountain youth stared at it. On one side, in raised gold, was the form of a serpent circling a globe, its tail in its mouth—the Midgard Serpent. He slipped a finger through the fold, opened the message, and squinted helplessly at the characters written in gold on the black inner surface.

"This scratching means nothing to me," he said.

The Empire man sniffed contemptuously. "I'll read it," he said, taking the missive. "It says, 'Follow the messenger to our quarters,' and it's signed *Margarita Imperii Regina*, which means Margaret, Princess of the Empire. Is that plain?" He handed back the note. "I've been looking an hour for you."

"Suppose I won't go," growled Hull.

"This isn't an invitation, Weed. It's a command."

Hull shrugged. He had small inclination to face Black Margot again, especially with his knowledge of the Harriers' plans. Her complex personality baffled and fascinated him, and he could not help fearing that somehow, by some subtle art, she might wring that secret from him. Torture wouldn't force it out of him, but those green eyes might read it. Yet—better to go quietly than be dragged or driven; he grunted assent and followed the messenger.

He found the house quiet. The lower room where Joaquin Smith had rested was empty now, and he mounted the stairs again steeling himself against the expected shock of Black Margot's presence. This time, however, he found her clothed, or half clothed by Ormiston standards, for she wore only the diminutive shorts and shirt that were her riding costume, and her dainty feet were bare. She sat in a deep chair beside the table, a flagon of wine at hand and a black cigarette in her fingers. Her jet hair was like a helmet of ebony against the ivory of her forehead and throat, and her green eyes like twin emeralds.

"Sit down," she said as he stood before her. "The delay is your loss, Hull. I would have dined with you."

"I grow strong enough on bread and cheese," he growled.

"You seem to." Fire danced in her eyes. "Hull, I am as strong as most men, but I believe those vast muscles of yours could overpower me as if I were some shrinking provincial girl. And yet..."

"And yet what?"

"And yet you are much like my black stallion Eblis. Your muscles are nearly as strong, but like him, I can goad you, drive you, lash you, and set you galloping in whatever direction I choose."

"Can you?" he snapped. "Don't try it." But the spell of her unearthly beauty was hard to face.

"But I think I shall try it," she cooed gently. "Hull, do you ever lie?"

"I do not."

"Shall I make you lie, then, Hull? Shall I make you swear such falsehoods that you will redden forever afterward at the thought of them? Shall I?"

"You can't!"

She smiled, then in altered tones, "Do you love me, Hull?"

"Love you? I hate—" He broke off suddenly.

"Do you hate me, Hull?" she asked gently.

"No," he groaned at last. "No, I don't hate you."

"But do you love me?" Her face was saintlike, earnest, pure, even the green eyes were soft now as the green of spring. "Tell me, do you love me?"

"No!" he ground out savagely, then flushed crimson at the smile on her lips. "That isn't a lie!" he blazed. "This sorcery of yours isn't love. I don't love your beauty. It's unnatural, hellish, and the gift of Martin Sair. It's a false beauty, like your whole life!"

"Martin Sair had little to do with my appearance," she said gently. "What *do* you feel for me, Hull, if not love?"

"I... don't know. I don't want to think of it!" He clenched a great fist. "Love? Call it love if you wish, but it's a hell's love that would find satisfaction in killing you!" But here his heart revolted again. "That isn't so," he ended miserably. "I couldn't kill you."

"Suppose," she proceeded gently, "I were to promise to abandon Joaquin, to be no longer Black Margot and Princess of the Empire, but to be only… Hull Tarvish's wife. Between Vail and me, which would you choose?"

He said nothing for a moment. "You're unfair," he said bitterly at last. "Is it fair to compare Vail and yourself? She's sweet and loyal and innocent, but you… *you* are Black Margot!"

"Nevertheless," she said calmly, "I think I shall compare us. Sora!" The fat woman appeared. "Sora, the wine is gone. Send the eldarch's daughter here with another bottle and a second goblet."

Hull stared appalled. "What are you going to do?"

"No harm to your little Weed. I promise no harm."

"But…" He paused. Vail's footsteps sounded on the stairs, and she entered timidly, bearing a tray with a bottle and a metal goblet. He saw her start as she perceived him, but she only advanced quietly, set the tray on the table, and backed toward the door.

"Wait a moment," said the Princess. She rose and moved to Vail's side as if to force the comparison on Hull. He could not avoid it; he hated himself for the thought, but it came regardless. Barefooted, the Princess Margaret was exactly the height of Vail in her lowheeled sandals, and she was the merest shade slimmer. But her startling black hair and her glorious green eyes seemed almost to fade the unhappy Ormiston girl to a colorless dun, and the coppery hair and blue eyes seemed water pale. It wasn't fair; Hull realized that it was like comparing candlelight to sunbeam, and he despised himself even for gazing.

"Hull," said the Princess, "which of us is the more beautiful ?"

He saw Vail's lips twitch fearfully, and he remained stubbornly silent.

"Hull," resumed the Princess, "which of us do you love?"

"I love Vail!" he muttered.

"But do you love her more than you love me?"

Once again he had recourse to silence.

"I take it," said the Princess, smiling, "that your silence means you love *me* the more. Am I right?"

He said nothing.

"Or am I wrong, Hull? Surely you can give little Vail the satisfaction of answering this question! For unless you answer I shall take the liberty of assuming that you love me the more. Now do you?"

He was in utter torment. His white lips twisted in anguish as he muttered finally, "Oh, God! Then yes!"

She smiled softly. "You may go," she said to the pallid and frightened Vail.

But for a moment the girl hesitated. "Hull," she whispered, "Hull, I know you said that to save me. I don't believe it, Hull, and I love you. I blame… her!"

"Don't!" he groaned. "Don't insult her."

The Princess laughed, "Insult *me?* Do you think I could be insulted by a bit of creeping dust as it crawls its way from cradle to grave?" She turned contemptuous green eyes on Vail as the terrified girl backed through the door.

"Why do you delight in torture?" cried Hull. "You're cruel as a cat. You're no less than a demon."

"That wasn't cruelty," said the Princess gently. "It was but a means of proving what I said, that your mighty muscles are well-broken to my saddle."

"If that needed proof," he muttered.

"It needed none. There's proof enough, Hull, in what's happening even now, if I judge the time rightly. I mean your Harriers slipping through their ancient sewer right into my trap behind the barn."

He was thunderstruck. "You… are you… you *must* be a witch!" he gasped.

"Perhaps. But it wasn't witchcraft that led me to put the thought of that sewer into your head, Hull. Do you remember now that it was *my* suggestion, given last evening there in the hallway? I knew quite well that you'd put the bait before the Harriers."

His brain was reeling. "But why… Why…?"

"Oh," she said indifferently, "it amuses me to see you play the traitor twice, Hull Tarvish."

* * * * * * * *

CHAPTER NINE
The Trap

THE PRINCESS stepped close to him, her magnificent eyes gentle as an angel's, the sweet curve of her lips in the ghost of a pouting smile. "Poor, strong, weak Hull Tarvish!" she breathed. "Now you shall have a lesson in the cost of weakness. I am not Joaquin, who fights benignly with his men's slides in the third notch. When *I* go to battle, my beams flash full, and there is burning flesh and bursting heart. Death rides with me."

He scarcely heard her. His gyrating mind struggled with an idea. The Harriers were creeping singly into the trap, but they could not all be through the tunnel. If he could warn them— His eyes shifted to the bell-pull in the hall beside the guard, the rope that tolled the bronze bell in the belfry to summon public gatherings, or to call aid to fight fires. Death, beyond doubt, if he rang it, but that was only a fair price to pay for expiation.

His great arm flashed suddenly, sweeping the Princess from her feet and crashing her dainty figure violently against the wall. He heard her faint "O-o-oh" of pain as breath left her and she dropped slowly to her knees, but he was already upon the startled guard, thrusting him up and over the rail of the stair-well to drop with a sullen thump below. And then he threw his weight on the bell-rope, and the great voice of bronze boomed out, again, and again.

But Black Margot was on her feet, with the green hell-sparks flickering in her eyes and her face a lovely mask of fury. Men came rushing up the stairs with drawn weapons, and Hull gave a last tug on the rope and turned to face death. Half a dozen weapons were on him.

"No... no!" gasped the Princess, struggling for the breath he had knocked out of her. "Hold him for me! Take him... to the barn!"

She darted down the stairway, her graceful legs flashing bare, her bare feet padding softly. After her six grim Empire men thrust Hull past the dazed guard sitting on the lower steps and out into a night where blue beams flashed and shots and yells sounded.

Behind the barn was comparative quiet, however, by the time Hull's captors had marched him there. A closepacked mass of dark figures huddled near the mouth of the ancient tunnel, where the bushes were trampled away, and a brown-clad file of Empire woods runners surrounded them. A few figures lay sprawled on the turf, and Hull smiled a little as he saw that some were Empire men. Then his eyes strayed to the Princess where she faced a dark-haired officer.

"How many, Lebeau?"

"A hundred and forty or fifty, Your Highness."

"Not half! Why are you not pursuing the rest through the tunnel?"

"Because, Your Highness, one of them pulled the shoring and the roof down upon himself, and blocked us off. We're digging him out now."

"By then they'll have left their burrow. Where does this tunnel end?" She strode over to Hull. "Hull, where does this tunnel end?" At his silence, she added. "No matter. They'd be through it before we could reach it." She spun back. "Lebeau! Burn down what we have and the rest we'll stamp out as we can." A murmur ran through the crowd of villagers that was collecting, and her eyes, silvery green in the moonlight, flickered over them. "And any sympathizers," she added coldly. "Except this man, Hull Tarvish."

File Ormson's great voice rumbled out of the mass of prisoners. "Hull! Hull! Was this trap your doing?"

Hull made no answer, but Black Margot herself replied. "No," she snapped, "but the warning bell was."

"Then why do you spare him?"

Her eyes glittered icy green. "To kill in my own way, Weed," she said in tones so cold that it was as if a winter wind had sent a shivering breath across the spring night. "I have my own account to collect from him."

Her eyes blazed chill emerald fire into Hull's. He met her glance squarely, and said in a low voice, "Do you grant any favors to a man about to die?"

"Not by custom," she replied indifferently. "Is it the safety of the eldarch's daughter? I plan no harm to her."

"It isn't that."

"Then ask it—though I am not disposed to grant favors to you, Hull Tarvish, who have twice laid hands of violence on me."

His voice dropped almost to a whisper. "It is the lives of my companions I ask."

She raised her eyebrows in surprise, then shook her ebony flame of hair. "How can I? I remained here purposely to wipe them out. Shall I release the half I have, only to destroy them with the rest?"

"I ask their lives," he repeated.

A curious, whimsical fire danced green in her eyes. "I will try," she promised, and turned to the officer, who was ranging his men so that the cross-fire of execution could not mow down his own ranks. "Lebeau!" she snapped. "Hold back a while."

She strode into the gap between the prisoners and her own men. Hand on hip she surveyed the Harriers, while moonlight lent her beauty an aura that was incredible, unearthly. There in the dusk of night she seemed no demon at all, but a girl, almost a child, and even Hull, who had learned well enough what she was, could not but sweep fascinated eyes from her jet hair to her tiny white feet.

"Now," she said, passing her glance over the group, "on my promise of amnesty, how many of you would join me?"

A stir ran through the mass. For a moment there was utter immobility, then, very slowly, two figures moved forward, and the stir became an angry murmur. Hull recognized the men; they were stragglers of the Confederation army, Ch'cago men, good fighters but merely mercenaries, changing sides as mood or advantage moved them. The murmur of the Harriers became an angry growl.

"You two," said the Princess, "are you Ormiston men?"

"No," said one. "Both of us come from the shores of Mitchin."

"Very well," she proceeded calmly. With a movement swift as arrow flight she snatched the weapon from her belt, the blue beam spat twice, and the men crumpled, one with face burned carbon-black, and both sending forth an odorous wisp of flesh-seared smoke.

She faced the aghast group. "Now," she said, "who is your leader?"

File Ormson stepped forth, scowling and grim. "What do you want of me?"

"Will you treat with me? Will your men follow your agreements?"

File nodded. "They have small choice."

"Good. Now that I have sifted the traitors from your ranks—for I will not deal with traitors—I shall make my offer." She smiled at the squat ironsmith. "I think I've served both of us by so doing," she said softly, and Hull gasped as he perceived the sweetness of the glance she bent on the scowling File. "Would you, with your great muscles and warrior's heart, follow a woman?"

The scowl vanished in surprise. "Follow you? *You?*"

"Yes." Hull watched her in fascination as she used her voice, her eyes, her unearthly beauty intensified by the moonlight, all on hulking File Ormson, behind whom the Harrier prisoners stood tense and silent. "Yes, I mean to follow me," she repeated softly. "You are brave men, all of you, now that I have weeded out the two cowards." She smiled wistfully, almost tenderly at the squat figure before her. "And you—you are a warrior."

"But..." File gulped, "...our others..."

"I promise you need not fight against your companions. I will release any of you who will not follow me. And your lands... it is your lands you fight for, is it not? I will not touch, not one acre save the eldarch's." She paused. "Well?"

Suddenly File's booming laugh roared out. "By God!" he swore. "If you mean what you say, there's nothing to fight about! For my part, I'm with you!" He turned on his men. "Who follows me?"

The group stirred. A few stepped forward, then a few more, and then, with a shout, the whole mass. "Good!" roared File. He raised his great hard hand to his heart in the Empire salute. "To Black... to the Princess Margaret!" he bellowed. "To a warrior!"

She smiled and dropped her eyes as if in modesty. When the cheer had passed, she addressed File Ormson again. "You will send men to your others?" she asked. "Let them come in on the same terms."

"They'll come!" growled File.

The Princess nodded. "Lebeau," she called, "order off your men. These are our allies."

The Harriers began to separate, drifting away with the crowd of villagers. The Princess stepped close to Hull, smiling maliciously up into his perplexed face. He scarcely knew whether to be glad or bitter, for indeed, though she had granted his request to spare his companions, she had granted it only at the cost of the destruction of the cause for which he had sacrificed everything. There were no Harriers any more, but he was still to die for them.

"Will you die happy now?" she cooed softly.

"No man dies happy," he growled.

"I granted your wish, Hull."

"If your promises can be trusted," he retorted bitterly. "You lied coolly enough to the Ch'cago men, and you made certain they were not loved by the Harriers before you killed them."

She shrugged. "I lie, I cheat, I swindle by whatever means comes to hand," she said indifferently, "but I do not break my given word. The Harriers are safe."

Beyond her, men came suddenly from the tunnel mouth, dragging something dark behind them.

"The Weed who pulled down the roof, Your Highness," said Lebeau.

She glanced behind her, and pursed her dainty lips in surprise. "The eldarch! The dotard died bravely enough." Then she shrugged. "He had but a few more years anyway."

But Vail slipped by with a low moan of anguish, and Hull watched her kneel desolately by her father's body. A spasm of pity shook him as he realized that now she was utterly, completely alone. Enoch had died in the ambush of the previous night, old Marcus lay dead here before her, and he was condemned to death. The three who loved her and the man she loved—all slain in two nights passing. He bent a slow, helpless, pitying smile on her, but there was nothing he could do or say.

And Black Margot, after the merest glance, turned back to Hull, "Now," she said, the ice in her voice again, "I deal with you!"

He faced her dumbly. "Will you have the mercy to deal quickly, then?" he muttered at last.

"Mercy? I do not know the word where you're concerned, Hull. Or rather I have been already too merciful. I spared your life three times... once at Joaquin's request at Eaglefoot Flow, once before the guardhouse, and once up there in the hallway." She moved closer. "I cannot bear the touch of violence, Hull, and you have laid violent hands on me twice. Twice!"

"Once was to save your life," he said, "and the other to rectify my own unwitting treason. And I spared your life three times too, Black Margot... once when I aimed from the church roof, once from the ambush in the west chamber, and once but a half hour ago, for I could have killed you with this fist of mine, had I wished to strike hard enough. I owe you nothing."

She smiled coldly. "Well argued, Hull, but you die none the less in the way I wish." She turned. "Back to the house!" she commanded, and he strode away between the six guards who still flanked him.

She led them into the lower room that had been the Master's. There she sat idly in a deep chair of ancient craftsmanship, lit a black cigarette at the lamp, and thrust her slim legs carelessly before her, gazing at Hull. But he, staring through the window behind her, could see the dark blot that was Vail Ormiston weeping beside the body of her father.

"Now," said the Princess, "how would you like to die, Hull?"

"Of old age!" he snapped. "And if you will not permit that, then as quickly as possible."

"I might grant the second," she observed. "I *might*."

The thought of Vail was still torturing him. At last he said, "Your Highness, is your courage equal to the ordeal of facing me alone? I want to ask something that I will not ask in others' ears."

She laughed contemptuously. "Get out," she snapped at the silent guards. "Hull, do you think *I fear you?* I tell you your great muscles and stubborn heart are no more than those of Eblis, the black stallion. Must I prove it again to you?"

"No," he muttered. "God help me, but I know it's true. I'm not the match for Black Margot."

"Nor is any other man," she countered. Then, more softly, "But if ever I do meet the man who can conquer me, if ever he exists, he *will* have something of you in him, Hull. Your great, slow strength, and your stubborn honesty, and your courage. I promise that." She paused, her face now pure as a marble saint's. "So say what you have to say, Hull. What do you ask?"

"My life," he said bluntly.

Her green eyes widened in surprise. "*You*, Hull? You beg your life? *You?*"

"Not for myself," he muttered. "There's Vail Ormiston weeping over her father. Enoch, who would have married her and loved her, is dead in last night's ambush, and if I die, she's left alone. I ask my life for her."

"Her troubles mean nothing to me," said Margaret of N'Orleans coldly.

"She'll *die* without someone... someone to help her through this time of torment."

"Let her die, then. Why do you death-bound cling so desperately to life, only to age and die anyway? Sometimes I myself would welcome death, and I have infinitely more to live for than you. Let her die, Hull, as I think you'll die in the next moment or so!"

Her hand rested on the stock of the weapon at her belt. "I grant your second choice," she said coolly. "The quick death."

CHAPTER TEN

Old Einar Again

BLACK MARGOT ground out her cigarette with her left hand against the polished wood of the table top, but her right rested inexorably on her weapon. Hull knew beyond doubt or question that he was about to die, and for a moment he considered the thought of dying fighting, of being blasted by the beam as he flung himself at her. Then he shook his head; he revolted at the idea of again trying violence on the exquisite figure he faced, who, though witch or demon, had the passionless purity and loveliness of divinity. It was easier to die passively, simply losing his thoughts in the glare of her unearthly beauty.

She spoke. "So die, Hull Tarvish," she said gently, and drew the blunt weapon.

A voice spoke behind him, a familiar, pleasant voice. "Do I intrude, Margaret?"

He whirled. It was Old Einar, thrusting his good-humored, wrinkled visage through the opening he had made in the doorway. He grinned at Hull, flung the door wider, and slipped into the room.

"Einar!" cried the Princess, springing from her chair. "Einar Olin! Are you still in the world?" Her tones took on suddenly the note of deep pity. "But so old... so old!"

The old man took her free hand. "It is forty years since last I saw you, Margaret... and I was fifty then."

"But so old!" she repeated. "Einar, have *I* changed?"

He peered at her. "Not physically, my dear. But from the stories that go up and down the continent, you are hardly the gay madcap that N'Orleans worshipped as the Princess Peggy, nor even the valiant little warrior they used to call the Maid of Orleans."

She had forgotten Hull, but the guards visible through the half open door still blocked escape. He listened fascinated, for it was almost as if he saw a new Black Margot.

"Was I ever the Princess Peggy?" she murmured. "I had forgotten... Well, Martin Sair can stave off age but he cannot halt the flow of time. But Einar... Einar, you were wrong to refuse him!"

"Seeing you, Margaret, I wonder instead if I were not very wise. Youth is too great a restlessness to bear for so long a time, and you have borne it less than a century. What will you be in another fifty years? In another hundred, if Martin Sair's art keeps its power? What will you be?"

She shook her head; her green eyes grew deep and sorrowful. "I don't know, Einar. I don't know."

"Well," he said placidly, "I am old, but I am contented. I wonder if you can say as much."

"I might have been different, Einar, had you joined us. I could have loved you, Einar."

"Yes," he agreed wryly. "I was afraid of that, and it was one of the reasons for my refusal. You see, I *did* love you, Margaret, and I chose to outgrow the torture rather than perpetuate it. That was a painful malady, loving you, and it took all of us at one time or another. 'Flame-struck', we used to call it." He smiled reflectively. "Are any left save me of all those who loved you?"

"Just Jorgensen," she answered sadly. "That is if he has not yet killed himself in his quest for the secret of the Ancient's wings. But he will."

"Well," said Olin dryly, "my years will yet make a mock of their immortality." He pointed a gnarled finger at Hull. "What do you want of my young friend here?"

Her eyes flashed emerald, and she drew her hand from that of Old Einar. "I plan to kill him."

"Indeed? And why?"

"Why?" Her voice chilled. "Because he struck me with his hands. Twice."

The old man smiled. "I shouldn't wonder if he had cause enough, Margaret. Memory tells me that I myself have had the same impulse."

"Then it's well you never yielded, Einar. Even you."

"Doubtless. But I think I shall ask you to forgive young Hull Tarvish."

"You know his name! Is he really your friend?"

Old Einar nodded. "I ask you to forgive him."

"Why should I?" asked the Princess. "Why do you think a word from you can save him?"

"I am still Olin," said the aged one, meeting her green eyes steadily with his watery blue ones. "I still carry Joaquin's seal."

"As if that could stop *me!*" But the cold fire died slowly in her gaze, and again her eyes were sad. "But you are still Olin, the Father of Power," she murmured. With a sudden gesture she thrust her weapon back into her belt. "I spare him again," she said, and then, in tones gone strangely dull, "I suppose I wouldn't have killed him anyway. It is a weakness of mine that I cannot kill those who love me in a certain way… a weakness that will cost me dear some day."

Olin twisted his lips in that skull-like smile, turning to the silent youth. "Hull," he said kindly, "you must have been born under fortunate stars. But if you're curious enough to tempt your luck further, listen to this old man's advice." His smile became a grin. "Beyond the western mountains there are some very powerful, very rare hunting cats called lions, which Martin Sair says are not native to this continent, but were brought here by the Ancients to be caged and gazed at, and occasionally trained. As to that I know nothing, but I do say this, Hull… go twist the tail of a lion before you again try the wrath of Black Margot. And now get out of here."

"Not yet, Hull," snapped the Princess. "I have still my score to settle with you." She turned back to Olin. "Where do you wander now, Einar?"

"To N'Orleans. I have some knowledge to give Jorgensen, and I am homesick besides for the Great City."

He paused. "I have seen Joaquin. Selui has fallen."

"I know. I ride to meet him tonight."

"He has sent representations to Ch'cago."

"Good!" she flashed. "Then there will be fighting." Then her eyes turned dreamy. "I have never seen the saltless seas," she added wistfully, "but I wonder if they can be as beautiful as the blue Gulf beyond N'Orleans."

But Old Einar shook his thin white hair. "What will be the end of this, Margaret?" he asked gently. "After Ch'cago is taken—for you will take it—what then?"

"Then the land north of the saltless seas, and east of them. N'York, and all the cities on the ocean shore."

"And then?"

"Then South America, I suppose."

"And *then*, Margaret?"

"Then? There is still Europe veiled in mystery, and Asia, Africa… all the lands known to the Ancients."

"And after all of them?"

"Afterwards," she replied wearily, "we can rest. The fierce destiny that drives Joaquin surely cannot drive him beyond the boundaries of the world."

"And so," said Olin, "you fight your way around the world so you can rest at the end of the journey. Then why not rest now, Margaret? Must you pillow your head on the globe of the planet?"

Fury flamed green in her eyes. She raised her hand and struck the old man across his lips, but it must have been lightly, for he still smiled.

"Fool!" she cried. "Then I will see to it that there is always war! Between me and Joaquin, if need be… or between me and anyone—*anyone*—so that I fight!" She paused panting. "Leave me, Einar," she said tensely. "I do not like the things you bring to mind."

Still smiling, the old man backed away. At the door he paused. "I will see you before I die, Margaret," he promised, and was gone.

She followed him to the doorway. "Sora!" she called. "Sora! I ride!"

Hull heard the heavy tread of the fat Sora, and in a moment she entered bearing the diminutive cothurns and a pair of glistening silver gauntlets on her hands, and then she too was gone.

Slowly, almost wearily, the Princess turned to face Hull, who had as yet permitted no gleam of hope to enter his soul, for he had experienced too much of her mockery to trust the promise of safety Old Einar had won for him. He felt only the fascination that she always bound about him, the spell of her unbelievable black hair and her glorious sea-green eyes, and all her unearthly beauty.

"Hull," she said gently, "what do you think of me now?"

"I think you are a black flame blowing cold across the world. I think a demon drives you."

"And do you hate me so bitterly?"

"I pray every second to hate you."

"Then see, Hull." With her little gauntleted fingers she took his great hands and placed them about the perfect curve of her throat. "Here I give you my life for the taking. You have only to twist once with these mighty hands of yours and Black Margot will be out of the world forever." She paused. "Must I beg you?"

Hull felt as if molten metal flowed upward through his arms from the touch of her white skin. His fingers were rigid as metal bars, and all the great strength of them could not put one feather's weight of pressure on the soft throat they circled. And deep in the lambent emerald flames that burned in her eyes he saw again the fire of mockery—jeering, taunting.

"You will not?" she said, lifting away his hands, but holding them in hers. "Then you do not hate me?"

"You know I don't," he groaned.

"And you do love me?"

"Please," he muttered. "Is it necessary again to torture me? I need no proof of your mastery."

"Then say you love me."

"Heaven forgive me for it;" he whispered, "but I do!"

She dropped his hands and smiled. "Then listen to me, Hull. You love little Vail with a truer love, and month by month memory fades before reality. After a while there will be nothing left in you of Black Margot, but there will be always Vail. I go now hoping never to see you again, but..." and her eyes chilled to green ice "...before I go I settle my score with you."

She raised her gauntleted hand. "This for your treachery!" she said, and struck him savagely across his right check. Blood spouted, there would be scars, but he stood stolid. "This for your violence!" she said, and the silver gauntlet tore his left check. Then her eyes softened. "And this," she murmured, "for your love!"

Her arms circled him, her body was warm against him, and her exquisite lips burned against his. He felt as if he embraced a flame for a moment, and then she was gone, and a part of his soul went with her. When he heard the hooves of the stallion Eblis pounding beyond the window, he turned and walked slowly out of the house to where Vail still crouched beside her father's body. She clung to him, wiped the blood from his cheeks, and strangely, her words were not of her father, nor of the sparing of Hull's life, but of Black Margot.

"I knew you lied to save me," she murmured. "I knew you never loved her."

And Hull, in whom there was no falsehood, drew her close to him and said nothing.

But Black Margot rode north from Selui through the night. In the sky before her were thin shadows leading phantom armies, Alexander the Great, Attila, Genghis Khan, Tamerlane, Napoleon, and clearer than all, the battle queen Semiramis. All the mighty conquerors of the past, and where were they, where were their empires, and where, even, were their bones? Far in the south were the graves of men who had loved her, all except Old Einar, who tottered like a feeble grey ghost across the world to find his.

At her side Joaquin Smith turned as if to speak, stared, and remained silent. He was not accustomed to the sight of tears in the eyes and on the cheeks of Black Margot.

(All conversation ascribed to the Princess Margaret in this story is taken verbatim from an anonymous volume published in Urbs in the year 186, called "Loves of the Black Flame." It is credited to Jacques Lebeau, officer in command of the Black Flame's personal guard.)

THE VORTEX BLASTER

E. E. SMITH, Ph.D.

The Lensman and the observer helped Storm into his heavily padded armor. Their movements were automatic—the ointment, the devices—THE Vortex Blaster!

SAFETY DEVICES that do not protect. The "unsinkable" ships that, before the days of Bergenholm and of atomic and cosmic energy, sank into the waters of the earth.

More particularly, safety devices which, while protecting against one agent of destruction, attract magnet-like another and worse. Such as the armored cable within the walls of a wooden house. It protects the electrical conductors within against accidental external shorts; but, inadequately grounded as it must of necessity be, it may attract and upon occasion has attracted the stupendous force of lightning. Then, fused, volatilized, flaming incandescent throughout the length, breadth, and height of a dwelling, that dwelling's existence thereafter is to be measured in minutes.

Specifically, four lightning rods. The lightning rods protecting the chromium, glass, and plastic home of Neal Cloud. Those rods were adequately grounded, grounded with copper-silver cables the bigness of a strong man's arm; for Neal Cloud, atomic physicist, knew his lightning and he was taking no chances whatever with the safety of his lovely wife and their three wonderful kids.

He did not know, he did not even suspect, that under certain conditions of atmospheric potential and of ground-magnetic stress his perfectly designed lightning-rod system would become a super-powerful magnet for flying vortices of atomic disintegration.

And now Neal Cloud, atomic physicist, sat at his desk in a strained, dull apathy. His face was a yellowish-gray white, his tendoned hands gripped rigidly the arms of his chair. His eyes, hard and lifeless, stared unseeingly past the small, three-dimensional block portrait of all that had made life worth living.

For his guardian against lightning had been a vortex-magnet at the moment when a luckless wight had attempted to abate the nuisance of a "loose" atomic vortex. That wight died, of course—they almost always do—and the vortex, instead of being destroyed, was simply broken up into an indefinite number of widely-scattered new vortices. And one of these bits of furious, uncontrolled energy, resembling more nearly a handful of material rived from a sun than anything else with which ordinary man is familiar, darted toward and crashed downward to earth through Neal Cloud's new house.

That home did not burn; it simply exploded. Nothing of it, in it, or around it stood a chance, for in a fractional second of time the place where it had been was a crater of seething, boiling lava—a crater which filled the atmosphere to a height of miles with poisonous vapors; which flooded all circumambient space with lethal radiations.

Originally published in Comet Stories, July 1941

Cosmically, the whole thing was infinitesimal. Ever since man learned how to liberate intra-atomic energy, the vortices of disintegration had been breaking out of control. Such accidents had been happening, were happening, and would continue indefinitely to happen. More than one world, perhaps, had been or would be consumed to the last gram by such loose atomic vortices. What of that? Of what real importance are a few grains of sand to an ocean beach five thousand miles long, a hundred miles wide, and ten miles deep?

And even to that individual grain of sand called "Earth"—or, in modern parlance, "Sol Three," or "Tellus of Sol", or simply "Tellus"—the affair was of negligible importance. One man had died; but, in dying, he had added one more page to the thick bulk of negative results already on file. That Mrs. Cloud and her children had perished was merely unfortunate. The vortex itself was not yet a real threat to Tellus. It was a "new" one, and thus it would be a long time before it would become other than a local menace. And well before that could happen—before even the oldest of Tellus' loose vortices had eaten away much of her mass or poisoned much of her atmosphere, her scientists would have solved the problem. It was unthinkable that Tellus, the point of origin and the very center of Galactic Civilization, should cease to exist.

BUT TO Neal Cloud the accident was the ultimate catastrophe. His personal universe had crashed in ruins; what was left was not worth picking up. He and Jo had been married… for almost twenty years and the bonds between them had grown stronger, deeper, truer with every passing day. And the kids It *couldn't* have happened… fate COULDN'T do this to him… but it had… it could. Gone… gone… GONE…

And to Neal Cloud, atomic physicist, sitting there at his desk in torn, despairing abstraction, with black maggots of thought gnawing holes in his brain, the catastrophe was doubly galling because of its cruel irony. For he was second from the top in the Atomic Research Laboratory; his life's work had been a search for a means of extinguishment of exactly such loose vortices as had destroyed his all.

His eyes focused vaguely upon the portrait. Clear, honest gray eyes… lines of character and of humor… sweetly curved lips, ready to smile or to kiss…

He wrenched his eyes away and scribbled briefly upon a sheet of paper. Then, getting up stiffly, he took the portrait and moved woodenly across the room to a furnace. As though enshrining it he placed the plastic block upon a refractory between the electrodes and threw a switch. After the flaming arc had done its work he turned and handed the paper to a tall man, dressed in plain gray leather, who had been watching him with quiet, understanding eyes. Significant enough to the initiated of the importance of this laboratory is the fact that it was headed by an Unattached Lensman.

"As of now, Phil, if it's QX with you."

The Gray Lensman took the document, glanced at it, and slowly, meticulously, tore it into sixteen equal pieces.

"Uh, uh, Storm," he denied, gently. "Not a resignation. Leave of absence, yes—indefinite—but not a resignation."

"Why?" It was scarcely a question; Cloud's voice was level, uninflected. "I won't be worth the paper I'd waste."

"Now, no," the Lensman conceded, "but the future's another matter. I haven't said anything so far, because to anyone who knew you and Jo as I knew you it was abundantly clear that nothing could be said." Two hands gripped and held. "For the future, though, four words were uttered long ago, that have never been improved upon. 'This, too, shall pass.'"

"You think so?"

Edward Elmer 'Doc' Smith, Ph.D. (1890 - 1965), author of the legendary *Lensman* and *Skylark* series' was one of the most popular SF authors of all-time and generally acknowledged as the 'Father of Modern Space Opera'. Smith's first book, *The Skylark of Space* (written between 1915 and 1919) was published in *Amazing Stories* in 1928 to universal acclaim, followed by two sequels, *Skylark Three* (1930) and *The Skylark of Valeron* (1934). But it was with the *Lensman* series (*Triplanetary, First Lensman, Galactic Patrol, Gray Lensman, Second Stage Lensman,* and *Children of The Lens*) that Smith forever changed science fiction. No writer before—and few since—wrote on such a vast scale. Spanning billions of years of galactic history, inconceivably vast distances, space battles involving literally millions of ships and weapons of super-science, multitudes of alien races, and galaxy-spanning organizations of evildoers the *Lensman* series set the standard for intergalactic adventure for decades and generations to come.

"I don't think so, Storm—I know so. I've been around a long time. You are too good a man, and the world has too much use for you, for you to go down permanently out of control. You've got a place in the world, and you'll be back—" A thought struck the Lensman, and he went on in an altered tone. "You wouldn't—but of course you wouldn't—you couldn't."

"I don't think so. No, I won't—that never was any kind of a solution to any problem."

Nor was it. Until that moment, suicide had not entered Cloud's mind, and he rejected it instantly. His kind of man did not take the easy way out.

After a brief farewell Cloud made his way to an elevator and was whisked down to the garage. Into his big blue DeKhotinsky Sixteen Special and away.

Through traffic so heavy that front-, rear-, and side-bumpers almost touched he drove with his wonted cool skill; even though, consciously, he did not know that the other cars were there. He slowed, turned, stopped, "gave her the oof," all in correct response to flashing signals in all shapes and colors—purely automatically. Consciously, he did not know where he was going, nor care. If he thought at all, his numbed brain was simply trying to run away from its own bitter imaging—which, if he had thought at all, he would have known to be a hopeless task. But he did not think; he simply acted, dumbly, miserably. His eyes saw, optically; his body reacted, mechanically; his thinking brain was completely in abeyance.

Into a one-way skyway he rocketed, along it over the suburbs and into the transcontinental super-highway. Edging inward, lane after lane, he reached the "unlimited" way—unlimited, that is, except for being limited to cars of not less than seven hundred horsepower, in perfect mechanical condition, driven by registered, tested drivers at speeds not less than one hundred and twenty-five miles an hour—flashed his registry number at the control station, and shoved his right foot down to the floor.

NOW EVERYONE knows that an ordinary DeKhotinsky Sporter will do a hundred and forty honestly-measured miles in one honestly measured hour; but very few ordinary drivers have ever found out how fast one of those brutal big souped-up Sixteens can wheel. They simply haven't got what it takes to open one up.

"Storm" Cloud found out that day. He held that two-and-a-half-ton Juggernaut on the road, wide open, for two solid hours. But it didn't help. Drive as he would, he could not outrun that which rode with him. Beside him and within him and behind him. For Jo was there. Jo and the kids, but mostly Jo. It was Jo's car as much as it was his. "Babe, the big blue ox," was Jo's pet name for it; because, like Paul Bunyan's fabulous beast, it was pretty nearly six feet between the eyes. Everything they had ever had was that way. She was in the seat beside him. Every dear, every sweet, every luscious, lovely memory of her was there... and behind him, just out of eye-corner visibility, were the three kids. And a whole lifetime of this loomed ahead—a vista of emptiness more vacuous far than the emptiest reaches of intergalactic space. Damnation! He couldn't stand much more of—

High over the roadway, far ahead, a brilliant octagon flared red. That meant "STOP!" in any language. Cloud eased up his accelerator, eased down his mighty brakes. He pulled up at the control station and a trimly-uniformed officer made a gesture.

"Sorry, sir," the policeman said, "but you'll have to detour here. There's a loose atomic vortex beside the road up ahead—

"Oh! It's Dr. Cloud!" Recognition flashed into the guard's eyes. "I didn't recognize you at first. You can go ahead, of course. It'll be two or three miles before you'll have to put on your armor; you'll know when better than anyone can tell you. They didn't tell us they were going to send for *you*. It's just a little new one, and the dope we got was that they were going to shove it off into the canyon with pressure."

"They didn't send for me." Cloud tried to smile. "I'm just driving around—haven't my armor along, even. So I guess I might as well go back."

He turned the Special around. A loose vortex—new. There might be a hundred of them, scattered over a radius of two hundred miles. Sisters of the one that had murdered his family—the hellish spawn of that accursed Number Eleven vortex that that damnably incompetent bungling ass had tried to blow up... Into his mind there leaped a picture, wire-sharp, of Number Eleven as he had last seen it, and simultaneously an idea hit him like a blow from a fist.

He thought. *Really* thought, now; cogently, intensely, clearly. If he could do it... could actually blow out the atomic flame of an atomic vortex... not exactly revenge, but... By Klono's brazen bowels, it would work—it'd *have* to work—he'd *make* it work! And grimly, quietly, but alive in every fiber now, he drove back toward the city practically as fast as he had come away.

IF THE Lensman was surprised at Cloud's sudden reappearance in the laboratory he did not show it. Nor did he offer any comment as his erstwhile first assistant went to various lockers and cupboards, assembling meters, coils, tubes, armor, and other paraphernalia and apparatus.

"Guess that's all I'll need, Chief," Cloud remarked, finally. "Here's a blank check. If some of this stuff shouldn't happen to be in usable condition when I get done with it, fill it out to suit, will you?"

"No," and the Lensman tore up the check just as he had torn up the resignation. "If you want the stuff for legitimate purposes, you're on Patrol business and it is the Patrol's risk. If, on the other hand, you think that you're going to try to snuff a vortex, the stuff stays here. That's final, Storm."

"You're right—and wrong, Phil," Cloud stated, not at all sheepishly. "I'm going to blow out Number One vortex with duodec, yes—but I'm *really* going to blow it out, not merely make a stab at it as an excuse for suicide, as you think."

"How?" The big Lensman's query was skepticism incarnate. "It can't be done, except by an almost impossibly fortuitous accident. You yourself have been the most bitterly opposed of us all to these suicidal attempts."

"I know it—I didn't have the solution myself until a few hours ago—it hit me all at once. Funny I never thought of it before; it's been right in sight all the time."

"That's the way with most problems," the Chief admitted. "Plain enough after you see the key equation. Well, I'm perfectly willing to be convinced, but I warn you that I'll take a lot of convincing—and someone else will do the work, not you."

"When I get done you'll see why I'll pretty nearly have to do it myself. But to convince you, exactly what is the knot?"

"Variability," snapped the older man. "To be effective, the charge of explosive at the moment of impact must match, within very close limits, the activity of the vortex itself. Too small a charge scatters it around, in vortices which, while much smaller than the original, are still large enough to be self-sustaining. Too large a charge simply rekindles the original vortex—still larger—in its original crater. And the activity that must be matched varies so tremendously, in magnitude, maxima, and minima, and the cycle is so erratic—ranging from seconds to hours without discoverable rhyme or reason—that all attempts to do so at any predetermined instant have failed completely. Why, even Kinnison and Cardynge and the Conference of Scientists couldn't solve it, any more than they could work out a tractor beam that could be used as a tow-line on one."

"Not exactly," Cloud demurred. "They found that it could be forecast, for a few seconds at least—length of time directly proportional to the length of the cycle in question—by an extension of the calculus of warped surfaces."

"Humph!" the Lensman snorted. "So what? What good is a ten-second forecast when it takes a calculating machine an hour to solve the equations... Oh!" He broke off, staring.

"Oh," he repeated, slowly, "I forgot that you're a lightning calculator—a mathematical prodigy from the day you were born—who never has to use a calculating machine even to compute an orbit... But there are other things."

"I'll say there are; plenty of them. I'd thought of the calculator angle before, of course, but there was a worse thing than variability to contend with..."

"What?" the Lensman demanded.

"Fear," Cloud replied, crisply. "At the thought of a hand-to-hand battle with a vortex my brain froze solid. Fear—the sheer, stark, natural human fear of death, that robs a man of the fine edge of control and brings on the very death that he is trying so hard to avoid. That's what had me stopped."

"Right... you may be right," the Lensman pondered, his fingers drumming quietly upon his desk. "And you are not afraid of death—now—even subconsciously. But tell me, Storm, please, that you won't invite it."

"I will not invite it, sir, now that I've got a job to do. But that's as far as I'll go in promising. I won't make any superhuman effort to avoid it. I'll take all due precautions, for the sake of the job, but if it gets me, what the hell? The quicker it does, the better—the sooner I'll be with Jo."

"You believe that?"

"Implicitly."

"The vortices are as good as gone, then. They haven't got any more chance than Boskone has of licking the Patrol."

"I'm afraid so," almost glumly. "The only way for it to get me is for me to make a mistake, and I don't feel any coming on."

"But what's your angle?" the Lensman asked, interest lighting his eyes. "You can't use the customary attack; your time will be too short."

"Like this," and, taking down a sheet of drafting paper, Cloud sketched rapidly. "This is the crater, here, with the vortex at the bottom, there. From the observers' instruments or from a shielded set-up of my own I get my data on mass, emission, maxima, minima, and so on. Then I have them make me three duodec bombs—one on the mark of the activity I'm figuring on shooting at, and one each five percent over and under that figure—cased in neocarballoy of exactly the computed thickness to last until it gets to the center of the vortex. Then I take off in a flying suit, armored and shielded, say about here..."

"If you take off at all, you'll take off in a suit, inside a one-man flitter," the Lensman interrupted. "Too many instruments for a suit, to say nothing of bombs, and you'll need more screen than a suit can deliver. We can adapt a flitter for bomb-throwing easily enough."

"QX; that would be better, of course. In that case, I set my flitter into a projectile trajectory like this, whose objective is the center of the vortex, there. See? Ten seconds or so away, at about this point, I take my instantaneous readings, solve the equations at that particular warped surface for some certain zero time..."

"But suppose that the cycle won't give you a ten-second solution?"

"Then I'll swing around and try again until a long cycle *does* show up."

"QX. It will, sometime."

"Sure. Then, having everything set for zero time, and assuming that the activity is somewhere near my postulated value..."

"Assume that it isn't—it probably won't be," the Chief grunted.

"I accelerate or decelerate—"

"Solving new equations all the while?"

"Sure—don't interrupt so—until at zero time the activity, extrapolated to zero time, matches one of my bombs. I cut that bomb loose, shoot myself off in a sharp curve, and Z-W-E-E-T—POWIE! She's out!" With an expressive, sweeping gesture.

"You hope," the Lensman was frankly dubious. "And there you are, right in the middle of that explosion, with two duodec bombs outside your armor—or just inside your flitter."

"Oh, no. I've shot them away several seconds ago, so that they explode somewhere else, nowhere near me."

"*I* hope. But do you realize just how busy a man you are going to be during those ten or twelve seconds?"

"Fully." Cloud's face grew somber. "But I will be in full control. I won't be afraid of anything that can happen—*anything*. And," he went on, under his breath, "that's the hell of it."

"QX," the Lensman admitted finally, "you can go. There are a lot of things you haven't mentioned, but you'll probably be able to work them out as you go along. I think I'll go out and work with the boys in the lookout station while you're doing your stuff. When are you figuring on starting?"

"How long will it take to get the flitter ready?"

"A couple of days. Say we meet you there Saturday morning?"

"Saturday the tenth, at eight o'clock. I'll be there."

AND AGAIN Neal Cloud and Babe, the big blue ox, hit the road. And as he rolled the physicist mulled over in his mind the assignment to which he had set himself.

Like fire, only worse, intra-atomic energy was a good servant, but a terrible master.

Man had liberated it before he could really control it. In fact, control was not yet, and perhaps never would be, perfect. Up to a certain size and activity, yes. They, the millions upon millions of self-limiting ones, were the servants. They could be handled, fenced in, controlled; indeed, if they were not kept under an exciting bombardment and very carefully fed, they would go out. But at long intervals, for some one of a dozen reasons—science knew *so* little, fundamentally, of the true inwardness of the intra-atomic reactions—one of these small, tame, self-limiting vortices flared, nova-like, into a large, wild, self-sustaining one. It ceased being a servant then, and became a master. Such flare-ups occurred, perhaps, only once or twice in a century on Earth; the trouble was that they were so utterly, damnably *permanent*. They never went out. And no data were ever secured: for every living thing in the vicinity of a flare-up died; every instrument and every other solid thing within a radius of a hundred feet melted down into the reeking, boiling slag of its crater.

Fortunately, the rate of growth was slow—as slow, almost, as it was persistent—otherwise Civilization would scarcely have had a planet left. And unless something could be done about loose vortices before too many years, the consequences would be

really serious. That was why his laboratory had been established in the first place.

Nothing much had been accomplished so far. The tractor beam that would take hold of them had never been designed. Nothing material was of any use; it melted. Pressors worked, after a fashion: it was by the use of these beams that they shoved the vortices around, off into the waste places—unless it proved cheaper to allow the places where they had come into being to remain waste places. A few, through sheer luck, had been blown into self-limiting bits by duodec. Duodecaplylatomate, the most powerful, the most frightfully detonant explosive ever invented upon all the known planets of the First Galaxy. But duodec had taken an awful toll of life. Also, since it usually scattered a vortex instead of extinguishing it, duodec had actually caused far more damage than it had cured.

No end of fantastic schemes had been proposed, of course; of varying degrees of fantasy. Some of them sounded almost practical. Some of them had been tried; some of them were still being tried. Some, such as the perennially-appearing one of building a huge hemispherical hull in the ground under and around the vortex, installing an inertialess drive, and shooting the whole neighborhood out into space, were perhaps feasible from an engineering standpoint.

They were, however, potentially so capable of making things worse that they would not be tried save as last-ditch measures. In short, the control of loose vortices was very much an unsolved problem.

NUMBER ONE vortex, the oldest and worst upon Tellus, had been pushed out into the Badlands; and there, at eight o'clock on the tenth, Cloud started to work upon it.

The "lookout station," instead of being some such ramshackle structure as might have been deduced from the Lensman's casual terminology, was in fact a fully-equipped observatory. Its staff was not large—eight men worked in three staggered eight-hour shifts of two men each—but the instruments! To develop them had required hundreds of man-years of time and near-miracles of research, not the least of the problems having been that of developing shielded conductors capable of carrying truly through five-ply screens of force the converted impulses of the very radiations against which those screens were most effective. For the observatory, and the one long approach to it as well, had to be screened heavily; without such protection no life could exist there.

This problem and many others had been solved, however, and there the instruments were. Every phase and factor of the vortex's existence and activity were measured and recorded continuously, throughout every minute of every day of every year. And all of these records were summed up, integrated, into the "Sigma" curve. This curve, while only an incredibly and senselessly tortuous line to the layman's eye, was a veritable mine of information to the initiate.

Cloud glanced along the Sigma curve of the previous forty-eight hours and scowled, for one jagged peak, scarcely an hour old, actually punched through the top line of the chart.

"Bad, huh, Frank?" he grunted.

"Plenty bad, Storm, and getting worse," the observer assented. "I wouldn't wonder if Carlowitz were right, after all—if she ain't getting ready to blow her top I'm a Zabriskan fontema's maiden aunt."

"No periodicity—no equation, of course." It was a statement, not a question. The Lensman ignored as completely as did the observer, if not as flippantly, the distinct possibility that at any moment the observatory and all that it contained might be resolved into their component atoms.

"None whatever," came flatly from Cloud. He did not need to spend hours at a calculating machine; at one glance he *knew*, without knowing how he knew, that no equation could be made to fit even the weighted-average locus of that wildly-shifting Sigma curve. "But most of the cycles cut this ordinate here—seven fifty-one—so I'll take that for my value. That means nine point nine oh six kilograms of duodec basic charge, with one five percent over and one five percent under that for alternates. Neocarballoy casing, fifty-three millimeters on the basic, others in proportion. On the wire?"

"It went out as you said it," the observer reported. "They'll have 'em here in fifteen minutes."

"QX—I'll get dressed, then."

The Lensman and the observer helped him into his cumbersome, heavily-padded armor. They checked his instruments, making sure that the protective devices of the suit were functioning at full efficiency. Then all three went out to the flitter. A tiny speedster, really; a torpedo bearing the stubby wings and the ludicrous tail-surfaces, the multifarious driving-, braking-, side-, top-, and under-jets so characteristic of the tricky, cranky, but ultra-maneuverable breed. But this one had something that the ordinary speedster or flitter did not carry; spaced around the needle beak there yawned the open muzzles of a triplex bomb-thrower.

More checking. The Lensman and the armored Cloud both knew that every one of the dozens of instruments upon the flitter's special board was right to the hair; nevertheless each one was compared with the master-instrument of the observatory.

THE BOMBS arrived and were loaded in; and Cloud, with a casually-waved salute, stepped into the tiny operating compartment. The massive door—flitters have no airlocks, as the whole midsection is scarcely bigger than an airlock would have to be—rammed shut upon its fiber gaskets, the heavy toggles drove home. A cushioned form closed in upon the pilot, leaving only his arms and lower legs free.

Then, making sure that his two companions had ducked for cover, Cloud shot his flitter into the air and toward the seething inferno which was Loose Atomic Vortex Number One. For it was seething, no fooling; and it was an inferno. The crater was a ragged, jagged hole a full mile from lip to lip and perhaps a quarter of that in depth. It was not, however, a perfect cone, for the floor, being largely incandescently molten, was practically level except for a depression at the center, where the actual vortex lay. The walls of the pit were steeply, unstably irregular, varying in pitch and shape with the hardness and refractoriness of the strata composing them. Now a section would glare into an unbearably blinding white puffing away in sparkling vapor. Again, cooled by an inrushing blast of air, it would subside into an angry scarlet, its surface crawling in a sluggish flow of lava. Occasionally a part of the wall might even go black, into pockmarked scoriae or into brilliant planes of obsidian.

For always, somewhere, there was an enormous volume of air pouring into that crater. It rushed in as ordinary air. It came out, however, in a ragingly-uprushing pillar, as—as something else. No one knew—or knows yet, for that matter—exactly what a loose vortex does to the molecules and atoms of air. In fact, due to the extreme variability already referred to, it probably does not do the same thing for more than an instant at a time.

That there is little actual combustion is certain; that is, except for the forced combination of nitrogen, argon, xenon, and krypton with oxygen. There is, however, consumption: plenty of consumption. And what that incredibly intense bombardment impinges up is... is altered. Profoundly and obscuredly altered, so that the atmosphere emitted from the crater is quite definitely no longer air as we know it. It may be corrosive, it may be poisonous in one or another of a hundred fashions, it may be merely new and different; but it is no longer the air which we human beings are used to breathing. And it is this fact, rather than the destruction of the planet itself, which would end the possibility of life upon Earth's surface.

* * * * * * * *

IT IS difficult indeed to describe the appearance of a loose atomic vortex to those who have never seen one; and, fortunately, most people never have. And practically all of its frightful radiation lies in those octaves of the spectrum which are invisible to the human eye. Suffice it to say, then, that it had an average effective surface temperature of about fifteen thousand degrees absolute—two and one-half times as hot as the sun of Tellus—and that it was radiating every frequency possible to that incomprehensible temperature, and let it go at that.

And Neal Cloud, scurrying in his flitter through that murky, radiation-riddled atmosphere, setting up equations from the readings of his various meters and gauges and solving those equations almost instantaneously in his mathematical-prodigy's mind, sat appalled. For the activity level was, and even in its lowest dips remained, far above the level he had selected. His skin began to prickle and to burn. His eyes began to smart and to ache. He knew what those symptoms meant; even the flitter's powerful screens were not stopping all the radiation; even his suit-screens and his special goggles were not stopping what leaked through. But he wouldn't quit yet; the activity might—probably would—take a nose-dive any instant. If it did, he'd have to be ready. On the other hand, it might blow up at any instant, too.

There were two schools of mathematical thought upon that point. One held that the vortex, without any essential change in its physical condition or nature, would keep on growing bigger. Indefinitely, until, uniting with the other vortices of the planet, it had converted the entire mass of the world into energy.

The second school, of which the forementioned Carlowitz was the loudest voice, taught that at a certain stage of development the internal energy of the vortex would become so great that generation-radiation equilibrium could not be maintained. This would, of course, result in an explosion; the nature and consequences of which this Carlowitz was wont to dwell upon in ghoulishly mathematical glee. Neither school, however, could prove its point—or, rather, each school proved its point, by means of unimpeachable mathematics—and each hated and derided the other, loudly and heatedly.

And now Cloud, as he studied through his almost opaque defenses that indescribably ravening fireball, that esuriently rapacious monstrosity which might very well have come from the deepest pit of the hottest hell of mythology, felt strongly inclined to agree with Carlowitz. It didn't seem possible that anything *could* get any worse than that without exploding. And such an explosion, he felt sure, would certainly blow everything for miles around into the smitheriest kind of smithereens.

The activity of the vortex stayed high, 'way too high. The tiny control room of the flitter grew hotter and hotter. His skin burned and his eyes ached worse. He touched a communicator stud and spoke.

"Phil? Better get me three more bombs. Like these, except up around..."

"I don't check you. If you do that, it's apt to drop to a minimum and stay there," the Lensman reminded him. "It's completely unpredictable, you know."

"It may, at that... so I'll have to forget the five percent margin and hit it on the nose or not at all. Order me up two more, then—one at half of what I've got here, the other double it," and he reeled off the figures for the charge and the casing of the explosive. "You might break out a jar of burn-dressing, too. Some fairly hot stuff is leaking through."

"We'll do that. Come down, fast!"

Cloud landed. He stripped to the skin and the observer smeared his every square inch of epidermis with the thick, gooey stuff that was not only a highly efficient screen against radiation, but also a sovereign remedy for new radiation burns. He exchanged his goggles for a thicker, darker, heavier pair. The two bombs arrived and were substituted for two of the original load.

"I thought of something while I was up there," Cloud informed the observers then. "Twenty kilograms of duodec is nobody's firecracker, but it may be the least of what's going to go off. Have you got any idea of what's going to become of the energy inside that vortex when I blow it out?"

"Can't say that I have." The Lensman frowned in thought. "No data."

"Neither have I. But I'd say that you better go back to the new station—the one you were going to move to if it kept on getting worse."

"But the instruments..." the Lensman was thinking, not of the instruments themselves, which were valueless in comparison with life, but of the records those instruments would make. Those records were priceless.

"I'll have everything on the tapes in the flitter," Cloud reminded.

"But suppose..."

"That the flitter stops one, too—or doesn't stop it, rather? In that case, your back station won't be there, either, so it won't make any difference." How mistaken Cloud was!

"QX," the Chief decided. "We'll leave when you do—just in case."

AGAIN IN air, Cloud found that the activity, while still high, was not too high, but that it was fluctuating too rapidly. He could not get even five seconds of trustworthy prediction, to say nothing of ten. So he waited, as close as he dared remain to that horrible center of disintegration.

The flitter hung poised in air, motionless, upon softly hissing under-jets. Cloud knew to a fraction his height above the ground. He knew to a fraction his distance from the vortex. He knew with equal certainty the density of the atmosphere and the exact velocity and direction of the wind. Hence, since he could also read closely enough the momentary variations in the cyclonic storms within the crater, he could compute very easily the course and velocity necessary to land the bomb in the exact center of the vortex at any given instant of time. The hard part—the thing that no one had as yet succeeded in doing—was to predict, for a time far enough ahead to be of any use, a usably close approximation to the vortex's quantitative activity. For, as has been said, he had to over-blast, rather than under-, if he could not hit it "on the nose:" to under-blast would scatter it all over the state.

Therefore Cloud concentrated upon the dials and gauges before him; concentrated with every fiber of his being and every cell of his brain.

Suddenly, almost imperceptibly, the Sigma curve gave signs of flattening out. In that instant Cloud's mind pounced. Simultaneous equations: nine of them, involving nine unknowns. An integration in four dimensions. No matter—Cloud did not solve them laboriously, one factor at a time. Without knowing how he had arrived at it, he knew the answer; just as the Posenian or the Rigellian is able to perceive every separate component particle of an opaque, three-dimensional solid, but without being able to explain to anyone how his sense of perception works. It just *is*, that's all.

Anyway, by virtue of whatever sense or ability it is which makes a mathematical prodigy what he is, Cloud knew that in exactly eight and three-tenths seconds from that observed instant the activity of the vortex would be slightly—but not too far—under the coefficient of his heaviest bomb. Another flick of his mental trigger and he knew the exact velocity he would require. His hand swept over the studs, his right foot tramped down, hard, upon the firing lever; and, even as the quivering flitter shot forward under eight Tellurian gravities of acceleration, he knew to the thousandth of a second how long he would have to hold that acceleration to attain that velocity. While not really long—in seconds—it was much too long for comfort. It took him much closer to the vortex than he wanted to be; in fact, it took him right out over the crater itself.

But he stuck to the calculated course, and at the precisely correct instant he cut his drive and released his largest bomb. Then, so rapidly that it was one blur of speed, he again kicked on his eight G's of drive and started to whirl around as only a speedster or a flitter can whirl. Practically unconscious from the terrific resultant of the linear and angular accelerations, he ejected the two smaller bombs. He did not care particularly where they lit, just so they didn't light in the crater or near the observatory, and he had already made certain of that. Then, without waiting even to finish the whirl or to straighten her out in level flight, Cloud's still-flying hand darted toward the switch whose closing would energize the Bergenholm and make the flitter inertialess.

Too late. Hell was out for noon, with the little speedster still inert. Cloud had moved fast, too; trained mind and trained body had been working at top speed and in perfect coordination. There just simply hadn't been enough time. If he could have got what he wanted, ten full seconds, or even nine, he could have made it, but…

IN SPITE of what happened, Cloud defended his action, then and thereafter. Damnitall, he *had* to take the eight-point-three second reading! Another tenth of a second and his bomb wouldn't have fitted—he didn't have the five percent leeway he wanted, remember. And no, he couldn't wait for another match, either. His screens were leaking like sieves, and if he had waited for another chance they would have picked him up fried to a greasy cinder in his own lard!

The bomb sped truly and struck the target in direct central impact, exactly as scheduled. It penetrated perfectly. The neo-carballoy casing lasted just long enough—that frightful charge of duodec exploded, if not exactly at the center of the vortex, at least near enough to the center to do the work. In other words, Cloud's figuring had been close—very close. But the time had been altogether too short.

The flitter was not even out of the crater when the bomb went off. And not only the bomb. For Cloud's vague forebodings were materialized, and more; the staggeringly immense energy of the vortex merged with that of the detonating duodec to form an utterly incomprehensible whole.

In part the hellish flood of boiling lava in that devil's cauldron was beaten downward into a bowl by the sheer, stupendous force of the blow; in part it was hurled abroad in masses, in gouts and streamers. And the raging wind of the explosion's front seized the fragments and tore and worried them to bits, hurling them still faster along their paths of violence. And air, so densely compressed as to be to all intents and purposes a solid, smote the walls of the crater. Smote them so that they crumbled, crushed outward through the hard-packed ground, broke up into jaggedly irregular blocks which hurtled, screamingly, away through the atmosphere.

Also the concussion wave, or the explosion front, or flying fragments, or something, struck the two loose bombs, so that they too exploded and added their contribution to the already stupendous concentration of force. They were not close enough to the flitter to wreck it of themselves, but they were close enough so that they didn't do her—or her pilot—a bit of good.

The first terrific wave buffeted the flyer while Cloud's right hand was in the air, shooting across the panel to turn on the Berg. The impact jerked the arm downward and sidewise, both bones of the forearm snapping as it struck the ledge. The second one, an instant later, broke his left leg. Then the debris began to arrive.

Chunks of solid or semi-molten rock slammed against the hull, knocking off wings and control-surfaces. Gobs of viscous slag slapped it liquidly, freezing into and clogging up jets and orifices. The little ship was hurled hither and yon, in the grip of forces she could no more resist than can the floating leaf resist the waters of a cataract. And Cloud's brain was as addled as an egg by the vicious concussions which were hitting him from so many different directions and so nearly all at once. Nevertheless, with his one arm and his one leg and the few cells of his brain that were still at work, the physicist was still in the fight.

By sheer force of will and nerve he forced his left hand across the gyrating key-bank to the Bergenholm switch. He snapped it, and in the instant of its closing a vast, calm peace descended, blanket-like. For, fortunately, the Berg still worked; the flitter and all her contents and appurtenances were inertialess. Nothing material could buffet her or hurt her now; she would waft effortlessly away from a feather's lightest possible touch.

Cloud wanted to faint then, but he didn't—quite. Instead, foggily, he tried to look back at the crater. Nine-tenths of his visiplates were out of commission, but he finally got a view. Good—it was out. He wasn't surprised; he had been quite confident that it would be. It wasn't scattered around, either. It *couldn't* be, for his only possibility of smearing the shot was on the upper side, not the lower.

HIS NEXT effort was to locate the secondary observatory, where he had to land, and in that too he was successful. He had enough intelligence left to realize that, with practically all of his jets clogged and his wings and tail shot off, he couldn't land his little vessel inert. Therefore he would have to land her free.

And by dint of light and extremely unorthodox use of what jets he had left in usable shape he did land her free, almost within the limits of the observatory's field; and having landed, he inerted her.

But, as has been intimated, his brain was not working so well; he had held his ship inertialess quite a few seconds longer than he thought, and he did not even think of the buffetings she had taken. As a result of these things, however, her intrinsic velocity did not match, anywhere near exactly, that of the ground upon which she lay. Thus, when Cloud cut his Bergenholm, restoring thereby to the flitter the absolute velocity and inertia she had had before going free, there resulted a distinctly anti-climactic crash.

There was a last terrific bump as the motionless vessel collided with the equally motionless ground; and "Storm" Cloud, vortex blaster, went out like the proverbial light.

Help came, of course; and on the double. The pilot was unconscious and the flitter's door could not be opened from the outside, but those were not insuperable obstacles. A plate, already loose, was sheared away; the pilot was carefully lifted out of his prison and rushed to Base Hospital in the "meat-can" already in attendance.

And later, in a private office of that hospital, the gray-clad Chief of the Atomic Research Laboratory sat and waited—but not patiently.

"How is he, Lacy?" he demanded, as the Surgeon-General entered the room. "He's going to live, isn't he?"

"Oh, yes, Phil—definitely yes," Lacy replied, briskly. "He has a good skeleton, very good indeed. The burns are superficial and will yield quite readily to treatment. The deeper, delayed effects of the radiation to which he was exposed can be neutralized entirely effectively. Thus he will not need even a Phillips's treatment for the replacement of damaged parts, except possibly for a few torn muscles and so on."

"But he was smashed up pretty badly, wasn't he? I know that he had a broken arm and a broken leg, at least."

"Simple fractures only—entirely negligible." Lacy waved aside with an airy gesture such small ills as broken bones. "He'll be out in a few weeks."

"How soon can I see him?" the Lensman-physicist asked. "There are some important things to take up with him, and I've got a personal message for him that I must give him as soon as possible."

Lacy pursued his lips. Then:

"You may see him now," he decided. "He is conscious, and strong enough. Not too long, though, Phil—fifteen minutes at most."

"QX, and thanks," and a nurse led the visiting Lensman to Cloud's bedside.

"Hi, Stupe!" he boomed, cheerfully. "'Stupe' being short for stupendous, not 'stupid'."

"Hi, Chief. Glad to see somebody. Sit down."

"You're the most-wanted man in the Galaxy," the visitor informed the invalid, "not excepting even Kimball Kinnison. Look at this spool of tape, and it's only the first one. I brought it along for you to read at your leisure. As soon as any planet finds out that we've got a sure-enough vortex-blower-outer, an expert who can really call his shots—and the news travels mighty fast—that planet sends in a double-urgent, Class A-Prime demand for first call upon your services.

"Sirius IV got in first by a whisker, it seems, but Aldebaran II was so close a second that it was a photo finish, and all the channels have been jammed ever since. Canopus, Vega, Rigel, Spica. They all want you. Everybody, from Alsakan to Vandemar and back. We told them right off that we would not receive personal delegations—we had to almost throw a couple of pink-haired Chickladorians out bodily to make them believe that we meant it—and that the age and condition of the vortex involved, not priority of requisition, would govern, QX?"

"Absolutely," Cloud agreed. "That's the only way it could be, I should think."

"So forget about this psychic trauma... No, I don't mean that," the Lensman corrected himself hastily. "You know what I mean. The will to live is the most important factor in any man's recovery, and too many worlds need you too badly to have you quit now. Not?"

"I suppose so," Cloud acquiesced, but somberly. "I'll get out of here in short order. And I'll keep on pecking away until one of those vortices finishes what this one started."

"You'll die of old age then, son," the Lensman assured him. "We got full data—all the information we need. We know exactly what to do to your screens. Next time nothing will come through except light, and only as much of that as you feel like admitting. You can wait as close to a vortex as you please, for as long as you please; until you get exactly the activity and time-interval that you want. You will be just as comfortable and just as safe as though you were home in bed."

"Sure of that?"

"Absolutely—or at least, as sure as we can be of anything that hasn't happened yet. But I see that your guardian angel here is eyeing her clock somewhat pointedly, so I'd better be doing a flit before they toss me down a shaft. Clear ether, Storm!"

"Clear ether, Chief!"

And that is how "Storm" Cloud, atomic physicist, became the most narrowly-specialized specialist in all the annals of science: how he became "Storm" Cloud, Vortex Blaster—the Galaxy's only vortex blaster.

The End

SAUCY BLAINE:

DEADFEAR

ART AND STORY © RON WILBER • 10

OUT IN THE DEPTHS OF SPACE, AN INTERGALACTIC TRADE FREIGHTER HAS BECOME THE FOCUS OF A MYSTERY— EVERYONE STATIONED THERE HAS DIED OF FRIGHT.
WHAT IS THE CAUSE? WILL SAUCY BLAINE, THE BRAVE SPACE PATROL HEROINE, BECOME A VICTIM OF THIS STRANGE CURSE?

SAUCY LOCATES THE MYSTERY SHIP AND MOVES IN TO DOCK WITH IT.
AS SAUCY MAKES HER WAY THROUGH THE FREIGHTER SHE NEVER NOTICES A WEIRD CREATURE IN THE DARKNESS.
WITHOUT WARNING, THE ODD BEAST BURIES THE TIP OF ITS POINTED TAIL INTO SAUCY BLAINE'S THIGH.
OUCH! WHAT?!!! OMIGOSH. I FEEL DIZZY... I...
ZEECH IS CONCERNED AS SAUCY'S ASPECT CHANGES INTO ONE OF TERROR.
OUR PET HAS DONE IT'S WORK ON THE FAMOUS SAUCY BLAINE!
A LUCKY BREAK!
2.

IT HAS STUNG ME AS WELL!
IT IS GOOD THAT WE CARRY PLENTY OF ANTIDOTE ON OUR BELTS!
ZEECH GRABS A VIAL.
OW!
SAUCY'S HEARTRATE HAS INCREASED WITH HER LEVEL OF TERROR. SHE COULD DIE OF FEAR.
ZEECH PREPARES TO USE THE ANTIDOTE.
HE MUST SAVE HIS FRIEND.
MY HEAD IS CLEARING, THANK YOU, ZEECH.
THOSE FIENDS USE THAT CREATURE TO KEEP THIS SHIP OPEN FOR THEMSELVES.
TIME TO SHUT THEIR OPERATION DOWN!
3.

SO THAT'S IT, SPACE SMUGGLERS!
SAUCY BLAINE'S RAY-GUN BLASTS ONE OF THE CRIMINALS, AND THE OTHERS ARE QUICK TO SURRENDER.
LATER-
QUITE FASCINATING, AN ANIMAL THAT KILLS IT'S PREY BY INJECTING THEM WITH A SERUM PRODUCING INTENSE FEAR.
WE MUST STUDY THIS!
I HOPE YOU UNDERSTAND, SAUCY.
THAT'S ALRIGHT ADMIRAL, I THINK I GOT THE POINT!
THE END

RON WILBER is, simply, a unique artist whose technique and talent has developed in quantum leaps over 20-plus years of illustrating science fiction, fantasy, pulp heroes, and more... He truly is one of the finest illustrators who ever placed ink on paper.

I've followed his work over many years... from *Echoes* to *Golden Perils* to all the other myriad pulpzines and books that he's lent his talent to... And then he disappeared...

I ALWAYS HAD heard about "The Controversy" regarding Wilber's artwork; the semi-nude pieces where an actual female nipple is shown, his scantily-clad heroines, and the rest... but it all seemed so ridiculous to me. Most of the world's greatest artistic creators paid tribute and homage to the wonderful female, and male, forms. To me, there is a difference between nudity and pornography... Ron Wilber never crossed that line, and the outcry against his work truly baffles me to this day.

When I first began working with Ron myself, I quickly realized that he's not only talented, but a true gentleman as well... and even though he was considered an "outcast", he continued with his passion for ART...

He told me something, on the phone one day, that I will never forget...

"Drawing is like breathing to me. I can't NOT do it."

SO EVEN when his work was criticized, he still continued on his path, following his true calling as an illustrator of stories... And it's my very proud pleasure to present this portfolio of Ron Wilber's artwork... Many of these pieces have never been published, or even seen by anyone, before now...

Savor them... for like all fine art, it will touch your soul, and inspire your imagination... And for an artist, that is the best legacy they can leave behind...

They say a picture speaks a thousand words...

Ron Hanna

STARTLING
ECHOES
27
PRESENTS
FADING
SHADOWS!
© WILBER • 86

©WILBER·89
ART©WILBER·86
"THE GRUESOME THING WITH ITS WEAVING TENTACLES STOOD BESIDE THE GIRL... ON THE OTHER SIDE STOOD A DEFORMED MONSTER... A SHARPENED METAL PIPE INSERTED IN THE VICTIM'S SIDE." FROM "THE CITY CONDEMNED TO HELL." THE OCTOPUS
©WILBER·03

©WILBER

©WILBER•92

©WILBER•91

40
BLACK BOOK
ECHOES
MAGAZINE
abyrinth
of MONSTER
A SPICY MYSTERY
BASED ON A STORY BY ROBERT LESLIE BELLEM
ART AND STORY ©RONALD WILBER 1970
Shadowed
pages
a gift for the Shadow!
©WILBER 91
MING
DWAN
FROM THE
Shadow
"TEETH OF THE DRAGON"

©WILBER•95

©WILBER·04

These illustrations and many more are showcased in THE AMAZING ART OF RON WILBER, also available from Wild Cat Books.

CASK
Reprinted from "Pulp Winds," © 2009 by William Michael Mott, www.mottimorphic.com

Of Ages

Wm. Michael Mott and Gerald W. Page

In aeons to come the Great Old Ones shall rise among the stars.
And to some worlds Azathoth and Cthulhu, Shub-Niggurath and
Tsathoggua, ai, even all the others, shall bring strange life.
But to more shall they bring strange death.

~ The Blessings of Haon-Dor

I.

BUTTER. I smelled butter, slightly rancid. My body was a stiff bar of pain as I sought to roll over. Dim recollections of a night ill-spent came back to me, of a barroom floor covered with discarded shuka-shells, reeking of buttery pistachio-nuttiness and alcohol-laden vomit. I seemed to recall a barstool coming down, barely dodging it, then the satisfying, spongy crunch of lips with teeth behind them, under my fist…

I rolled over. There was long red hair all over the bed. The hair was attached to a head, which was attached to a curvaceous, sheet-clutching body.

Now I remembered… some of it. The foul buttery smell was the residue of shuka gunk in my hair. I was in a seedy flophouse on Barbalos in a city called Jaguan, and the woman I'd met the night before at the *Corsair's Junket*, an equally seedy dive near

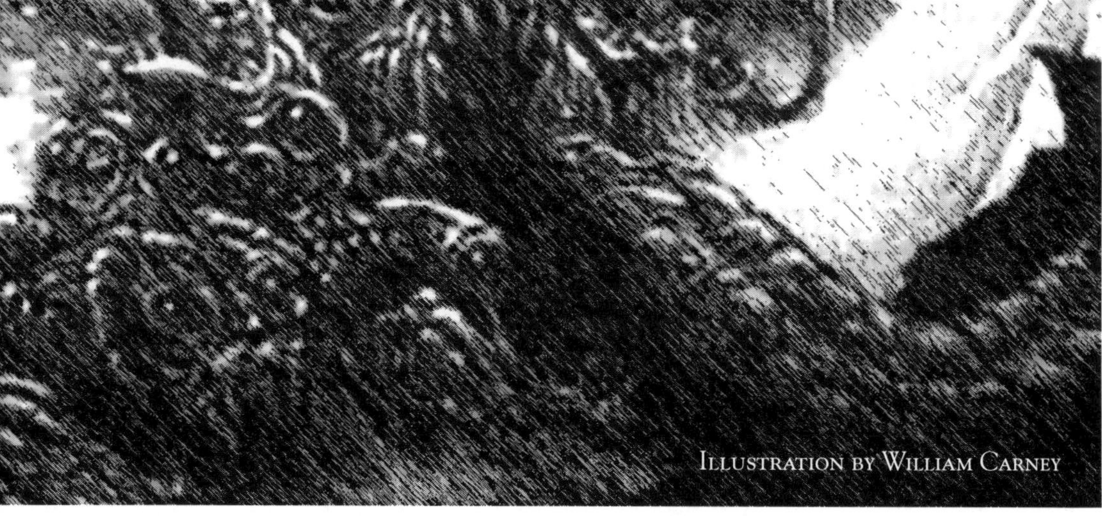

Illustration by William Carney

the spaceport. We'd hit it off. How the fight started, I couldn't remember. Some guy who said he was her ex-boyfriend. She said she never saw him before…

I recalled more details and became more alert. The Authoritators might be looking for me even now. I hoped I hadn't killed anybody; I didn't think I had, anyway.

Then the hair moved.

Not all of it, just a stray lock. It curled up on itself and seemed to climb over another lock. The body, the head the hair was attached to, didn't move at all.

I gave that a few moments' thought and began to believe her about never having seen the guy who said he was her ex. If what I suspected was true, most of her exes were probably dead.

I eased out of bed and hit the shower, hoping to get out of her room before she woke up.

When I came back she was sitting on the bed, already dressed. She wore an expensive looking blue shirt and dark shorts, ideal for bar-crawling, but with a black util belt and a blaster on her hip. She could have been just another rich girl slumming, dressed like that. *What was her name, anyway?*

She raked me with an appreciative eye and I went for my clothes. I waved toward the bathroom. "You gonna take a shower?"

She shook her head, came close. She smelled good, not a hint of reek on her. "No time—we've work to do today. Do you remember what you promised to do for me last night, when you took my money?"

I grimaced. "I was drunk. I'll give you your money back—"

"You already spent it. The food, the booze, the fight… You had to pay off the owner of Corsair's, remember? You've probably got half of it left. So how about it, tough guy?"

If I'd paid off the bar owner, then it wasn't too likely I was in trouble with the law.

"Okay, whatever. A deal's a deal. So, fill me in again?" I hoped it was honest, though I knew that wasn't any too likely. I added, "Medusa."

"How ever did you figure that out?" There was as much resignation as sarcasm in her tone; she wasn't surprised I knew.

"When I woke up. I saw your hair move."

The corners of her mouth curved into an expression that was half smile, half resignation. She reached up and straightened my collar, looking at me with those weird green eyes of hers.

"I'm a half-breed, all right? My mother was *Shambleaux*, my father a human. Born on Earth, just like you. Of course I never knew him."

"Of course," I said. "And just why am I alive?"

"I don't have the gift. A lot of the time with us half-breeds it's like that."

I went to the bed and retrieved my blaster from beneath the pillow, where I'd hidden it just in case, and my ten-inch dirk from where it jutted from beneath the mattress. The knife I put in my boot, where it disappeared. A pair of korambits was already concealed in the large and seemingly-ornate buckle of my belt.

She nodded, and went to the window. What was her name again? Damn. It would come to me, I knew.

She may have been a half-breed, but she lived up to the best qualities of both species. On some worlds her kind were killed as a matter of course, but here on the Barb they were tolerated, even sought after by some, as long as they weren't of the vampiric variety.

"Listen Cromwell, it's simple. Nobody else will go in there with me. The place is crawling with Solipsid assassins. Those things know no fear…" She shuddered slightly, or was it trick of the light from the twin suns rising outside the window?

Gerald W. Page sold his first story, "The Happy Man" to John W. Campbell for *Analog* (formerly *Astounding Science Fiction*) and it appeared in the March, 1963 issue. Since then he has published scores of science fiction, fantasy, humor and mystery stories in magazines like *Mike Shayne Mystery*, *Spaceway*, *Magazine of Horror*, *Startling Mystery*, *Weirdbook*, *Whispers*, *The Magazine of Fantasy and Science Fiction*, *Planetary Stories*. *Pulp Spirit*, *Wonderlust* and others, as well as several anthologies in the United States, Great Britain, Japan,, Hungary and elsewhere, including *Introducing SF* edited by Brian Aldiss, various volumes of E.J. Carnell's *New Writings in Science Fiction*, Richard Davis's *Space*, *When the Black Lotus Blooms* edited by Elizabeth Saunders, and Michael Bishop's *Light Years and Dark*.

As an editor he worked for *TV Guide* for twenty years, and in the stfantasy field was the editor of *Witchcraft & Sorcery*, edited *Years Best Horror Stories* for DAW Books in the 1970s, *Nameless Places* for Arkham House, and co-edited *Heroic Fantasy* with Hank Reinhardt. In addition to his own stories, he has collaborated with Robert E. Howard, Jerry Burge, Wm. Michael Mott and Michael Bishop.

"Of course not, since they don't believe that anyone or anything else really exists." I shook my head as I finished strapping on my gear. "Or so I've heard. Okay, we're going. Do you want breakfast first?"

She shook her head. "No, but you do. Our late-night activity was nourishment enough for me."

"I thought you didn't have the gift."

"The one I don't have is the one that kills you. I got most of the others."

"Right." Part of me was starting to remember some of them from last night. "Well, we'll stop for whatever we can find, and hope for coffee. And I need some influx to cure this hangover. You can fill me in on the rest of the details on the way."

As we hit the streets of Jaguan we drew only a few curious glances. Since I'm a mercenary and wanted on half of the human worlds, this was a refreshing change. Barbalos was a pretty fast-and-loose sort of world, kind of a 23rd century version of a frontier town, being on the edge of the Glory Hole and all.

The long-haired chick beside me looked human enough at first glance, even gorgeous in an eerie sort of way. She filled me in, speaking lowly, but I still somehow heard her husky, sexy voice through the noise of the crowd.

Apparently she, and in fact her whole unit, had lost a very valuable item that was on its way to a powerful person in the planetary government. Or maybe it wasn't the planetary government because she was fairly careful not to explain what sort of unit she had been in, and who it answered to. They were assigned to protect this chunk of something called "The Nova Texts" as it was transferred from one of the Living Ships—that was her wording—to the Spaceport Transit Authority, and they had it lost it in a strange and humiliating way. Of her entire unit of twelve, she was the sole survivor, Lt.... What the *HELL* was her name?

Anyway, they were in the process of moving the rock when something fell on them like a blanket, like darkness, like clinging, stinging cobwebs. While they'd gagged and struggled, someone or something took the fragment. When the stuff dissipated, or maybe even crawled away, Sherantha (*that* was her name!) was the only survivor, probably because she wasn't completely human herself, and had some sort of immunity to whatever had killed them. All of her buddies, male and female, were dead and horribly desiccated.

As she lay immobilized on the pavement, she had an impression of wide fibers, multiple, pattering feet of strange shape and size. She was overwhelmed by a petroleum-carrion-sulfur stench that left her retching when it was all over. She figured that since her hybrid cytoplasm was significantly different from that of her human counterparts (Shambleau were of Martian extraction, sort of molluskan humanoids with vampiric tendencies), she had not been as adversely affected by whatever had killed everyone else.

The whole thing smacked of the Great Old Ones to me. But this far out from Earth, and nowhere near the Lantern? It seemed unlikely, despite my suspicion.

She was given a week to get the relic back, or face some pretty stiff punishment. She heard rumors about the Adlans and their servants, the Solipsids, making a big score, so she sought me out, bringing her life's savings with her and a promise to split the reward.

Now, I reached out and stopped her in mid-sentence, turning her to face me.

"You look like a damned socialite. The first thing we've got to do is get you some street clothes, like these." I gestured at my

---

Wm. Michael Mott is the author and illustrator of *Pulp Winds*, the long-awaited collecton of short fiction, verse, and Forteana. With introductions by Walter Bosley, Brad Steiger, and Gerald W. Page, these tales will take you from the antediluvian world to lost cities beneath the earth, onward to other planets around distant stars, and even to the Dark Ages, the Old West and the High Seas. New twists on mythos and madness are intermeshed and presented in these yarns of terror and adventure!

In addition to being the author of the new book he is also the author of the satirical fantasy novel *Pulsifer: A Fable* and its sequel, *Land of Ice, A Velvet Knife* (recently re-released in one authorized volume as the *Pulsifer Saga Omnibus Edition*, from TGS Publishers) as well as the non-fiction books *Caverns, Cauldrons, and Concealed Creatures* and *This Tragic Earth: The Art and World of Richard Sharpe Shaver.*

His website is at www.mottimorphic.com. Book links, artwork, and audio interviews from a variety of radio shows can found there.

spaceman's outfit: thick synthetic denim jeans, baggy black long-sleeved shirt, black leather vest, spacer's brown boots almost to my knees. She looked me over and nodded.

"Yeah, I guess if I dress like this no one will take me seriously, will they?" She looked around, spotted a shop across the street. "Let's try that place—but I'm out of credits. You'll have to spot me some and let me pay you back."

"Story of my life," I said. We dashed across the street, thick with pedestrians both Terran and non-terran. She slipped into the shop while I loitered around out front.

I looked up as a big transport, lifting into space, cast a long, lingering shadow over the whole scene, almost as dark as an earthly night. A figure darted out of a nearby alley, wrapped in form-concealing robes and hood, as if chasing the darkness, and said something in a half-whisper, as it passed:

"There are doors best left unopened. Remember!"

Then he, she, or it was gone, following in the retreating shadow of the transport.

Ten minutes later, Sherantha came out in her new clothes, and we stepped back out onto the street. For some reason I said nothing of the hooded whisperer. Things were getting weirder by the minute… She blinked in the pink haze of Algol, variable twin suns which were still at their dimmest. There would be no need to put on the sun suits and shades for a couple of days. Barbalos orbited Algol B which was also orbited by the larger, dimmer Algol A, and the distance from both stars was just enough to be safe for life, and to make for some interesting atmospheric effects at times. I still wasn't used to looking up to see the ribbon of fire flickering between the two suns as the denser star A siphoned off plasma from B. Algol was the star's Terran name and means "the demon" in Arabic, and from Earth, the system was the Eye of The Gorgon in the constellation Medusa. Given my current partner, that seemed appropriate.

I'd been on Barbalos for six Terran months, getting as far as possible from the wars on Earth. After fighting the Shoggoth Horde in Iowa, I figured I deserved a break, but then I was sidetracked by the Oort Offensive, and spent a year fighting various creepy-crawlies in Sol's outer shell. And now, just when I was getting used to the relative peace and quiet of this world, this chick comes along…

What the hell, I thought. I was getting bored anyway. I sneaked a look at her as we headed for the Adlan section. She was a stunning looker, no doubt about it, and only this far out from Earth could I have met such an exotic beauty. Plus, the reward for recovery of the fragment was half a million GC, which would leave me with a cool quarter mil once the job was done.

Sherantha now wore an outfit much like my own, with plenty of room for both movement and to accommodate her not inconsiderable charms. Her weapon was concealed beneath a free-hanging blue shirt; her jeans were dark gray, and were not tucked into her black boots. I guessed that those boots carried a few surprises as well. Her step was brisk, and she shot me a wary glance as we reached the edge of the Shafts, the oldest part of town.

The bulge of my blaster, a Walther 9mm plasma combo holstered between my arm and ribs, was reassuring weight. And the long bundle jutting over my shoulder was not really surveying equipment, despite the case markings, but a disruptor-katana, illegal on most worlds and in all conflicts which did not involve the Great Old Ones. It had seen me through many a tight scrape. I felt relatively secure in terms of armament. The diskatana was one of the most effective weapons in the human arsenal.

I hoped I wouldn't need it.

I also carried a standard survival kit on the back of my belt. I hoped I wouldn't need it, too.

Before us the streets became terraces leading downward. Alleyways which were ramps as well twisted away in all directions. Adlans, mysterious and not much given to interaction with Terrans, disliked bright light, so they preferred subterranean dwellings. Their equally mysterious humanoid servants, the Solipsids, were their link with the sunlit world most of the time.

"You sure you know where you're going?"

She nodded. "Pretty sure. Sure enough. Glzttakkket supposedly has increased his, its security tenfold." The alien name rolled off her tongue with ease. "It must have come by something valuable. Glzttakkket is not only the biggest crook in town, but also the most cautious"

"So how do we get in? After all, we're armed." I stepped more carefully in the growing gloom, for we were well below the level of the rest of the city already. Around us, bluish lamps glowed in walls and on posts. She laughed lowly.

"I've set up a meeting. He's... *It's* expecting us."

I stopped right there. "What the hell? Why all the secrecy, why bother to change clothes? Why hire me?"

She laughed, her eyes glowing faintly and catlike in the gloom. "I needed a bodyguard to watch my back while I dicker. This will be a meeting of mutual respect, at least at this point in the game. They won't try to take our weapons, at least not at first..."

I snorted. "Yeah, right. First move toward my stuff and there's going to be slime flying. I've half a mind to head back topside right now."

She called my bluff by just looking at me, her eyes alien and amused at the same time.

The air was musty, almost moldy, and from what I knew, the place was more mazelike further down. "Do you really know your way around down there?"

"I've memorized all the maps. But you haven't, so it's in your best interest to see to that nothing happens to me." She started off.

I shrugged and followed after her.

By the time we got into the caverns proper, I was pretty well lost. Sherantha seemed to know where she was going, though, stepping surely in the gloom. It was obvious she'd done more than just memorize maps.

A rag-wrapped figure bustled past, with a chitinous clicking as it went. Buildings loomed all around, to merge with the ceilings over the streets. The architecture was cube like, simplistic, and starkly eerie. Lights occasionally glowed within windows. Robed, hooded figures, more or less identical to the one that I'd seen earlier, became more frequent. Sherantha indicated them with a gesture of one hand.

"Adlans. Semi-human scum. Don't get too close to them, they may be diseased."

I nodded. The Adlans were an unusual race, and some rumors said that they were somehow akin to humanity, perhaps the descendants of proto-humans that had been taken from Earth to the stars in the distant past. No one knew for sure who the ancient race would have been that spread them across several dozen worlds, but many ancient star-faring races were prime suspects. The Adlans themselves held that they were, in fact, the ancestors of humanity on Earth, and that they had left the planet ages before to escape both a series of cataclysms and a sun which had grown poisonous to life. They did have a strong aversion to the direct light of most suns, and an affinity for subterranean warrens; but they were so secretive, so furtive, dealing with others through lackeys and representatives, that little was known about them other than superficially. They were rumored to possess an ancient technology that was so esoteric as to almost seem like magic, and to be masters of illusion and deception. Truth to tell, they had already been present on many of the worlds "discovered" by Terran explorers over the last two centuries, including Barbalos 62, which they called by a name hardly pronounceable by an earthman; and the original pit-city of Jaguan had been there for untold ages before their ostensible human cousins arrived, to build it up and out.

No one knew how they had come to so many worlds, nor their servants which humans called Solipsids; Adlan spaceships had yet to be found. This bit of information the Adlans doggedly kept to themselves, if they even remembered the truth of it.

I was not looking forward to dealing with them, but mentally I shrugged. A job was a job, and good-paying work was hard to find this far from the war zones. Rumors on many worlds held that the Adlans were a race of despotic perverts, thieves, and abductors of women and children. Some said that they were so genetically damaged that they scarcely resembled whatever species they had originally been, most being addicted to hellish drugs and even more hellish machines for both pleasure and pain. They were the goblins to frighten children on a score of worlds, and their greed was legendary.

After many long paths and twisting turns, we found ourselves before a large stone facade, covered with bas-relief images of contorted humanoid figures, and worse things. I didn't look too close, but scanned the shadows within the tall, deep entrance. Most of the subterranean pedestrians had long since become scarce, and the silence was uncanny. Suddenly, a very human-sounding wail rang out, seemingly from the depths of the structure before us. I exchanged a dubious look with Sherantha, then stepped up to the portal.

"There are doors best left unopened," the creature had told me. The words were still fresh in my ears.

Sherantha reached out and pressed the alert button, but we heard nothing from inside. We stood looking at one another uneasily.

Somewhere there was the hint of another wail, almost a sigh of pain or pleasure, barely heard. Then the door slid open silently, and a dim-lit corridor was before us. A voice issued from an unseen speaker:

"Enter, guests."

I went in first, not too fast, followed by Sherantha. The door slid shut almost silently behind us. Dim lights with a bluish tint gleamed in wall-sockets, giving the hallway the look of a dim blue tube. Ahead could be seen doorways, leading off to each side; the voice spoke again, with a touch of humor, or sarcasm.

"Proceed."

We moved ahead, and a doorway to our left opened abruptly, with a slightly warmer radiance pouring out. Peering around the jamb, we found a large chamber, sumptuously furnished, which we entered with more than a touch of caution.

Robed figures ranged both sides of the room. At the far end was a huge seat, half-throne and half-divan, upon which yet another robed figure lounged. On the walls, flat panels of luminous material displayed writhing, sculptural images of an abstract nature. Slowly we approached the focal point of the room, the figure upon the divan.

This figure rose up languorously, to regard us from beneath a gray robe. A soft voice that could be either a boy or a woman broke the stillness.

"Welcome to the underworld of your nightmares… Sherantha os Sullin, and of course, Malcolm Cromwell." Seeing my obvious surprise, a lilting laugh followed. "Yes, Cromwell, you are well-known here. Those angry blue eyes, those black brows… When you set foot on the surface of this world it was known to us—the hero of the Battle of Boise, and the Assault on Devil Reef."

"You know me," I said, "but I don't know you."

"Indeed. Those who fight effectively against the Great Old Ones are of interest to us, as those entities have been our foes since the sinking of civilizations long-forgotten on our mutual home-world… But then again, there are those among your kind who say that we are just as bad."

"We've come to deal," Sherantha said pointedly. "Your message said that you know something about the stolen Nova Text fragment. You want a favor from us in return for—what? The fragment, or information?"

"Patience, succubus," the figure replied. "We arranged for the name of Cromwell to be mentioned in your presence, and to catch your ear; we have need of the services of the both of you."

"Okay," I said. "But I like to see who, or what, I'm dealing with, before we even begin to talk business—"

The figure stood with a serpentine ease. A slender hand threw back the hood, and we looked upon what seemed at first glance to be a woman of startling, dusky beauty. Her face was heart-shaped, her lips full; her eyebrows arched, and her brown eyes a trifle larger than usual, with enormous pupils. Her black hair tumbled about her head, widow-peaked and exotic. Yet something in the cast of her features seemed unnatural, wrong…

I couldn't place the wrongness of it, but she was gorgeous. Around us, the fifteen or so other Adlans in the room pushed back their hoods…

"I am called Naoleen," she stated with a slight bowing of her head. "Through our agents I'm known as Glzttakkket, and as a male—so you are being accorded a rare honor, one that will cost you your lives if you reveal it."

Some of them were possessed of the same ethereal beauty, but the others were monstrous to look upon. Deformities both subtle and blatant, twisted bone structure, misshapen features, and the hint of worse beneath some of the robes… I tried to ignore them and concentrate on the woman—for she was a woman, apparently—before us.

"I will tell you a story," she began. "More, perhaps, than we Adlans have shared with your kind since you flung yourselves recklessly into the stars. We are kin, you see, your kind and ours, though the kinship is distant, and branched apart ages ago."

Seeing our interest, she continued, as others brought us high-backed chairs and we cautiously sat. "Our kind has been on Earth all along, at least until very recently; slowly, surely, we have evacuated the home planet, due to what we saw as the adverse effects of solar radiation. Your golden ages, your mythical memories—such were our histories, our beginnings. We were nearly immortal, and our civilization spanned the world—until a rogue planet of huge size passed too close to the Earth and brought with it cataclysms of unprecedented scope, continent-sweeping tsunamis, the fall of a canopy of liquid water above the planet that sheltered it from harmful radiation, along with the final devastation of the fall of a lesser moon... Your myths remember these events as the Flood, as Ragnarok, and as the Day of Judgment..."

She reseated herself. Her eyes, her voice, her face had a hypnotic quality. "Atlantis, Lemuria, Valusia, Hyperborea... all of these ancient realms and others were kingdoms in our crown. We watched our distant cousin, humanity, rise from the ape, to stride red-handed across a surface world we had long abandoned; we saw ages undreamed of, when science turned to sorcery and cataclysmic aftershocks, spaced by eons, destroyed your fledgling civilizations again and again. We watched, sometimes guiding, sometimes hindering, as you rose from stone-wielding savages to city-states, and we used you as a resource, as a genetic bounty, as we saw fit, over the millennia." She laughed again.

My mind reeled at what she described. "So what were you, 'ancient astronauts'?" My tone was skeptical, but somehow I knew that she was telling the truth. Her story explained much in terms of mysteries which still baffled humankind.

"You could say that," she replied. "Actually, our culture was ancestral to yours. When we realized that the intrusive dark planet had altered the magnetic field and hence the radiation of the sun, we also realized that our near-immortality was at an end. Some of us hid as long as we could beneath the surface; the crust of old Earth is even now honeycombed with our tunnels, our highways, our all-but-dead cities. Others began leaving the planet at once, to look for new worlds to inhabit, worlds with suns of a friendlier nature. Few were found. For a while we embarked on an interbreeding program with humanity, which your kind remember as liaisons with Olympians, with fairies, and with devils. This kept us going, some of us more than others..." She nodded at those around us. "We still need a fresh genetic infusion, now and then.

"At any rate, we left the planet by several means. We would come back, from time to time, to plunder the treasures of our past, technological marvels of which mankind on the surface was and still is utterly unaware. Earth became a tomb to be looted, and our vessels were seen by your kind for centuries, only adding to the awe and fear in which you held us. Finally, about an earth-century past, our evacuation was complete—and then your species discovered the various types of spacedrives, and suddenly you were out here among us! Obviously, this was to our advantage to some extent, as we have always viewed humanity as a resource, and by coming to us among the nearer stars you saved us a trip or two 'home', when the need arose.

"On some worlds our type has all but degenerated into insane, lust-driven robots. Any few who might still remain on Earth, lurking beneath the crust, are of this type. Untold centuries of inbreeding, of self-inflicted alterations, of strange radiations and... habits, have taken their toll. On your world, such degenerate types were known as 'trolls', 'dero', and 'goblins'. Those of us who had a friendlier attitude toward humanity, and who fought off degradation as long as possible, were known as the 'good people,' the 'light elves,' the 'tero'. But even we are slowly succumbing to inevitability: our very genes have become senile, treacherous and worn out beyond repair. Only by interbreeding with fresh human stock do we even continue our existence and delay extinction; on those worlds where human stock is scarce, and minds and bodies have gone into madness, the Adlan race has degenerated into forms that shock even us."

"So what does this have to do with the Nova Text fragment, and with us?" Sherantha eyed the other woman suspiciously.

"Very simple," Naoleen replied. "We know where the fragment is. We can help you reach and retrieve it—but you must do us a favor in turn."

"I knew that we'd pay for story-time," I muttered. "So, spill it— What's the rest of the picture?"

"We were not the first sentient beings on Earth," Naoleen continued. "Before our race arose, there were darker, more ancient, more fierce races. Species. Forms." She shook her head almost in disgust. "Cromwell, you know them well enough; you call them the Old Ones. Cthulhu, Yog-Sothoth, Tsathoggua, Hastur… We, too, fought them in ages past, before your kind climbed down from the trees to strike two rocks together. The Serpent-Men of Valusia, those offspring of Yig, the druj, gnophkeh, dholes, meego, ghuls, the voormis, and other servant-races of the Old Ones were our foes. Acting as 'gods' and guides, we helped mankind in its infancy to fight these same creatures, to continue our age-old battle; you see, when we delved beneath the surface of the planet, we intruded into *spaces* where such beings had encapsulated themselves, awaiting an appointed *time* of resurgence. The wars we fought beneath the Earth—with shoggoths, with the spawn of Shudde-M'ell, with horrors that even you could not imagine—raged on for millennia! In plumbless N'kai, gray-litten Y'quaa, in Pav, in K'n-yan, Agharti, Muria, Nifleheim and Tartarus; beneath the seas and under the poles, we fought. We even ventured into the transdimensional Vale of Pnath, beneath the crust and outside of contiguous space, to fight the massive bholes, ancestors of the accursed dholes and the cousins of Shudde-M'ell and Cthulhu himself. Beneath Thule we shattered the Voorish domes in Deep Dendo, at a terrible cost to ourselves. We set seals in places, some of which may still hold, using a quantum science that your kind would still call magic… On Mars, too, our wars raged."

A chill ran down my spine. "What are you saying?" But I already knew the answer.

"The thieves you seek are servants of the Old Ones. Reaching through a tunnel, a breach in the cosmos, they came here, from some unguessable chasm beneath the distant

Earth, and took the relic. There is something they greatly need, in that object—perhaps a key to their victory, at least on Earth, and possibly among the stars. They opened one of the doors that we ourselves use upon occasion, and shuddered through and back again. Only when certain alignments exist, between stars, planets, and matter dark and light, between fields of thought and probability, is such a thing possible… And currently we are in such a time of possibility." She leaned forward, almost hungrily. "Are you willing to walk a crooked road, and retrieve your lost item?"

Sherantha was looking at her with a strange intensity. I shrugged. "What's your angle? What's in it for you?"

The Adlan smiled. "We are always eager to recover treasures from our home world and our past. We know where the servants of the Old Ones have taken your relic. We can help you reach it, without having to resort to the time and trouble of space-travel. While you are there, you will also retrieve something for us." It seemed that she momentarily cast a wary eye about the room, and her own kind. "There are those among our own who oppose this—who fear the Old Ones so much that they've lost all courage, and would give up to their minions everything we left behind. They think that our time in the universe is done. But while I rule this enclave, my word determines our course of action in all things." Again, she looked about, this time a bit defiantly.

I realized then that the Adlan on the street above was a subversive, someone opposed to her plans. Was he or she here, in this very room? Which one could it be? I really didn't want to take a good hard look at any of them.

"But first," she continued, rising again and gliding forward, "we must make certain that you are up to the task. So… Defend yourselves!"

This imperative was simultaneous with a rustle from all sides as a number of robed figures rushed us. There was no time for thought, only for action, and I rose and ducked a blow from a club that had been pulled from beneath a robe, struck the assailant with a blow to the carotid with my forearm, wheeled while kicking out at an attacker from the rear and feeling a kneecap or something similar break and slide away, and drew the diskatana on my back. I thumbed on the switch and the edge came alive with a deep hum, and death was laughing nearby, waiting for me to send him some playmates.

Sherantha had downed an attacker and drawn her blaster. Naoleen's voice rang out:

"Enough!" The degenerate humanoids drew back, and she stepped closer, nodding appreciatively. "You can put your weapons away! You have the vigor that we lack for such an enterprise. We had to be sure, you understand."

I didn't. It seemed wasteful and stupid, pointless grandstanding.

Around us, the other Adlans were dragging away their injured comrades. Neither Sherantha nor I had put our weapons away. "Maybe I'll just kill you now, for the hell of it," I growled.

"You would be evaporated instantly," Naoleen replied calmly. "There are a score of unseen weapons trained on you. So, do we have a deal? You will also be rewarded with money, in addition to everything else you'll get out of the exercise."

"How much?" Sherantha asked, reluctantly reholstering her gun. She was gorgeous, feline, predatory when aroused by either passion or strife.

"Two-hundred thousand CG apiece, or half-a million stads. Your choice."

I flicked off the katana and re-sheathed it. "Okay, let's do this. But I assume that our money will be waiting when we get back?"

"Of course. But now for your part. You have to retrieve something for us."

"Which is?"

"A box, a metal casket of sorts. About a yard long, a foot wide and deep. Made of a greenish alloy, covered in ancient symbols. You will find it near where you will find the fragment, because the fragment was stolen by the guardians of the box."

"Gee, what a co-inkydink." I glanced at Sherantha and she was as suspicious as I was. "And why do agents of the Old Ones have this box, and what's inside?"

"That's none of your concern," Naoleen retorted with a tone of anger. "You wouldn't be able to open it anyway. Let's just say that the contents offer hope to a dying race—and your fragment of the Nova Texts may hold the key to opening it, or so the Old Ones believe. What they seek is what we seek, but for different reasons; we seek to reinvigorate our once-proud race and genetic code, while they seek something that will allow them to propagate substantially on this plane of existence, without human or animal agency to hybridize with—something that they currently cannot do."

"Kind of like the Adlans," Sherantha observed. "Alright, we'll do it. But we want a guide through this wormhole or whatever is, 'cause we're not going alone to be stranded by treachery."

"Some of our Solipsids will accompany you—they ask no questions and obey us without hesitation. They will do the same for you, if I tell them to."

I shook my head. "Not good enough. I want at least one Adlan to come along also. Nothing ventured, nothing gained..."

She laughed. "Of course. Two of our people will accompany you, along with myself!"

I couldn't argue with that.

II.

BEFORE US the darkness pulsated. It throbbed, both visibly and in some indescribable, sensed way. The stone frame around it was covered in strange bas-relief figures, much like those I'd seen on Earth beneath Boise, and in the warrens of the shoggoths before we filled them with plasma and scorched them back to the depths.

Door number two.

It did not look inviting and I began to have second thoughts. We were ten: Sherantha and myself, Naoleen, two other robed Adlans, and five Solipsids, their lean, chitinous hides glistening in the dim light, their six eyes like black stones, mandibles twitching. The Adlans were a male and female, both apparently ashamed enough of their physical appearance in our presence to decide to keep themselves mostly covered. The lumpy-featured male was named Muton Revash, and the female was called simply Jeera. The Adlans and their insectoid servants were all heavily armed with both guns and blades, though none of the weapons were familiar to me. I cleared my throat and all except the Solipsids shot me a glance.

"I've never traveled by...whatever this is, before. How safe is it, anyway?'

"It's a safe as walking down the streets of the Shafts that you took to come here," Naoleen wryly replied. Even when being a smart-ass, she exuded a powerful sexuality. She now wore a flattering pair of tight pants, and a tunic roomy enough to allow her ample attributes some space to breath. She also wore a belt with a variety of devices attached to it. "Not exactly a wormhole *outside*, but another type of pathway between points within our continuum. Humans are only beginning to grasp this concept, but all bodies in space—planets, suns, and so on—have an astral sleeve of sorts, an envelope that they create by the interaction of their mass upon the local gravity field—which is itself an unseen side of space-time. We have detected a trail, a residual stain, left by the agents of the Old Ones; they came and went *outside*, but we can approximate, perhaps even duplicate, their path, by moving sideways, yet inside. This is Adlan science, old when Egypt was young." She added, "Egypt – back on Earth."

She favored us with a smile, as if that was a joke. Then she said, looking at Sherantha, "This isn't exactly the witch-space of Nyarlathotep's minions. At least, their hounds do not roam it looking for interlopers to devour."

I said, "Whatever you say." Sherantha gave me a look that seemed cool on the surface, but I could see something in her eyes. Possibly it was apprehension but it seemed to me more likely it was anticipation. "You ready?"

She nodded. "Lead on, Naoleen."

Naoleen stepped toward the pulsing darkness. "This way, then," she said. She carried a metallic staff with a bulb at the end, and I wondered if it were a weapon. The next second, she had vanished into the inky blackness set into the wall.

Muton Revash followed her, along with two of the Solipsids. Then I stepped up, Sherantha close behind, and slipped into the complete unknown—

Maybe the bravest thing I've ever done. Probably the most stupid.

The darkness was total, complete—but I could *see*. It was like being inside a photographic negative, in three dimensions; the constraints were narrow, with perceptual nothingness to all peripheries. Utter, deafening silence. The tunnel, for lack of a better term, twisted away, up and down, and ahead I could see those who had preceded me, colored in reverse, moving against darkness yet visible, with Naoleen's black-tipped staff here glowing a sickly white. Somehow I knew that object was leading us along this strange road between worlds.

I glanced back and was startled to see the most complete and frightening blackness I'd ever seen, right on my heels. I reached back, and someone took my hand—Sherantha. Apparently she could see me, since I was in front of her. I gave her hand a squeeze and then looked forward again.

It was like being disembodied and damned, I guess, and it seemed to go on for hours—or minutes. Ahead, Naoleen finally paused, holding the staff firmly before her, and motioned for everyone to pass her by. The other Adlan and the two Solipsids did so, and popped out of sight like bursting bubbles; without pausing I joined them, glad to leave this intergalactic colon, actually grateful for the wave of nausea I suddenly felt. Soon the whole group stood together, and Naoleen stepped through to join us.

We looked about in fascination. One of the Adlans had produced a lantern of some sort, too dim for my tastes, and this provided some degree of relief against the darkness. The gravity felt different here, and somehow I knew that I was back on Earth, or I should say, under its surface—a six-month trip in... how long?

The air was too dry, yet strangely fetid. We stood in a weirdly-angled gallery of some sort, a sloping tunnel that led off into even greater depths. Naoleen clicked some studs on her staff and it became implanted in the solid stone; behind us, a hole of strange whiteness, dim and non-reflective and the opposite end of the transpatial tube, hung open in the air, with the tunnel creeping away into blackness behind it. Apparently the technology of the staff maintained the open passage between worlds. It was also apparent that it was in our best interest to see to that Naoleen, the one person who knew how to use the device—as far as Sherantha and I knew anyway—had to be protected at all costs.

Naoleen took a hand-held device from her belt and a small console lit up. "We're somewhere beneath North America—well, Hyperborea. What you would call Greenland." She sighed in relief. "Thank your god that we did not end up in Arag-Kolat, or N'kai! Still, I'm not sure just *whose* domain we've entered…"

I pulled my blaster from its holster and a multi-light from my kit. "So let's go. The sooner we find this damned box, the sooner we can get out of here. Maybe we can even get back to Barbalos before they even know we've been here."

I tried not to show just how nervous I was. We were deep in the Old Ones' territory, in a part of the Earth which had been reclaimed by them for decades! I didn't even know which slimy tyrant had laid claim to this place again, but it was as likely to be Sathogwa as any. I'd learned in school that Hyperborea had once been his stomping-grounds, and there was no reason to assume that he wouldn't want it back…

Down that strange tunnel we went, the way sometimes broad, sometimes narrow. The walls and floor were strangely angled, as if not designed for terrestrial biology or locomotion, and we sometimes half-slid as we went along, still trying to move quietly.

"So where are we going?" Sherantha's whisper echoed strangely in the twisting tunnel, almost seeming to be magnified back at us by the weirdly angled walls.

Naoleen, a foot in front of me, shrugged. "In truth, this is our first journey sideways in space. When I left the Earth, centuries ago, we tended to use more conventional methods of space travel. We were afraid to use this ancient technology. We have forgotten much but desperation calls for desperate acts! All I know is that we are close to the origination and destination of those who came to Barbalos and took your fragment…"

Sherantha, now by my right shoulder, scowled. "You mean you gambled with our lives—"

"Life is a gamble!" Naoleen retorted. "Death is the stakes! You worry about your individual fate, while the survival of my race, my species, may very well rest on this venture!"

Sherantha was silent, her Medusa-eyes glowing greenly in the dark. Now we moved in silence, save for the shuffle of our collective tread, the scraping of clothing and limbs, our breathing.

The acrid-fetid odor in the air grew stronger. Wordlessly I took the lead, and Naoleen did not object, but did motion for the Solipsids to come up near my back. They were the ever-obedient shock-troops, after all. The smell was similar to that of the subterranean petroleum bogs in which shoggoths were known to wallow and swarm, and it meant trouble.

A foul, steady wind began to blow in our faces. My light, set on dim, still gave plenty of illumination to our darkness-sensitized eyes. To the Adlans, it was probably like a beacon. To the offspring of the Old Ones, it would be an alarm, perhaps even physically painful to some of them, depending on which end of the spectrum I had it set on. Currently I had it set in a low-daylight mode.

Something scraped wetly, suckingly, ahead. Suddenly the tunnel was filled with blackness—

A ropy blackness, like a ball of mating anacondas. Red eyes and red mouths throughout. Thrashing, writhing, rolling forward. I glimpsed what looked like a huge hoof sliding forward, heard the scrabbling of others, as the stench nearly made me retch…

"A child of Shub-Niggurath!" Naoleen hissed. Then the thing surged forward as if invited by her words.

I emptied ten anti-matter rounds into the thing, then switched to the plasma-beam setting. Tiny implosions of blinding whiteness, not loud, and the thing bucked and heaved, filling the tunnel like a clog in a drain. The plasma then raked it with orange heat, and it began to shrivel, like a spider on a hot log. I switched back to the imploders and finished it off.

The whole encounter had lasted twenty seconds. Already it melted away into a licorice sludge. Warily, we moved forward and around a bend.

The tunnel widened and sloped downward. A vastness loomed ahead, a massive cavern that had to be miles across.

We killed our lights and peered cautiously down. An eerie glow lit the place, coming apparently from a thick carpet of lichen-like stuff on walls and floor. The place was a maze of flowstone and formations, and bloated, dome-like structures jutted throughout. Further on, a massive black pile of something loomed, an artificial structure of some sort, dark stone lit by the lichen-stuff… a city.

A dim thrumming came from that pile, a chanting…

"Ia! Shub-Niggurath! Ia! Gof'nn hupadgb Shub-Niggurath! Dhol-kk ptahan ftaghn! Ia! Ia! Cthulhu R'lyeh wgah-nagh fhtagn!"

I shuddered. I hated that unhuman chanting crap more than I hated classical rap.

The landscape below us seemed deserted—Apparently we had encountered a lone guard of some sort. Everything seemed to be in the city-structure, and some sort of preternatural hoe-down was underway. I turned to Naoleen.

"Time to use your Solipsids. Send them down to scout it out, and see if they can find the fragment and the box!"

She nodded, and motioned to the bipedal crustaceans. They moved smoothly down the slope, each with a small beige packet strapped to their torsos, their exoskeletons shifting in color and pattern as they went, matching the environment flawlessly. Handy critters, and they didn't even look back…

The chanting continued sonorously, thrumming with a deep timbre of hundreds or even thousands of voices. *"Ia! Shub-Niggurath! Ia! Gof'nn hupadgb Shub-Niggurath! Dhol-kk ptahan ftaghn! Dhol-kk ptahan ftaghn! Ia! Ia!"*

"They're calling the dholes," Naoleen observed. "That may take a while, if they're only getting started."

"Do you know what dholes are?" Sherantha asked, coming up beside me. She stood just close enough to betray her fear.

"Never seen one, but I've heard of 'em," I replied. "Worm-things, with teeth. Pale and big, lots of different sizes. Usually hungry." I think I shuddered.

She shot me a curious look. "You handled that other creature well enough."

"I prefer the horrors I already know," I said. And the war back on Earth had introduced me to plenty. "That was a shoggoth, a child of Shub-Niggurath. But dholes? I don't know enough about them to be overly-confident."

The chanting took on a deeper tone now, with a deeper, granitic voice added to it, presumably that of Shub-Niggurath herself or another Old One, chanting: *"Ia! Ubbo-Sathla! Ia! Ubbo-Sathla kptakn ftaghn! Ubbo-Sathla wgah'nagl fhtagn! Ia! Ia!"*

Naoleen shuddered, a look of shock momentarily on her face, then moved closer as well, the other two Adlans crouched right behind her. "They're mounting some sort of major offensive. Look, see those long formations hanging from the ceiling? Nutrient-clusters, probably used to be human and animal life. Shoggoths feed on those if they have to, and I'm sure that the siblings of that thing you killed could do so as well... But not the dholes, I'm guessing. Our histories indicate that they prefer living meat…"

"The Adlans have fought the dholes, many times over the ages. The Earth is in for a major assault—they're up to something big. Shub-Niggurath herself must be there," she nodded toward the citadel, "and the dholes are being called up from deeper parts of the subterranean and other-dimensional regions. We must be somewhere in the vicinity of Y'qaa, well beneath the site of the dead volcano Voormithadreth—which would, in this age, be greatly altered, if not gone entirely. We should be under massive glaciers, and possibly even a frozen inland sea."

"Greenland is right in the middle of Old One territory, so they're getting ready for an offensive," I said. "But against which region? My guess would be Boston—it's already an island of humanity in a largely-lost zone. Or maybe something bigger…"

Below us there was movement, as roiling, clattering shoggoths began to enter the cavern from other tunnels and head for the citadel. They looked like black clouds, like elongated black tumbleweeds at this distance. Naoleen shook her head.

"This is bigger than taking one human city! Listen—if we are near Y'qaa, that would explain both the theft of your fragment and their—insistence—on finding and holding the container that we seek. Somewhere below us, probably not far, Ubbo-Sathla the Primal One lies, guarding in his chaotic idiocy the Elder Keys, which even the Old Ones require and cannot yet obtain! Those Keys hold the secret to an ultimate power, an ability to completely transcend all space, time, and dimensional barriers—to master and rule not just this universe, but all universes!"

It made sense, in a way. It explained much. "Maybe that's why the Old Ones came to the Earth in the first place," I whispered. "To find these Keys and use them."

Naoleen nodded. "You're learning. Yes, that is well known in some circles. The Keys are actually encoded data tablets, which when activated would reveal the underlying holographic nature of all reality, in all its forms. They are artifacts of a greater and separate reality, perhaps the reality from which this one sprang, or by which it was itself created. The Keys allow complete access, movement, and control of all realms of existence, even of Time itself; and if the Old Ones gain access to them, then all worlds are doomed. Not just Earth."

It didn't paint a pretty picture. First, I knew that they would consolidate their power on Earth and throughout the Solar System; then from there ripple outward as they had before, throughout trans-dimensional space-time. Cthulhu would be brought out of stasis, and the whole kit and kaboodle would be released and roaming at will. Game Over.

"So how do the fragment and container figure into this?" Sherantha asked.

"The Nova Texts contain information that was lost to the Old Ones before they ever invaded Earth in its infancy," Naoleen explained. "One of the Great Old Ones destroyed a planet which was in fact one solid mass of crystallized knowledge, created by the Elder Gods in the Prime. The Old One Ezindont fragmented not just the planet but the whole system, by tripping a self-destruct device which was left there specifically to keep her kind from taking ownership of the Texts. They were flung out from their supernova star, generally along the Shaddrun Veil, and every now and then fragments are found. Apparently," and here she lowered her voice with passion, "...there is something of great importance in your particular fragment of a fractured world, information that they need to bring some plan to fruition.

"I suspect," she continued, "that the container is the other half of the equation. My distant ancestors—whom you would call Atlanteans, or tero, or light elves—discovered it long ago, after a long battle beneath the Earth with the Sons of Yig, perhaps in this very region. They recognized, by a few of the glyphs, that it contains an artifact of vast potency, something having to do with total racial or species regeneration, rebirth, and conquest. They may think they need it, but we need it worse... and we have the technology to read the Nova Text fragment, since we long ago learned to utilize the crystalline structure of the Earth and other worlds to store a near-infinity of data."

The dim chanting from the city, never born of human throats, began to rise to a crescendo. The cavern almost quaked with it, and I noticed that the lichen-like stuff growing a few yards away actually seemed to quiver or pulsate in... What? Excitement? Anticipation? I looked at my companions and saw that they too, had noticed.

"Ia! Shub-Niggurath! Ia! Gof'nn hupadgb Shub-Niggurath! Dhol-kk ptahan ftaghn! Dhol-kk ptahan ftaghn! Ia! Ia!" The same chant as before, but louder, more insistent. *"Ia! Shub-Niggurath! Ia! Dhol-kk ptahan ftaghn! Ia! Ia!"*

Something unpleasant was happening in the cavern below, as if things could look any worse. The air above the basaltic edifice began to congeal, to thicken like semi-transparent syrup, in an area the size of a city lev-bus. The region roiled like clouds, grew thicker, sludgy, sent forth pseudopods to grope downward—

"Back! Hide your eyes!" I hissed. "That bitch Shub-Niggurath is here, and she may sense our attention if we're looking directly at her as she comes through!"

Hastily we slid back on our bellies, faces turned away from the blasphemous spectacle. I caught a last glimpse of the blackness, the writhing, many-legged thickness, as it continued to grow and descend—

Then the ground began to shake in earnest, and I knew we were in deep shit.

"The dhole is coming through!" Naoleen yelled, not even bothering to lower her voice in the sudden uproar. We risked a look over the edge of the slope, to see that the cavern floor was erupting in numerous places, and huge, snouted, worm-like things, pale as milk and as long as telephone poles, were bursting through. They raised their eyeless heads and quested about hungrily, then turned their attention, one by one, to the city.

There were scores of them, and more were coming up. From our vantage the cavern looked like it was filling up with giant, writhing maggots, as big around as horses and rhinos. They heaved their quivering, slug-like bulks forward, toward the source of the chanting, and their dark mistress Shub-Niggurath.

I looked at the others. Sherantha wore a look of both fascination and disgust, and I wondered if her Shambleau genes sensed some sort of kinship with those things. For a second I wasn't so sure that I wanted to sleep with her anymore—but I got over that with another look at her. Naoleen had a fervent, fanatical look in her eye, and Jeera, gaunt-featured and dark-eyed, looked terrified beneath her pale locks. Muton Revash was stoic, but his knuckles were almost as white as the dholes, he gripped his blaster so tightly.

"What now?" I asked Naoleen. "If the stuff we're after is in that city or fort or whatever it is, we're screwed. I don't know about the rest of you, but I'm not crashing Shubby's birthday party! I didn't bring the right present!"

She laughed. "Don't worry, we brought enough presents for everybody." She pointed.

One of the Solipsids was returning. It slid up and over the rise like a cricket, and chattered something to the Adlans. The bundle it had worn was missing. Naoleen grinned.

"We have a few surprises for the Old Ones, now placed around the cavern. Ss-tinik here tells me that they've isolated the fragment of the Text by its gluon-pulse radiation—it's not even in the walls, but is in one of the dome-things not too far away from here. As for the casket— Well, it would be in the tallest structure, probably, because the closer to the sun it is, even if buried beneath miles of ice and stone, the more efficacious its effects are believed to be. *She* probably knows that, if we do…"

"Solipsids are great climbers, like cockroaches, right?" Sherantha interjected.

Naoleen nodded, as another of the five Solipsids slid over the rim and into the tunnel. She chattered something to it and it departed again. It, too, was missing its packet of goodies. She then turned to Sherantha. "He'll gather his brethren to try and scale the walls and get the box. It's probably on top of the pentagonal tower at the right, almost against the wall. See, no windows anywhere, and the platform is probably some sort of altar… As for us, well, Ss-tinik will lead one or two of us to the fragment—" …And here she looked at Sherantha and me.

"Okay, I didn't come along for the sights," I grumbled. Cautiously I looked into the huge cavity below, to see that nearly all of the dholes had vanished. A few still slithered toward the structure, but were soon lost in the shadow of weirdly-angled entrances. Ss-tinik crept forward and I followed, motioning for Sherantha to stay behind for now.

The ground crawled beneath our feet, the lichen-stuff quivering like a bed of sea anemones, their pulpier parts making tiny smacking sounds. They squashed flat underfoot but sprang back once we'd passed, and even through my boots I felt like I was treading on spongy flesh. Rapidly we went down the slope, with no servants of the Old Ones in sight; the dome-like structures, resembling giant puffball mushrooms, came near. The Solipsid veered to the left and we skirted the structures for a hundred yards, to at last draw up before a particularly large specimen, squat and brooding.

I drew my katana but didn't thumb on the disruptor edge. With a weapon in each hand I followed the nonhuman, with the chanting from the citadel vibrating through my feet and into my legs, into my head and chest from the very walls. I steeled myself for conflict as we reached the puffball.

"Ubbo-Sathla kptakn ftaghn! Ubbo-Sathla wgah'nagl fhtagn! Ia! Ia!" Still the abominable call rang out, a summons to an Idiot God of Filth, wallowing in some worse hell than this one…

There was no obvious entrance, but the thing was bifurcated along one side, resembling a gigantic woman's cleavage. I sensed that this was the entrance, so I approached it with the blade held forward, and gently probed at the crevice.

This had the effect of setting the whole thing to quivering like jelly, sentiently it seemed, but it did not open. I thumbed on the disruptor switch and chopped into it like butter, and the deja vu smell of rancid, rotten dairy products, came out with a blast of wet air as the opening split. The sides of the aperture fell back in accordion-fashion, and inside I could see a dark rounded object in the midst of a mound of slimy tissues, like some perversion of oyster and pearl—

Door number three…

Spear-like teeth as long as my forearm sprouted from the sides of the opening and the whole mass lunged at me, trying to engulf me in its maw. I staggered back, slashing with my sword; except for the fact that the thing was rooted in the stone floor of the cavern, I would have been lunch. The mouth snapped shut and the thing began to quiver and quake. Around us, the other pod-things began to behave in a similar manner.

Again it lunged at me, blindly. Swift as a darting swallow, the Solipsid leapt inside, grasped the Nova Text fragment, and tossed it out. The creature was already halfway out when the maw snapped shut with a grinding, crushing force.

Bug juice everywhere. Holstering my pistol I grabbed up the fragment and hauled ass, dodging the lunging mushroom-things on all sides, hurdling the smaller ones, and heading for the tunnel. Somewhere, a weird honking started, barely audible above the chanting of the ritual of the Old Ones….

I made the mistake of looking back. Dholes were emerging from the city like great white maggots, and heading in my general direction. I started up the slope and smelled the foul sewer funk of shoggoth in the air, but didn't look back again. Above me, the beams of Sherantha's blaster and the weapons of the Adlans leaped out with a crackle, striking targets behind and below me. I scrambled over the top and hit the dirt, then turned to look at the spectacle below.

I thumbed off the charged blade and resheathed it, drawing my pistol. The cavern was quickly becoming a seething mass of unholy activity, as a host of insanely structured beings began to pour from the structure. A score of dholes was already nearing our tunnel, and others were on their way to other parts of the cavern, wriggling like obese albino serpents among the pod-dome creatures, which attacked them indiscriminately when they ventured too close. A horde of shoggoths surged across the cavern floor, pullulating and joining, merging into symbiotic clumps of ropy tendrils, snakelike limbs, black, hoofed legs, and screaming mouths, to break loose again in new configurations or individual creatures, whichever they might have been.

The shoggoths began to fall upon the pod-things in a frenzy, ripping them to shreds, searching for an egg-like fragment they would no longer find…

The chanting suddenly stopped.

The ground began to quake in a serious way, as *something* began to push its way up from beneath the basaltic structure, something black and tarry and bubbling and *alive*. It began to seep out from beneath the walls, to flow out through the entranceways, a giant plasmodium-thing crawling out from the ultimate bottom of some ultimate rock. Simultaneously Shub-Niggurath herself rose huge as a small hill within the walls, having apparently devoured her nearest worshippers and co-summoners, ready to consummate some grisly ritual or union with the Primal Thing that was the Idiot Demiurge, Ubbo-Sathla.

Still we fired at the growing army of obscenities that assaulted the slope before us.

"We've got to go!" Sherantha yelled. "We have the fragment—"

"Not yet!" Naoleen snarled. "The Cask of Ages is still within our grasp—"

"May have to give that one up," I answered. "We can't fight off this filth forever!"

As if to prove me wrong, a stalactite grew suddenly from the tunnel entrance before us, color-shifted, became a Solipsid hanging by one arm, and dropped. The creature carried a long, dark greenish-black object under one arm. Naoleen laughed wildly.

"See! We have succeeded! Their ritual is ruined—Watch!"

In the cavern Shub-Niggurath was getting ready to get her groove on, having assumed a hugely receptive form of extreme ugliness above the citadel walls. Beneath the She-Goat of a Thousand Heats, a titanic pseudopod of vaguely phallic proportions was taking shape as Ubbo-Sathla continued to grow, and to blindly seek, by instinct, an unholy and frankly, disgusting union with the Slut from the Stars…

The demiurge from below met with that which had summoned him/it. Grasping several strangely-angled turrets and crenellations, Shub-Niggurath made herself ready for her paramour. Long, black, rubbery, hairy tentacles sought out the highest pentagonal point, questing for the long container, while other limbs strained downward from the outer walls, expectantly awaiting a certain data-fragment—

Shub-Niggurath groped in vain.

Ubbo-Sathla, still an Idiot, began to combine procreation with predation. It threw quivering sheets of cohesive black slime about the equally-black, many-legged and –armed form of Shub-Niggurath, and whatever weird pleasure was in progress turned to pain! In an instant the two were locked in not a lovers' embrace but in violent conflict, and the walls, towers and turrets began to smash and fall, crushing those of Shubby's minions who were too close to the battle.

This collapse had the effect of driving shoggoths and dholes alike toward various tunnel entrances in even greater numbers, including ours. Naoleen barked commands to her Adlan subordinates, and they detached control devices from their belts. She turned to Sherantha and me with a sadistic smile.

"We Adlans still have our science. Watch!"

Around the cavern, figures began to appear, a fairy-tale army of ever-growing proportion. There were Amazon giantesses in leather armor, brigades of barbarian swordsmen and lancers, half-reptilian men with pikes of weird metal; spacemen of a type unknown to me, with baroque or angular costumes and blazing weapons. As if by spontaneous generation their ranks began to swell, and they fell upon the shoggoths and dholes with unbridled fury and joy—

"Now we run!" Naoleen yelled, and she turned, followed by her companions and the lone Solipsid, carrying the box. Sherantha and I didn't argue, but brought up the rear post-haste.

I looked back, to glimpse a gigantic section of the cavern ceiling, knocked loose by the thrashings of the Old Ones, falling like the Hammer of God upon them both. A massive, pig-like dhole-head filled the tunnel, as the creature sought to force its bulk through. Behind it rose thrashing, ropy black limbs.

As we ran, I yelled in the general direction of the back of Naoleen's head. "Who—? What—? How did—?"

"Adlan illusion!" She replied with a cackle. "The Solipsids planted crystals containing holograms of Adlan armies dead for twenty-thousand Terran years! But it won't take the shoggoths long to figure out the trick, and dholes are mostly blind—"

She didn't have to say any more. We rushed up the path, relieved to finally see the white square of the space-time rift, and plunged into it without hesitation. Naoleen grabbed up the implanted staff and brought up the rear, effectively sealing the way behind us.

Door number four.

Through that netherworld passage, we ran. Again the altered perception, the displaced senses, the claustrophobic tightness of the path; for hours, or minutes, or seconds, it was hard to tell for how long, we fled that conflict on an increasingly-distant world.

We came through the portal with such abruptness that we tumbled together in an embarrassing heap, the Solipsid alone springing free and steady, still carrying its prize. Naoleen came through last, landing right in my lap; for an ancient progenitor of the human race type, she smelled, and felt, pretty much like any other woman, curves and soft spots and firmness in all the right places. We rolled about awkwardly until we got to our feet, to find Sherantha looking at us with a knowing, sardonic look in her green cat's eyes.

"What?" I said.

III.

"SHUB-NIGGURATH won't die that easily," Naoleen said.

We were in the same large chamber as before, surrounded by seventy or eighty Adlans. Nearby, Jeera and Mutan Revash held one another; apparently they were spouses or mates or whatever the hell an Adlan would call such a partnership.

Sherantha clung to my arm as we looked at the objects before us. Occasionally her hair moved, as if of its own volition, and brushed my cheek.

On a long table were the two objects we'd gone through space, time and hell to collect.

In the here and now, they didn't look all that impressive; just a chunk of what looked to be rock, shaped a bit like an old-fashioned jar or vase, covered over the top with a hard cap of some mossy looking material, and an oblong thing somewhat like a box, a very old box, marked with angular, vaguely kanji-looking incisions. Didn't look like much to me, but then again, I never was much into antiques.

The leader of the Adlans continued. "She would simply have been forced out of our continuum by the conflict, or perhaps back to one of her subterranean realms on Earth, like Arag-Kolat beneath the Arabian sand. Ubbo-Sathla will by now have seeped back down to his eternal pool, where he still guards the lost secrets of the Elder Gods that he took long ago, and for which he was lobotomized and made guardian of that which he stole, by those from who he stole it."

"All's well that ends well," I observed. "So, when do we get our Nova Text fragment and our money?"

Sherantha elbowed me in the ribs.

"Soon enough. First, however, you will witness the rebirth of the Adlan race, as we were before the First Cataclysm, before the rise of Acheron and the First Age of Darkness! Before our descendant Kull sat on the Topaz Throne, and the surface-men reverted to barbarism and superstition!"

Two robed Adlans brought forth a strange device, a simple metal framework, into which they gingerly placed the Nova Text. Filaments grew out of the tubes and secured the stone, and the air was filled with a faint hum.

"For millennia the Adlans have ferreted out the secrets of the ages, the knowledge locked by nature herself in stone and mineral and crystal. We have embedded our own endless records in libraries of crystal and rock, on dozens of worlds, and have even left behind unknown centuries of holographic records in rocks that are now considered rubble by the current humans of Earth! We are fairly certain that we've decoded the markings on this fragment, as it seems not dissimilar to the markings on the Pnakotic Manuscripts..." Naoleen ran her hand over the device. "Observe."

A hologram sprang to life, a weirdly multi-dimensional image of shapes and forms and outrageous colors that hurt my eyes, so I looked away, mostly. The Adlans gathered about in interest, babbling in their own language, a few of them taking notes.

"Of course!" Naoleen exclaimed. Mutan Revash stepped forward and adjusted the device, until the hologram bathed the surface of the box. The jarring dimensions of the shapes and colors aligned, narrowed into beams, and fit into a number of the glyphs on the Cask of Ages. All of the symbols on the container began to glow an unpleasant red...

"Now we unlock the secret of perfect and eternal rejuvenation!" Naoleen yelled at me with a wild grin. I took Sherantha's hand and began to back away.

"She can send us a check," I said to my business partner. She didn't argue as I pulled her toward the exit, a sinking feeling in my gut.

"They've forgotten about the Nova Text fragment," said Sherantha, going to it and ripping the filaments away and lifting it out of the framework.

She was right. The Adlans ignored her. They were too absorbed by the Cask of Ages.

Door number five, best left Unopened...

The top of the container became molten and evaporated. Inside was deep blackness.

Blackness came out.

We barely made it to the spaceport as the city fell behind us, sucked into the ravenous maw that had once been the Shafts. Stealing a jumper at gunpoint, I forced Sherantha aboard and we lifted off, the levs straining to break the pull of the oozing, bubbling, growing, gravitational entity that had reached out from the box, to finish off the last of the Adlan Race on Barbalos. We had scarcely escaped the collapsing headquarters of the Adlans, and had raced up paths and streets that had seemed to be sliding and twisting back down the way we had come; around us figures struggled, staggered, and fell, to go rolling or sliding off into the growing blackness behind us.

As we finally pulled free of planetary drag, I watched Barbalos disappear into a black maelstrom of something alive and growing and hungry and enraged. Not many people on the ground made it offworld, and as we hit low orbit, we looked at the viewers to see tendrils of darkness snaking out across the southern continent like rivers of ink. Anyone who wasn't in space is filling the belly, or whatever, of a frustrated elder thing in a supreme snit.

It was three days before I was even willing to look at the navigation tank and consider landing. Sherantha seemed to know exactly where she wanted to go, however. A small world off the beaten paths. I never even learned the name of the star we went to.

Six hours later, I saw my first Living Ship.

IV.

THE SHIP was named *Arthur Jermyn* and I didn't get a very good look at it. I didn't see the outside of it either, that day, and I still haven't. We went up to it from the ground through another type of interdimensional passage apparently generated by *Arthur Jermyn* himself. Sherantha called it step-down. *How many types of Witch Space were there?* I found myself wondering.

But the big surprise wasn't the ship, it was what waited there for us. Or who.

Hugh Ambroce was just under six feet, with broad shoulders and a deep chest. He had a relaxed way about him that almost made you take it for softness. But when he moved he moved like a cat. He had thick reddish blonde hair that looked like a lion's mane combed back from his forehead.

I'd run into him before. He was one of the few men I'd think twice about standing toe-to-toe with and slugging it out, even in my boxer days. Fortunately, we'd always been on the same side.

He was wearing civilian clothes now but when I knew him back on Mars, he'd worn the uniform of a brigadier general in special ops. Not that I knew him socially, me being a grunt and all, but I saw him around and I heard the stories they told about him. If they were only half true, he was something, and a lot more than any other general I ever heard about, including a lot more dangerous. Once I was with a patrol that got far enough into the Drylands to see Jekkara, and he sat in on our debriefing, saying nothing, but making notes now and again. He'd asked me to copy a Martian map we'd gotten a glimpse of, but I noticed even then that he sized me up as we spoke. He was a natural-born soldier, that guy, always assessing situations, enemies, friends, and potentials.

He was one of the few brass I'd ever really respected. And then, suddenly, I realized this was the guy Sherantha had been working for all along—which raised some questions about her.

Sherantha had filed a report as soon as we dropped out of hyperspace, but General—I mean Mr. Ambroce asked her to give it again, verbally. He listened politely—no military formality now—and asked a few questions.

We'd talked about it, Sherantha and me. And we came to a conclusion.

Why is it that the Great Old Ones don't often get together anymore and rub bellies? Why no recent offspring? Could it be that something—or someone—else is needed, and is missing?

What do you call a third sex? He? She? Heesh?

Whoever or whatever it is, it's pissed. And once it's covered Barbalos, the call will go out, you can bet your ass. I mean, it's been locked up for a billion years, with no action whatsoever, and pretty soon it'll be looking for love in only the Wrong Places.

Sherantha ended her report by offering that theory and the general—he will always be the general to me—listened politely and didn't offer any contradiction.

But he glanced at me, only for a second, and it was the same scary look I remembered from before.

"A sort of sexual coefficient?" he said, looking back at her. "Interesting, and it might actually be true. We'll be studying it, among other problems." He rubbed his nose.

We were in a comfortable room that I'd been told was inside a living ship but it didn't look like any guts I'd ever seen. It was dark paneled, with a desk behind which Ambroce was sitting, and a couple of chairs, which was where Sherantha and I sat. The walls had a couple of star charts and some photos, several of them showing Ambroce and a gorgeous Asian woman I later found out was his wife. A lot of things had changed since Mars.

"Describe that box again," he told her. She did and then he looked at me and said, "Is that how you saw it?"

It was Mars all over again. I was so cowed I had to force each syllable individually. "Pretty much. I suppose I could draw it but I wouldn't be able to get the markings right."

"As I recall you did all right with the Martian writing on that map," he said.

"That was different. I knew I was on a mission and would have to make a report then. And I'd seen Aihai before."

"Fair enough. Does that mean you could still handle going on missions, Mr. Cromwell?"

I'm not sure what he saw on my face, though I know what was going on in my stomach. Hell, I *still* hadn't had that vacation yet!

He smiled and went on. "Here's what we think happened. We hold with a slightly different interpretation of the Nova Text origin than the Adlans do. We don't believe that they're fragments of a world but objects that were on a world that was destroyed. But their theory is interesting and we will investigate it. The Nova Texts were originally created by an Elder God called Zazarin and intended to contain a wealth of information, much of it related to the Great Old Ones. Zazarin was attacked by the Great Old One Ezindont and the result was the nova of the star around which orbited the planet they were on. Only the Nova Texts survived. Thousands of them, perhaps millions. The cataclysm destroyed Zazarin, but it's believed Ezindont survived—trapped in one of the fragments. Most fragments are pretty much like what you saw—roughly jar-shaped. But not all. Some of them might even be box shaped."

"Whoa," I said. "You can't think—"

"We can and do," he went on. "We think the box the Adlans wanted was not quite the box they believed it was, but another Nova Text fragment. We think it was the one that held Ezindont. So, now Ezindont is back and we—people like Sherantha and me—have to do something about it. In short, Mr. Cromwell, how would you feel about a really, really dangerous job, working with Sherantha, and for me? I can promise good pay, travel to interesting places, and probably a short lifespan."

He slid a whiskey decanter and glass my way and I took them. Sherantha gave me that half-lidded cat-eyed look, and the prospect began to appeal to me.

"First, some R and R," I grumbled, lifting the amber nectar to my lips. "My last vacation was shot all to hell."

The End

Startling Stories presents

A GOLDEN AGE COMICS REPRINT

KENTON OF THE STAR PATROL

BY THE YEAR 3750 MANKIND HAD BRANCHED OUT FROM THE SOLAR SYSTEM TO THE STARS. TO POLICE THESE VAST AREAS, THE *STAR PATROL* WAS BORN! SOMETIMES A SHIP FLASHED OUT OF THE VOID, FILLED WITH *PLUNDERING PIRATES* FROM AN *UNKNOWN GALAXY*. SUCH A RAIDER WAS THE *BETAXON SIG*, FILLED WITH STRANGE CREATURES-- THE *FLANN*, WHO WANTED PRECIOUS URANIUM. *DAVE KENTON* DREW AN *ASSIGNMENT IN DEATH* WHEN HE RODE THE SPACEWAYS TO TRACK DOWN-- *THE ALIEN RAIDERS!*

THE ALIEN SHIP FIRST APPEARED OFF TITAN, SATURN'S LARGEST MOON, WHERE RICH URANIUM MINES WERE WORKED BY CONSOLIDATED PLANETS--

AS THE GUARDS START TO RUN, DEADLY LIGHT BEAMS DRIVE DOWN THROUGH THE THIN ATMOSPHERE, FREEZING THEM IN THEIR TRACKS...

BATES AND O'HARA, FROZEN SOLID! WHAT.. WHAT IS THAT THING?
NEVER MIND WHAT IT IS! START FIRING!
MAN THE REPULSERS!
CLANG A LANG

SLOWLY THE ALIEN SHIP DROPS TOWARD TITAN, ITS HEAVY WEAPONS SPOUTING DEATH-DEALING BEAMS!
WE ARE SMASHING THEM, ONE BY ONE!

THE COLD BEAMS SILENCED THEIR WEAPONS AND THE SLEEP-GAS RENDERED THE HUMANS UNCONSCIOUS...
WE WILL NOT ONLY GET URANIUM, BUT SLAVES AS WELL! IT IS GOOD!

OUR ROBOTS WORK WELL, BUT NOT NEARLY AS EFFICIENTLY AS HUMANOIDS WILL! AND WE WILL NEED MANY WORKERS TO REFIT OUR ROCKETS FOR INTERSTELLAR TRAVEL BY SIHIL! WE HAVE MADE A RICH HAUL!

AS THE GREAT ALIEN SHIP POINTS ITS NOSE OUTWARD TOWARD THE RIM OF THE SOLAR SYSTEM... AND THE STARS BEYOND—
THE HUMANOIDS SEEM TO BE FREEZING, COMMANDER. WE OF FLANN LIKE ZERO TEMPERATURES, BUT THE HUMANS WILL DIE!
VERY WELL. SEAL THE PRISON CHAMBERS, AND RAISE THE HEAT TO FIFTY ABOVE ZERO!

AS THE FLANN SPACESHIP ZOOMS OUTWARD, A STAR PATROL CRUISER HOVERS OVER THE RAVAGED TITAN...
STAR PATROL CRUISER BANTAM CALLING BASE! CLEAR LANES FOR VITAL MESSAGE! CALLING BASE! CLEAR LANES! CLEAR LANES! VITAL! VITAL!

AND AT THE PATROL ACADEMY, IN MARSOPOLIS...
RUSH THIS TO COMMAND OFFICER O'LEARY. VITAL! FULL PRIORITY-
CHECK, SIR! AT ONCE!
2

IT'S ABOUT THE RAIDS ON TITAN. WE'VE LOST TEN SHIPS, AND MORE THAN A THOUSAND MEN! SOMEBODY IS RAIDING TITAN FOR URANIUM AND SLAVES, BUT WHO IS DOING THE RAIDING WE DON'T KNOW!

THE CONVICTS RACE TO THE UPPER LEVELS, WHERE THE TURRET BATTERIES ROAR DEFIANCE AT THE ALIEN INVADERS- FOR A LITTLE WHILE ONLY...
BY JUPITER! THOSE FORCE RAYS BLAST EVERYTHING THEY TOUCH!

MY ONLY CHANCE TO SURVIVE IS TO FALL-PRETEND TO BE HIT, AND THEN HOPE THAT THESE RAIDERS, WHOEVER THEY ARE, FORGET ABOUT ME...

THEY'RE GOING PAST ME! THEY THINK I'M DEAD! THEY'LL BE SEEKING URANIUM AND SLAVES! IF I'M GOING TO DO ANYTHING AT ALL, I'VE GOT TO DO IT NOW!

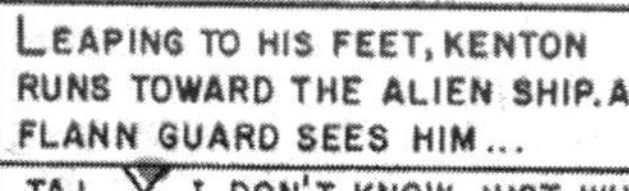
LEAPING TO HIS FEET, KENTON RUNS TOWARD THE ALIEN SHIP. A FLANN GUARD SEES HIM...
TAJ SKITT BANTI!
I DON'T KNOW JUST WHAT THOSE WORDS MEAN, BROTHER- BUT I KNOW IT ISN'T ANY SHOUT OF WELCOME!

...SO I'D BETTER GET RID OF YOU IN A HURRY!

NOW TO FIND A PLACE TO HIDE AWAY IN HERE- AHH! THAT BOAT OUGHT TO BE JUST THE THING---!

THEIR RAID COMPLETED, THE ALIENS BLAST AWAY FROM TITAN, BOUND TOWARD THEIR HOME PORT, SOMEWHERE ON THE RIM OF THE SOLAR SYSTEM...
HERE WE GO! BRR... IT'S PLENTY COLD IN THIS LIFEBOAT! MUST BE FIFTY BELOW ZERO IN HERE...
4

GOT TO GET SOMETHING TO... KEEP WARM! BRRRR...MAYBE THIS STORAGE COMPARTMENT--A BLANKET! JUST THE THING! I'LL WRAP MYSELF UP IN IT.

FOR HOURS, DAVE KENTON LIES COLD AND NUMB. THROUGH THE METAL WALLS OF THE TINY SHIP, HE HEARS SIGNAL GONGS CLANG--HEARS THE FORWARD JETS ROAR INTO LIFE--FEELS THE SLOW PROGRESS OF THE SPACESHIP ENTERING A PLANET'S MAGNETIC TUG. THEN THERE IS THE THUMP OF THE ALIEN SHIP SINKING INTO ITS LAUNCHING CRADLE.
CLANGGG

THEY'VE GONE! NOW'S MY CHANCE TO GET OUT...BUT FIRST I HAVE TO GET SOME ALIEN CLOTHES THAT WILL KEEP ME WARM IN THIS ARCTIC COLD!

ALONE IN THE SPACESHIP'S LABORATORY, KENTON WORKS WITH INSULATED WIRE AND SMALL, POWERFUL BATTERIES TO MAKE HIMSELF A SET OF ELECTRIC CLOTHES...
THIS WORKS ON THE SAME PRINCIPLE AS THE ELECTRIC BLANKET. NOT ONLY WILL IT KEEP ME WARM IN THIS SUB-ZERO TEMPERATURE, BUT IT WILL SERVE AS A DISGUISE, AFTER I STUFF THE EXTRA SLEEVES WITH CLOTH.

I CAN PASS FOR AN ALIEN EXCEPT FOR A CLOSE INSPECTION! HMMM... FIRST THING TO LOOK FOR IS A MUSEUM...

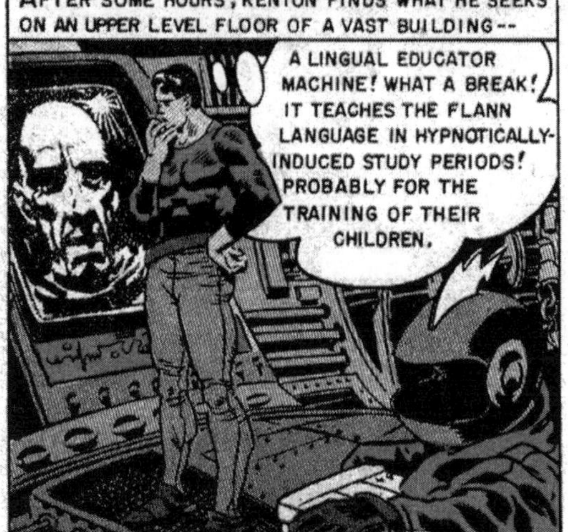
AFTER SOME HOURS, KENTON FINDS WHAT HE SEEKS ON AN UPPER LEVEL FLOOR OF A VAST BUILDING--
A LINGUAL EDUCATOR MACHINE! WHAT A BREAK! IT TEACHES THE FLANN LANGUAGE IN HYPNOTICALLY-INDUCED STUDY PERIODS! PROBABLY FOR THE TRAINING OF THEIR CHILDREN.

HOUR AFTER HOUR, KENTON STUDIES THE FLANN LANGUAGE. HE TOILS ON, MOVING FROM SCREEN TO SCREEN, LEARNING THE ACCUMULATED WISDOM OF THE FLANN--WHEN SUDDENLY, BEHIND HIM, A DOOR OPENS...
THE FLANN CAME TO THE SOLAR SYSTEM FROM THEIR OWN WORLD OVER A THOUSAND YEARS AGO! THEY'RE COMPOSED OF SILICON ATOMS RATHER THAN CARBON ATOMS, AS MANKIND IS--HUH! THAT OUGHT TO MEAN SOMETHING TO ME--BUT WHAT?
5

YIII! IF I HADN'T SEEN THE REFLECTION OF THAT OPENING DOOR IN THE GLASS OF THE VISI-SCREEN, I'D BE BLASTED INTO MOLECULES RIGHT ABOUT NOW! JUST WHEN I WAS GETTING TO KNOW YOU FLANN PEOPLE TOO...

YOU FLANN CAME FROM SOME-WHERE OUT BEYOND ANDROMEDA GALAXY, MORE THAN A THOUSAND YEARS AGO! YOU LANDED ON THE COLDEST PLANET IN THE SYSTEM, PLUTO—

ON PLUTO, YOU BUILT YOUR CITY, DEVISED NEW WEAPONS—WITH THE CONQUEST OF THE ENTIRE SOLAR SYSTEM IN MIND! THAT MAKES THIS SO MUCH SWEETER MUSIC TO MY EARS!

THE FLANN HAVE BEEN RAIDING THE URANIUM MINES ON TITAN TO GET ENOUGH ATOM BOMBS TO BLAST THE EARTH—STONGEST OF ALL PLANETS—OUT OF EXISTENCE! THEY'RE READY TO MOVE INWARD TOWARD EARTH RIGHT NOW--AND I'M TOO FAR AWAY TO SEND ANY KIND OF WARNING!

AS KENTON RACES THROUGH THE CITY OF FLANN, SEEK-ING SOME MEANS OF ESCAPE, ARMED GUARDS DISCOVER THEIR FALLEN COMRADE...
A MAN FROM EARTH, YET HE SPOKE THE LANGUAGE OF THE FLANN! HE HIT ME--ALMOST WITH THE KICK OF A FORCE RAY!
AN EARTH SPY LOOSE IN FLANN CITY! WE'LL SOUND THE ALARM-- ALERT ALL PATROLS!

MINUTES LATER, ON THE STREETS OUTSIDE--
ATTENTION, ALL PERSONNEL! REPORT AT ONCE TO H.Q. AN EARTH SPY IS AT LIBERTY! REPORT AT ONCE TO BE CODED AND CERTIFIED! ATTENTION...
THEY'VE GOT ME THERE! IF I DON'T REPORT, A POLICE PATROL WILL BLAST ME...IF I DO REPORT, A CITY GUARD WILL DO THE SAME THING! WHAT DO I DO NOW?

AN EXPLOSIVE BULLET BLASTS THE SIDE OF THE STONE BUILDING, INCHES FROM KENTON'S FACE...
PARROWWW
THEY'VE SEEN ME! I'VE GOT TO FIND COVER SOMEWHERE!
6

ONE OF THOSE BULLETS ISN'T GOING TO MISS, PRETTY SOON! THERE MUST BE SOMEWHERE TO TURN--BUT WHERE? OH-OH HERE COME THREE MORE IN FRONT...

ONE GOOD BODY BLOCK WILL CHECK YOU...

GOT TO TAKE A CHANCE...DIVE IN HERE! YIII!--THAT ONE WAS CLOSE!

WHAT THE--! THIS SLIDE IS COVERED WITH ICE... AND IS IT COLD! BRRR... HEY--I KNOW WHAT I'M IN! I'M INSIDE A GIGANTIC AIR-CONDITIONING VENT! ONE OF THE VENTS THAT KEEPS FLANN CITY AS COLD AS THAT SPACESHIP WAS...!

I COULDN'T STOP ON THAT CHUTE...IT WAS COVERED WITH ICE... NOW WHERE AM I GOING...?

THIS GLASS DIDN'T CUT ME, BUT I--HEY! GLASS! SURE, THAT'S THE ANSWER TO THE COLD AND TO THE FLANN'S SILICON CONSTRUCTION! WHY DIDN'T I THINK OF THIS BEFORE?

THE AIR-CONDITIONING ENGINES MUST BE FAR BELOW! IF I REMEMBER THE LAYOUT OF THE CITY FROM THOSE BLUEPRINTS I STUDIED BACK AT THE MUSEUM, I'M IN THE MAIN WEATHER-CONDITIONING BUILDING RIGHT NOW....
7

THIS TIME EXPLOSIVE BULLETS FLY AWAY FROM PATROL CAPTAIN KENTON—WITH THE DEADLY ACCURACY OF AN EXPERT MARKSMAN! IN A MATTER OF SECONDS, HE IS THE ONLY MAN ALIVE IN THE GREAT CONTROL ROOM...

AS THE THERMOMETER RISES TO THE DANGER MARK AND BEYOND, SWEAT POURS OFF KENTON'S BODY! HE RIPS HIS UNIFORM TO SHREDS! HIS LUNGS PANT FOR AIR! UP, UP, UP GOES THE TEMPERATURE!

THIS INSULATED ROOM IS THE ONLY THING KEEPING ME... ALIVE! AND EVEN THIS INSULATION CAN'T TAKE MUCH MORE OF... THIS! IF I DON'T TURN OFF THE POWER, THIS HEAT WILL BAKE ME TO A CRISP...

FOR ONE HOUR THE TEMPERATURE OF FLANN CITY RISES TO INCRED-IBLE HEIGHTS! STEAM SPURTS FROM AIR VALVES! EXPLODING WATER MAINS BURST UNDER PRESSURE! AND THEN, EVEN DAVE KENTON CAN STAND NO MORE...

JUST... MADE IT... BEFORE I BLACKED OUT! GOT THE FUR-NACES BANKED... BUILDING UP COLD NOW, AS BEFORE... INSTEAD OF THAT... AWFUL HEAT...

THE FLANN HAVE TURNED INTO GLASS! SINCE GLASS IS FORMED OF SILICON, FUSED BY HEAT, THE INTENSE HEAT FUSED THE SILICON IN THEIR BODIES... CHANGED THEIR MOLECULAR STRUCTURE FROM FLUID SILICON TO HARD SILICON... OR... GLASS!

MIRROR MAGIC

BY RON HANNA

GUMMITCH WAS a superkitten… no more.

EVEN AFTER several years had passed, he retained his consciousness and memory of that day when he had flung his spirit, yet not his mind, into the blackness that was the human Sissy's body and soul. He had no regrets. He had protected his human charges from her evil. Baby was now grown into a young teenager away at boarding school, and he rarely saw him anymore. He still bore the slight scars from the hat pin that had been scratched into his face by Sissy, but as that was in the "bad times", and now they lived in "good times", they were never mentioned. In fact, Gummitch believed that with Sissy's new enlightenment there really was no reason to remember those awful, dark days. Old Horsemeat and Kitty-Come-Here had retired into a comfortable middle-age where they took great pleasure in relaxing in front of a fireplace, petting Gummitch with loving human hands, stroking his fur while Gummitch purred, and perhaps even they didn't remember the events of that night when Sissy, in her dark madness, had attempted to harm Baby, whom Gummitch protected with the greatest sacrifice of all. His spirit.

Sissy had grown up and began a new life once Gummitch's spirit had entered her through the practice of mirror magic, which was only one of many types of special talents that all cats and kittens possessed. It was a selfless sacrifice on Gummitch's part, and even though he was fated to remain the only cat to never achieve his potential, it had been worth it. Despite what many people may believe, cats are not totally self-absorbed creatures, involved only with following their own paths, oblivious to humankind. They cared, they loved, and yes, they even are capable of sacrificing their own selves for the greater good. Gummitch had no regrets.

But he was older now, by many years, and at times it seemed he could not remember things as well as he used to. He definitely had trouble walking now, what with arthritis and old age setting in. His electrical, shining fur had become dull and flat. He had been losing weight, even with the good meals that his owners had fed him. Ashurbanipal and Cleopatra, the other two household felines, had departed from this mortal coil a couple of years ago, leaving Gummitch alone. Of course, there was the occasional squirrel or bird that Gummitch loved to chase, but along with his growing infirmities, even that pleasure was now denied him. Mostly, he just limped along, sometimes staring up into the night skies, seeing the vastness of the stars, and despaired that he would never reach them.

SISSY HAD gone on to become a Veterinarian, and a very good one too, and Gummitch had always suspected that it was because she owed her salvation to him, even though she never spoke about it. She still could not play the "Owl Eyes" game, one of Gummitch's favorite pastimes, and so his big, round yellow eyes felt as alone as his soul was empty. But he knew it was because of the guilt she felt, and what had happened the last time they had locked their eyes upon each other and Gummitch used the Springing Space-Time and Mirror Magic to defeat her evil intentions of harming the infant Baby. But since that transformation, she had gone on to become a fine, loving human who cared deeply about Gummitch, and who always gave him a hug and treats when she visited her family. Although she didn't visit often—she was often in her veterinary laboratory working to save the lives of many varied creatures—she always remained a high-spirited and loving person. The type of person that Gummitch was meant to be.

THE DAYS grew longer. Gummitch grew more tired. His sense of balance, once beautiful to behold, was no longer as stable as it used to be. And sometimes he found himself not remembering what he had just eaten for dinner—or was it breakfast?—or even that he occasionally "missed" while doing his business in the litter box. But sometimes—only at some times—he could still remember the books he was planning on writing, the verbal discourses he would have with humans, and the great expeditions he would have gone on, yet these were fleeting memories. Perhaps he had Catzheimer's Disease, which was a dreadful way to end his days, as even though his body may still function, his mind would be gone, and he would wither away until he passed on into the death that awaits every creature. When he thought of this, Gummitch would crawl into a dark closet, alone, and both cry and purr his way into a deep and dark sleep.

Gummitch would still pass by the heavy mirrors on the wall, and glance—he could never look straight into them again—at the Gummitch Double that resided within the Mirror World. With the inky blackness that now infested his spirit, he no longer cared about being taken over by the entity on the other side of Reality. He had been leading such a dull and dark life for so long that these things didn't matter anymore. He was sure that the Gummitch Double was just as stricken and destitute as he had become. And even when he occasionally touched paws with his Mirror Double, he still felt the coldness that pierced the barrier of the Other World. Yes, all thoughts of happiness were gone... all that was left were shadows and his own cold, unfeeling reflection. As he once knew that his Higher Change was approaching—only to be stopped by the black spirit within young Sissy—Gummitch became increasingly aware that his days were soon to come to an end. And at this point, he welcomed it. For far too long he had been a trapped soul, bound by blackness, and there was no escaping that fact... He was dying.

SEVERAL DAYS later, after increasingly nightmarish dreams of death, and with no dreams of hope, Gummitch was awakened from his fitful sleep by Sissy, who had come to visit Old Horsemeat and Kitty-Come-Here. The little girl, now grown, was talking with her parents, and even in his drowsiness, Gummitch heard the words.

"Mom... Dad..." Sissy was saying, "I know you love our good old Gummitch, but just look at him! I didn't graduate from Vet School not to know when an animal is in misery and..." she hesitated, "...should be put to sleep."

"But, darling," Old Horsemeat said, "are you sure? I know he's not in the best of shape, but..."

"No, dad", Sissy continued, "He's nothing but skin and bones. His blood levels show increased toxicity in his renal glands. His kidneys are failing, his bones are showing massive signs of osteoporosis, and his quality of life is, well, about as bad as it can be. Plus, he's showing signs of dementia as well as other neurological symptoms. Would YOU like to live like that? Of course you

---

Ron Hanna I've been reading since I was 3 years old and have always had a life-long passion for books of all kinds. I started writing my own adventure stories to amuse myself when I was about 10, and recently my mother actually found one of those tales and sent it to me. Wow, that really brought back memories! As I grew older I began writing, with some occasional painting, in other genres but never really pursued it as much as I should have. Later, when I began publishing the *Secret Sanctum* fanzine I actually revived my writing by doing a parody series of *Pinky & The Brain* (an animated TV series) versus various pulp heroes. I really enjoyed them, but I just never could seriously concentrate on my writing while being a publisher as well... But about a year ago I read Fritz Leiber's story "Space-Time For Springers" and after that, well, I just had to write a sequel to it... It was written with passion, respect, and much love and I hope you enjoy reading it as much as I enjoyed writing it!

wouldn't! Both you and Mom have specifically requested in your wills that you not be kept alive by artificial means, and at least for animals, we have the benefit of Euthanasia when the owners deem that their pets' lives are better off dead, rather than living in pain and torment. I became a Veterinarian to HELP animals, and you know I love Gummitch…" Here she hesitated. "He… he… SAVED me! You both know that when I was younger, I was not a good person… but Gummitch, well, he… he DID something that lifted something… something BAD from me! YOU KNOW IT!" Sissy was almost screaming now, and old Gummitch was now wide awake, because when Sissy raised her voice, it could wake the dead!

"Dear…" Kitty-Come-Here started to say, "you know we don't talk about…"

"It doesn't matter if we ever talked about it, it's TRUE… and I will not see my Gummitch die slowly and painfully!" Sissy was very emphatic in her tone. "Now… Dad, I want you to get your old terry-cloth bathrobe, the one that Gummitch still loves to sleep on, and I want you to let me take him to my Hospital... and I will put him out of his misery with all the love and care I can. Trust me, he'll feel no pain. The injections (with hat-pins? thought Gummitch) will be given in separate doses, with the first one being a pain-killer so that he'll never even feel the final ones that will free him from suffering at last. C'mon, Mom... Dad... you know it's time. In your hearts, you know it's time." (Yes, it is, Gummitch thought to himself).

"Well… OK, darling, I guess we know you're right, but…" Kitty-Come-Here started to sniffle and cry, and Old Horsemeat put his arms around her tenderly, then went to the closet, picked up his old bathrobe, wrapped Gummitch in it, and handed him to Sissy.

"Make sure he doesn't suffer, Sissy", Old Horsemeat said, "We all love that crazy cat, but you're right. It's time."

"Don't worry, dad." Sissy replied, "I won't." And she took hold of Gummitch, wrapped in his birthing robe from many years ago, and headed out to her car.

GUMMITCH DIDN'T much like the antiseptic smell of the Vet's office, and the stainless steel table was cold. Cold as death itself, cold as his spirit. But Sissy did something special for him. She placed the terry-cloth robe on the floor and placed Gummitch on it. The feeble cat looked up and was amazed to see a large mirror placed against the wall, and he saw the Gummitch Double, old and tired as was he, reflected in it. He glanced up and saw Sissy draw up some clear liquid in a syringe, and then she pulled something out of a drawer—a piece of paper it looked like—and then she bent down and cradled Gummitch in her arms.

"My kitty," she spoke softly, "…my wonderful little cat… I know what you did so many years ago. I spent my entire life after that evil episode just so I could reach this moment." She started to cry. "You gave me your spirit when you crossed the space-time and entered me. You saved me… and I know it cost you dearly. You see, when your so very special essence entered me, I knew the things that you knew. I saw your dreams and hopes and desires. And I hope that here, at the end, I can help you the way you helped me."

Gummitch was confused, partly from his increasing Catzheimer's Disease, but also because he wasn't sure what she was talking about.

"I'm not really positive if this will work, because I only have deeply buried memories of that day, but here…" And then Sissy moved Gummitch's head towards the mirror, and to his surprise, she then placed a photograph in front of it—a photo of Gummitch as a very young kitten—and then she continued in a soft and loving voice…

"Look, Gummitch… Look at yourself as you once were." She then injected the syringe with a pain-relieving fluid into his veins.

Gummitch began to feel drowsy.

"Look at your picture… Look beyond the picture." Her voice was almost hypnotic and Gummitch could not resist her words.

"As you feel no pain, look into your past, through your picture and into the mirror." And Gummitch found he could do that! His gaze was failing but he seemed to see not only the picture that was himself, but through the picture into the mirror where the Gummitch Double resided!

"Now, my dearest friend," Sissy spoke for the last time, "I want you to use your powers and… SPRING! Use the Mirror Magic!"

And Gummitch, from the deepest recesses of his mind, those parts that had not yet fallen prey to old age… walked through his picture, touched paws with the Gummitch Double, and the Gummitch Double instantly flung his own spirit, through the mirror and photograph, and passed into the dying Gummitch.

Gummitch lay on the terry-cloth robe. His beautiful and loving heart had stopped beating at last.

Sissy thought to herself, "There are many primitive peoples that believe a person's soul is trapped in a photograph. And they never allow their picture to be taken. I've studied all my life to do this for you, my dearest kitty. I only hope it works."

She left the Hospital room… and cried for several days.

GUMMITCH RAN through the fresh grass in his new world, smelling all those wonderful odors of life, batting at squirrels, chasing butterflies, and stalking birds. He thought of wonderful things… of drinking coffee and becoming human… of writing books and going on exotic expeditions—and his heart was happy. His spirit was restored. His soul was whole again at last!

GUMMITCH WAS a superkitten… once more.

Dedicated to Fritz Leiber
In Honor of his Story
Space-Time For Springers

by CARLETON GRINDLE

Despite all appearances to the contrary, just how does a naive Star Guard get it through a space pirate's head that he's the one under arrest?

1.

IN A CLEARING on the small jungle-covered northern continent of an unclaimed planet in the Markel System, two saurian creatures were roasting a small human. The small human, though clearly no match for the larger creatures was struggling valiantly. But the fire was roaring in a pit the saurian pair had dug for that purpose, and their victim was already tied to the spit, or at least so tangled up in the ropes as to make no difference.

"We should probably have killed the thing before trying to cook it," the first saurian said.

"We should *certainly* have killed the thing first," said the other saurian, picking up a large, nearby rock. The victim was struggling on the ground next to the pit. The saurian lifted the rock high over the small creature's head. But the human twisted around in the nick of time and the rock crashed harmlessly to the ground, missing her entirely. By this time she was pretty much resolved to dying, but so angry that she had sworn not to die until she had somehow found a way to take one of her attackers with her.

"Hold her still!" shouted the saurian, reaching for another and larger rock.

"And have you crush my hands? The spit has a sharp end, kill her with that."

"She's tied to the spit."

"Loosely tied to it. Slide it out of the ropes, stab her, and we can slide it back in."

The saurian gave a snarl, but it reached for the spit and grasped it firmly in both hands, then pulled it out. He moved to the human and lifted the sharpened stick with the point toward his potential victim. He hesitated.

"Are you sure this isn't the one we're supposed to be hunting for?"

"The one we're hunting for is a male. This one's a female."

The first saurian lowered the stick. "Are you sure? How can you tell a thing like that?"

"I just can. Now hurry up and kill it. I'm starving."

The small human began to roll around even more furiously despite the way they had the ropes tangled around her limbs. The saurian again lifted the sharpened stick high and made ready to plunge it down as soon as it could get range of her but she was remarkably uncooperative—even for a human. She lashed out with her legs and drove the heels of her heavy boots against the saurian's ankles.

The saurian screamed and danced back away from the creature who sat up as if scrambling to her feet—which she could not do because of the way she was tangled in the ropes. The second saurian, ignoring the distress of his partner, grabbed her by the neck and tried to throw her down again. Somehow, this time she did scramble to her feet and drove her head straight at him, butting him right between the eyes.

It was a mistake. Her head was nowhere near as hard as the saurian's.

She suddenly saw more stars than she had seen through the ship's ports on the trip in to this planet. Sharp, fierce pain erupted through her skull. The strength ran out of her and her legs folded under so that she collapsed face down in the grass.

As from a great distance she heard one of the saurians say, "That's what we want. Hit her again, Qurlos. Hard. Quick."

Oh God, she thought. *I'm not getting to take either of these bastards with me.*

Then there was a noise, a loud one, and something heavy struck the ground beside her. She blinked her eyes into focus and was staring at what was probably Qurlos, lying right next to her, its tongue lolling out of the side of its snout, and its snake-like eyes staring at her blindly. "What the hell," she said and pulled back as far away from it as she could.

There was a repeat of the loud noise and something gave a loud, pained yelp and she rolled over in time to see the other saurian, four or five feet away, toppling like a tree. She could smell the scorched stench of its uniform and body as a small bolt of flame burst out of its chest, flickered a bit and then went out.

Suddenly a man—another human for God's sake—was bending over her, giving her a very concerned look, and saying, "Are you all right, ma'am?"

"Of course I'm not all right," she growled at him in a weak voice. "That pair of toad droppings are trying to kill my ass!"

"Well, technically," the man said, "they aren't. Not any more at least."

She was untangling herself from the ropes snarled around her arms and legs. It seemed easier now but when—refusing to let her rescuer help her up—she scrambled to a standing position, she somehow tripped and fell face down onto the grass again.

She tried to say something extremely unkind about the planet's ancestry, but there seemed to be a clump of grass in her mouth. She spit it out.

Her rescuer took her arm and helped her stand up. "Goddamn it, I'm not even supposed to be on this crappy planet," she growled. "No one is."

"So I understand," the man said. "But it seems pretty crowded just now."

She fixed him with her eyes. "So what the bloody hell are you doing here?"

"I was just about to ask you that."

"We can talk later," she said. "I suspect we need to get away from here."

"I rather think you're right," he agreed. "I think those two who had you were trying to head me off and found you more or less by mistake. The rest of their gang is coming up behind me, probably pretty fast, and certainly pretty angry."

She said, "Oh," and looked back the way he had come. There was nothing to see but orange jungle, with the occasional flash of grey, red and blue blossoms growing from the trees and vines. "I don't hear them, so we must have a lead on them."

"Maybe not as much a lead as you might think," he said.

He pointed up to where two things that looked like birds with bat-like wings, glided circles in the greenish sky. "Those aren't birds," he said, though it was hardly necessary.

"I know," she said. "I recognize the configuration. Those are Parak's scout ships."

"I think we need to get under cover of the jungle before more ships get here," he said.

"Can't argue with you on that," she said. "You must be really special to have the meanest, crappiest piece of scum in the Galaxy hunting for you."

"Well, I guess that's a fair assessment," he said, grabbing her by the arm and starting toward the nearest thicket. "But he's my old man, and when he gets pissed off at me, he always seems to get more pissed off than he does at most people. Which says a lot."

He was less guiding her than yanking her along as they plunged into the underbrush. His speed in this tangle was amazing, but the fact that he seemed to be able to not trip every two steps was even more amazing.

When she could find enough wind to manage words all she could come up with was, "So you're Parak, Junior?"

"Royce," he said. "Call me Royce. I hate being called 'junior.'"

"I don't care what you hate, *Junior*. Do you know who I am?"

"No ma'am," he said, somehow managing to make both of them avoid the trunk of a tree that loomed up suddenly in front of them.

"I'm Star Guard," she said. "That's bleeping Star Guard Division of Fugitive Tracking to you. Do you know how much reward there is for your capture?"

"Can't be much, ma'am," he said, not slowing down. "I'm not yet twenty-one, not for another whole week yet."

"Two bleeping thousand sur credits," she said. "Not even credits, bleeping sur credits. That's certainly enough to explain why your old man's whole crapping gang of mothergrinders is out after you."

"That's not it," Royce told her.

"And me…"

"By the way, just what do I call you?"

"What?"

"Your name—," he clarified.

"I know what jacking 'call you' means!" she snapped. And added: "Rhayla."

"Hello, Rhayla." He stopped suddenly, almost pulling her arm out of its socket. He pushed her behind a tree.

"They're catching up on us," he said.

Her eyes widened. "Who's catching up on us?"

"Them. The guys we're running from."

"Then let me rephrase my question. Who the crap are we running from? Oh, wait a minute. I know that. Your old man's thugs. In that case, why?"

"It's a long story," Royce said.

"Then *Reader's Digest* the crap out of it," she told him. "And hurry."

"If I have the time," he said, peering around the tree trunk and back along their trail. Back in that direction, Rhayla could hear something tromping through the underbrush.

"That's not them," he said.

It sounded like a herd of bleeping dinosaurs. She risked peering around the bole of the tree she was hiding behind to see what it was.

She saw nothing.

Then, suddenly, it crashed through the trees. Holy Mugwumps of Zeus! It was bigger than a herd of barfing elephants. Royce, peering around the other side of the trunk, said, "Way to go! I've wanted me one of them for just the longest time!" and took careful aim.

And missed.

2

DESPITE THE fact that Markel VII was pretty colorful as planets went, with its orange jungle and greenish sky and all, it didn't matter once you got under the canopy and into the heavy foliage. There it was dark, there it was shadows. There it was steaming and hot and she had to put up with Royce muttering to himself. He'd missed a target big as two houses and the damned thing had almost trampled them turning around so it could run away.

Now they were running away. Such was life.

"Why did you shoot at the thing if you couldn't hit it!" she yelled, even though he was less than two feet from her.

"I didn't want to throw away my knife," he said.

Suddenly he grabbed her elbow and pulled her to the left, almost jerking her arm out of its socket once again. She lost her footing and he dragged her until she found

Carleton Grindle has published sf and fantasy in Spaceway (edited by William Crawford, the man who published H.P. Lovecraft's first book), the American Perry Rhodan series (edited by Forrest J Ackerman), Witchcraft & Sorcery (edited by Gerald Page), and the anthology "When the Black Lotus Blooms" (edited by Elizabeth A. Saunders). He was born in Tennessee and now makes his home in Georgia.

it again, which she made a point of doing quickly before she really lost the arm.

They were running along a path at a right angle to their earlier course. She could hear the thing that was after them crashing through the jungle, smashing trees and scattering leaves and branches behind them. "I think we lost it," Royce said. "At least it'll take it a few hundred meters to slow down enough to turn."

They broke out of the jungle and were running along a ridge with a sloping side to the left of them.

"Down that way," Royce said, and emphasized his point by shoving her.

"Holy crap!" she yelped, somersaulting off the trail. He reached for her, missed and she kept tumbling, with him running after. At what might have been the bottom of the slope—it was hard to tell in this terrain—she came up hard against some bushes. The branches whipped at her face, but at least she was no longer rolling.

Royce caught up with her. "You were running too fast," he said, helping her to her feet. "You got to take it easy or you'll wear yourself out."

"Oh, shut up," she managed to say. He was pulling her across a clearing now, toward the shelter of some trees. He shoved her behind a tree trunk and said, "Hold up." For a second or two he gazed back the way they had come. "I think we lost that whatever-it-is."

"This is your home world and you don't even know what that thing was?"

"I'm an inhabitant, not an explorer. But I do know there are lots of dangerous animals here. I just don't know what all of them are. I never even saw that one, before."

"Oh, great," she said. "I'm running through the woods with a raccoon cap that doesn't even have a Daniel Boone under it!"

In the distance they could hear the monster still thrashing through the jungle but the sounds were growing fainter.

"He's either forgotten what he was chasing or he's found something better tasting to go after," Royce said.

"Maybe he's found your father's men. The mother-grinders who were chasing us, I hope."

"Maybe, but I don't think he was going in the right direction."

"By the way," she said. "You're under arrest."

"For what?"

"For being the son of a pirate."

"Being the son of a pirate! You're arresting me for *that*?"

"Not just any pirate. You're the son of Parak, the most notorious pirate in the galaxy. I'll come up with other and better charges, later," she snapped. And added: "Boy, it's really gotten quiet."

He stepped from behind the tree and surveyed their back trail a few moments. "Well, we lost the big critter. Maybe we lost Daddy's men, too.

"Oh, and by the way," he went on. "You can't *actually* arrest me because you don't have a gun."

"Sure I do," she said, reaching for her holster. "Oops!"

"It must have fallen out in all that running around through the jungle," he said. "Well, don't worry about it for now. I can find you a new one and you can arrest me then. But for now, I think we better keep going."

He started off through the jungle again.

They trudged on, following an animal trail that wove in and out of trees, bushes and other obstacles so that they probably went as far back and forth as they did forward.

She was thinking how she'd handle this infuriating situation when the time came that she could surreptitiously grab for her hideout gun. It was even more important to locate some sort of communication device that was capable of reaching stellar distances. Boy, was this planet going to burn. Or at least the pirates and other scum on it were. The planet itself looked too bleeping wet to burn.

"Whoa! Look out," Royce said.

She stopped before he could yank on her arm again. She was confused. The trail ahead of her looked all right.

"Don't step there," he said. "It's a pitfall."

"What? Oh," she said, jumping aside as she realized Royce was right.

"Hey, be careful," he told her.

"I am being careful," she growled. "What the bleep do you think I'm being?"

Embarrassingly, that was when she felt something tickle her ankles, then suddenly grab at them. For a brief moment she thought it was a snake, but then she realized it was a rope—a snare of some sort. It closed tightly on her ankles, yanked her feet out from under her and then lifted her up feet first with incredible speed that just managed to be fast enough so her head didn't slam the ground. "Oh, bloody, monkey-grinding *CRAP!*" she yelled.

"Well, fancy be! And what, pray tell, might we have here?" said a voice she didn't recognize.

She was hanging by her heels, swinging back and forth and looking at him upside down as a stranger lumbered out of some bushes. He was rather outlandishly garbed in mismatched clothes in too many too-bright colors, and he looked something like a bear.

"Lovo!" shouted Royce, happily. "I didn't know you were on this planet?"

"Then why were you looking for me?"

"Lovo?" Rhayla said. "Lovo the pirate?"

"At your service, ma'am," he said, blinking at her and tilting his head a bit, the better to see her.

"That does it!" she growled. "Get me down from here. And then put your hands up. You're both under arrest."

Lovo said, "It be seeming to me she has a piss-poor grasp of the situation, Royce."

3

"OH, SHE'S all right," Royce said. "But I do admit she can be a bit excitable. And by the way, we weren't looking for you. I'm the one being looked for."

"Who would be after you when she's available?" said Lovo. "Of course she's a human, and on the small side, but she has a nice shape to her." He eyed her appreciatively. "For a human, that is. I like the way her skirt be hanging down from her waist that way."

"It's a short skirt, too," Royce said. "But she's upside down right now and it'll hang differently when she gets down from there."

"You perverts!" Rhayla shouted.

"Is that a thong or panties she's wearing?" Lovo said. "Whirl her around a bit so I can tell."

"You crapping pervert! What the bleep does it matter to a mother-grinding bear what I'm wearing! Get me down from here!"

Lovo pulled a knife and walked over to a near-by tree where the rope that held Rhayla was tied off. He sliced the rope deftly and Royce barely managed to reach in time to prevent her from cracking her head open on the ground.

Royce loosened the rope around her ankles as Rhayla gave forth with a stream of inspired invective.

"She be spirited," said Lovo, approvingly. "I give her that."

"Oh, she's that all right," Royce said. "Now give me the story, buddy. What brings you back here? Didn't Daddy say he was going to parboil your balls and feed them to you if he ever saw you again?"

"I seem to recall he phrasing it a bit more colorfully, but that's it in the main. Where did you pick up the chickie-babe?"

Rhayla stood up, stamping her feet just to make sure they were still there. "You can shave off the 'chickie-babe' stubble, Pooh-bear and turn over your weapons. Then throw your hands up. You're under arrest. That goes for you too, Junior."

Lovo looked at Royce. "Junior?"

"It's a term of endearment back on Earth," Royce told him. "As for the rest of it, she must have hit her head despite my best efforts."

Lovo said. "She never hit her head. I know. I wasn't watching her cute little tail-feathers the whole time."

"Forget about my 'mugwumping' rear end and put your hands up!," she shouted.

"Oh, calm down," Royce said, beginning to lose patience with her. "We're not under arrest yet. You don't even have a gun on you."

"I always work with a back up," she said.

"I know." He bent down and reached into a clump of grass to pick something up. "It fell out of your boot while you were swinging back and forth." He hefted the gun. It was small and flat but had some solid weight to it.

She stooped down to reach into her right boot. "Crapping lobsters," she said. "Crapping mother-grinding lobsters!"

"Oh, calm down," Royce said. "You aren't going to arrest us, and that's final. Here's your gun back."

"Her gun back?" said Lovo. "Is that... er... no offense lad, but does that be the smartest thing to do and all?"

Royce handed her gun back to her anyway. “Put it away. You'll need every charge in it if Daddy's goons catch up to us. Which reminds me.” He turned to Lovo. “Just why did you come back?”

“Why, I be back to settle things with your old man. From ambush, preferably. I got me some loot stashed on this planet, assuming he hasn't found it and grabbed it up and all. That was the real reason he chased me off. ‘Cause he knew I had treasure hidden and he thought he might be having the time to find it with me gone. So now you tell me. Has he?”

“Not so far as I know. If you hid it, there's a good chance it's still hidden. Of course Daddy's not the only pirate who might have found it.”

“That be a chance I had to take,” said Lovo, nodding. “And while we be telling our life's yarns, why be it you're out here fleeing from your old man's minions?”

“He thinks I did him dirty,” Royce said.

“And knowing the two of you like I do, I've no doubt he's right,” Lovo said.

“Well, he has a case, but he's wrong to think it's such a big case. I don't mind it if he picks on mining ships or passenger liners or the like, but he was going to hit a hospital ship just to see what drugs it might carry. There're sick people on a hospital ship and they need the drugs. So I ratted him out. He found out, sort of, and got pissed off at me.”

“Found out, he did? I'll bet he found out. I'll bet he was swooping down on what he thought was a defenseless hospital buggy and all of a sudden out of nowhere a bunch of Star Guard gunships zip into space and heat things up. Is that it?”

“More or less.”

“And he takes that as un-son like of you, I be wagering.” Lovo nodded. “Under the circumstances I might be taking a thing like that rather poorly myself. And this thing?” He indicated Rhayla.

“She just showed up, kicking up a fuss and all.”

Lovo said, “My guess is she came here to arrest you and your old man.”

“I think that might be right.”

“Hello!” Rhayla said. “I'm right here, listening to every word. If you have a question about me, just ask.”

“Am I right about you being here to throw Daddy in jail?”

“You better believe it,” she snarled.

“In that case I don't have any more questions,” Royce said.

“And you too, now that I know where you are. And Lovo. Can't pass up an opportunity to bring in all three of you.”

“Of course you can't,” Royce said. “I wouldn't ask it of you. Neither would Lovo. But I have a feeling those guys who're after us will catch up with us if we just stand here. So we better get moving again.”

“You can't run off,” Rhayla said. “You're under arrest!”

“Now, now,” said Royce. “There'll be time for that later. We need to be moving in that direction.”

“What a monkey bleeping dry-dock you are,” she said. She looked around. “But you're probably right,” in a more subdued tone.

“Of course I am,” he said.

“Grind off,” she growled.

She turned and started off into the jungle but at once caught her toe on a stray root. She sprawled face first on the ground.

Lovo looked down at her. “*Ah*,” he said. “Thong.”

4

THE JUNGLE was lighter here, the trees not as tall, nor the braches as interwoven with one another. Through plentiful breaks they could see the sky here and there. After a while it became evident that Parak's planes were beginning to cluster their search-patterns in this area.

“Their detectors are picking us up,” Rhayla said.

“Then they must know exactly where we are,” Lovo said. “Why not just blow us out of existence?”

“I like to think it's because of me,” Royce said.

“From what I've seen of your personality, I doubt it,” Rhayla said. “More than likely it's me. I'm carrying a small masking device. They obviously have equipment good enough to detect our heat signatures but not good enough to pinpoint our location through them.”

“Or else they can't tell us from the local fauna,” said Lovo.

“Well,” Royce put in, “Whatever it is let's take advantage of it while we can.”

They spent the afternoon trudging deeper into the jungle. The shadows lengthened and the sky darkened. Then from out of the shadows men stepped, men who held weapons pointed at them. Royce gestured for Rhayla and Lovo to stop and stand beside him. The men came closer.

Finally, one of them said, "Royce? Is that you Royce? And you, Lovo?"

The speaker was about a head shorter than Royce, and Rhayla's first impression of him was "scrawny."

"So," say Lovo. "You really weren't looking for me."

"Doesn't mean I'm not glad to see you," Royce said.

"Royce, lad," the scrawny man said and came forward. He threw his arms around the boy and they greeted each other like lost brothers. Lovo glanced at Rhayla. "You intending to arrest these fellows too, sweetheart?"

"First good chance I get."

"Well put," he told her. "That'll likely be some time yet."

Royce brought the scrawny man over to Rhayla and said, "Rhayla, this is Transk. He's the one I was telling you about. No, belay that. He's the one I was going to tell you about when I got the time." He grinned sheepishly. "This is him!"

"Transk?" Another one who was on her list. "Wow, you got no one but celebrities on this planet, don't you?"

"I do believe the girl's wearing SG colors," Transk said.

"Pretty short skirt, though, right?" said Royce.

"Will you shut up about the skirt for crapping sakes?" Rhayla growled.

"She's here to arrest us all, especially me and Daddy."

"Is that a fact... Where's her task force?"

"One planet, one SG agent," Rhaya snarled.

"It might just be one planet," Royce said. "But there's at least two pirate crews here." He turned to Transk. "She's so good she just figured she'd come in and take all of us at one fell swoop and line us up in formation until the armada comes in."

Transk lifted both eyebrows. "Armada?"

"Well, bunch of ships," Royce confessed. "I don't really know how many there are, but it's got to be more than just a few. Look how many of us there are."

"I got me eight men," Transk admitted. "What's your old man's roster?"

"Close to eighteen armed guards, but he has some mechanics, field hands, a cook and so forth, maybe two dozen in all. He wouldn't want to rely on the household help, but they can hold guns if they have to. And the major domo is old Ratcliffe, you remember him, don't you?"

Transk smiled. "Not as well as he remembers me, I bet. Did he ever grow that hand back?"

"Heck, no," Royce said. "But he's got a nice, sharp titanium hook on the end of that arm, just waiting till he sees you again."

"I bet," Transk said, grinning. He might have said more then, but there was a crackling sound and the air around the man standing next to him took on a goldish tint. Transk gave a yowlp and hit the ground just in time so that the next shot was high of him. "They're not shooting like the household help," he said.

Royce had shoved Rhayla to the ground and was lying on top of her. She yelled for him to get off but he ignored her. Suddenly she felt a cold hand on her rear and thought it was Royce. But when she looked back she saw Transk smiling back at her and felt his fingers groping away. "Sorry," he said. "Just checking to see if you had any spare ammo charges."

"If I did, grind-face, that's not where I'd carry them."

She started to point her gun at him but he let go of her and rolled away into the underbrush. To Royce she snarled, "You pirates don't have any manners, do you?"

He blinked at her and said, "Did I just fart or something?"

"Never mind." She saw someone stick his head up over a bush and took a shot at it. He ducked in time but her blast took out a tree behind him; it came straight down on top of the poor man.

For a minute or so the air was thick with energy bolts. Trees and brush all around them were blowing up. Two or three people got hit early on, but everybody got as low to the ground as possible and the last half minute they were just wasting charge. The firing died down and everyone concentrated on not sticking his head up any higher than he had to.

"Not sure I like this at all," Royce muttered. "Heck, we could lay here for days never firing and never moving, until we run out of rations and have to back out."

Rhayla looked around. It was true. They were in a cleared out area with jungle close on all sides. There was plenty of cover from boulders and bushes although it was all combustible and Royce felt he could start a fire behind the opposition that would trap them, with just three well-placed shots. That would, however, send them running toward his position which wasn't what he wanted. He wanted them running in the other direction. He didn't dare start a fire in front of them, however because the wind was blowing toward him.

He looked at Rhayla. "We're in a real fix, aren't we?"

"Oh, shut up."

"Aren't you going to arrest them?"

He must have set a branch moving because someone from the other side fired a power bolt just a couple of feet over his head. He gave a nervous laugh and crawled back a few feet. Lowering his voice he said, "Rhayla? What say we crawl off in that direction over there."

He was indicating the place where the jungle looked thickest. She nodded, shoved her gun away and, keeping low to the ground, followed him.

Undoubtedly someone must have noticed them, but if so, it probably looked as if they were heading off to flank or surround the enemy. When they were sufficiently shielded by the trees, Royce got to his feet and Rhayla stood up next to him.

In a low voice he said, "I'm sorry, ma'am. I hope you don't think poorly of our hospitality and all."

"You're still under arrest."

"That's all right," Royce said. "But you seem to have lost your other prisoner. Lovo doesn't seem to have followed us this time."

She was grateful for that even if it did mean she wouldn't be able to take him in, but she didn't tell Royce that. She said, "How do we get to your old man's place from here?"

"You never got around to telling me where your ship is," he said.

"It was just a little four-man speedster," she said. Then, after a moment she added, "It got hit while I was landing it. It sort of… crashed after that."

"And you with not a scratch on you. How did you plan on taking Daddy and me back to jail?"

"I was going to confiscate one of his ships."

"Confiscate! You mean steal. Did it ever occur to you that inasmuch as Daddy chased off everybody else on this planet that he's more or less the legal government here? Or at least the closest thing we got to one. And you an officer of the law."

"He's a rogue government and this is a rogue planet," she said.

"And that's your story and you're sticking to it, huh?" He thought for a moment. "I can get you to our spaceport where you can find yourself a ship to steal, er, confiscate. I'll even help you with the access codes. But I won't take you to Daddy."

"I'm not leaving this planet empty handed," she said.

"You won't have to. You can take me back. Two thousand sur credits, remember?"

"You're giving yourself up?" She seemed genuinely astonished. "Why would you do a thing like that?"

"Well, he is my daddy," Royce said. "Besides, if he catches me, he'll have me hauled up in front of a firing squad."

"And what if I insist on arresting that crap-faced old pirate anyway?"

"You're arresting me not him, and you're going to do it even if I have to tie you up and carry you over my shoulder like a sack of potatoes. Now, don't go making that face. The spaceport is a lot closer than Daddy's stronghold."

"You don't understand—"

"And I don't care. Come along. I'm under arrest and I'm all you're getting whether you like it or not."

5

IT WAS A round-about trudge through the jungle because Royce insisted that they avoid other people—which was all right with her.

Daylight was beginning to fade by the time she spotted the ships through the foliage. They burst out of the jungle soon after into a large cleared area where two ships rested on launching cradles. One of them was Parak's private yacht. She recognized it from descriptions and photos in Parak's file.

"That means your old man's still on this grinding dirtball of a planet," she said. "He never goes anywhere in any other kind of ship if he can help it." A grin lit up her face. Royce would have taken it for an evil grin except he thought she had a really cute face. "I'm going to confiscate that one."

"What? He'll skin you alive!"

"He'll do more than that," she said. "He'll be so mad he won't be able to see straight. He'll follow after me. I can lead him into a trap."

"I hate to keep harping on this," he said. "But you're really just one person."

"You were right about the armada. It's poised in this system, in the asteroid cluster."

"Poised? Why not just flare in?"

"Because they don't know how big a bunch of mother-grinding pirates there is on this world. They're waiting for reinforcements. Another five ships. It'll take them another week to get here."

"Meanwhile you zoom in all on your lonesome."

"When you know me better you'll realize I'm not a bleeping patient person."

"Oh, I don't think I'll have to wait around for that. I spotted it as one of your chief characteristics the first minute I met you." He looked out across the field at his father's yacht. "It's a good choice, though. That other ship's just a cargo lugger, barely fit to ship warm fertilizer."

"Is it locked? The yacht, I mean."

"On this planet? Why would it be locked. Nobody here but a bunch of pirates."

"Is it or isn't it?"

"Don't fret none about it. I got all the necessary lock codes stored in my magnificent cranium."

"Then what are we standing here for?"

It was dark now, but the port lights were on. Rhayla drew her weapon and they crossed the field to the yacht's launching cradle without being challenged.

The airlock hatch was thrown back, leaving the lock invitingly open. Rhayla gestured with her gun. "You first," she told Royce, He went up the ladder and clambered in. She was right behind him.

The ship's lights were on. The inner hatch was as open as the outer one. Rhayla frowned. "It can't be maintenance or restocking of provisions. There's no service truck here. It's just like pirates to not have any concept of power conservation."

"It's better for us," he said. "We won't have to charge up the generators now. Might save us as much as an hour and a half."

She stepped into the passageway and looked aft, then forward. "Comfy enough," she said. "Does this place have a brig?"

"You don't need one."

"Sure I do. I need a place to store you while I go pick up your old man."

"Now wait just a minute," Royce said. "In the first place, getting into Daddy's stronghold is not going to be as easy as getting into this ship was. In the second place, not all of Daddy's men are out looking for me. But all of them are armed. There's a good chance you won't be able to get to him before they take you prisoner—or worse."

"My oath of office didn't say anything about only taking the easy jobs, scum pot."

"Did it mention using your head? Trying to get to him is too great a risk. Why not just take this ship back to where your friends are. You have all the information they need to plan an attack on the stronghold, including a full assessment of his strength so they won't have to hide behind a pack of asteroids until reinforcements arrive. Furthermore you have an important prisoner."

"It does sound tempting when you put it like that," she said.

"As well it should. What's your decision?"

She looked at him a long moment and then said, "Okay, let's get this bird off the nest."

She went back to the outer hatch and pulled in the ladder, then sealed up. Then she led Royce forward to the small control room where it took her about two minutes to power up and check the telltales. Royce sat in the copilot's chair. "When you show up, your Star Guard friends are going to be so proud of you."

"They're going to want to space me," she said. "They think I'm annoying, if you can believe that."

Royce started to tell her he believed it, but thought better of it. The automatic alarms buzzed softly throughout the ship and he could feel the kick-in of the ship's gravity system, which neutralized most of the effects of lift off and heavy acceleration.

The ship took off.

A few minutes later they were orbiting the planet and Rhayla was glowering at the astrogation equipment. Royce watched her closely and was sure she wasn't angry at the equipment, and that meant just one thing.

And sure enough, she abruptly announced, "We're going back," and reached for the control knob that would fire the braking rockets.

Royce caught her wrist. "Hold on there."

"I mean it, Royce. I'm in charge. Let go of me."

"Going back doesn't make any sense."

"I'm the captain."

"No you're not," he told her. "It's my daddy's spaceship, so that puts me in charge."

"I'm SG, moron. I confiscated the crapping thing."

"No you didn't. I gave you permission so you didn't confiscate anything. And that means I'm still in charge. You can't get into Daddy's stronghold without getting yourself caught again, so you can just forget about going back. You hear me? Forget it."

"Like hell."

"You tell him, babe," said a voice behind them. They looked around to see an older man holding a gun on them. It was a paralaser and could safely be fired inside the cockpit because it only effected things with nervous systems.

"Daddy!" Royce said. "What are you doing here?"

Rhayla's jaw dropped. "Daddy! Are you telling me this is your old man?"

"You came all this way and don't even know what he looks like?"

"He looks a lot younger in his mug shots," she said. "Mother-grinding hell!" she added with delight. She turned in her chair to face Parak. "Okay, you piece of monkey crap. You are under lobster grinding arrest. You hear that? Now hand over your weapon and sit down while I deliver you to the armada that's on its way to invade this crap-assed planet."

"Where do you find these dates?" Parak asked Royce.

"Oh, she's not a date, Daddy. I'm as much under arrest as you are."

"What the hell is this? Doesn't she know you're a snitch? She can't arrest you if you're a snitch, can she?"

"I'm not a snitch."

"Then where the hell did this armada she's talking about come from?" Parak said, waving his gun around for emphasis.

"It wasn't me," Royce insisted. "Heck, I never told anyone where you were hiding out."

"Well, it sure wasn't any of my crewmembers," Parak said. "Those guys are as loyal as the day is long."

"On the night-side of Mercury, maybe," Rhayla said. "We've had an informant in your gang for months. In fact, we have at least three and they don't even know about each other."

"Son of a bitch! Tell me who it was and I'll go back and skin the bastard alive."

"Didn't you hear me? You're under bleeping arrest. You can sort it out in court."

"Daddy, you might recall me telling you a month ago I thought Ratcliffe was acting weird."

"Yeah, and what's so unusual about that? Wait a minute… Ratcliffe?"

"Lucky guess," Rhayla said. "But remember, I said there was more than just the one. Now be a good sport about it and hand me your gun."

"Grind off, sister," Parak said. For emphasis he poked the muzzle of his gun to within an inch of the tip of her nose.

"Hey, that's no way to act when you're under arrest."

Royce reached over and took the gun out of her hand.

Her mouth gaped open a second and then she yelled, "Whose side are you on, anyway?"

Parak laughed and said, "Well, I guess blood is thicker than water." He stepped aside so they could pass him. "Get her out of that chair and let's take her back to the airlock, son. I'm going to give her a fair chance to hold her breath outside the ship until her chums get here."

"They're waiting for reinforcements," Royce said. "It might take them another week to get here."

"That's too bad. Oh, take her gun. It's a long way to the airlock."

Rhayla got out of the chair. Parak said, "I guess I was right. Blood is thicker than water."

"But it isn't as thick as your skull is, Daddy." And hit him over the head with Rhayla's gun. It was a small gun; he had to hit him twice.

After Parak was safely ensconced in one of the storage lockers, Royce wandered back up to the control deck and sat down next to Rhayla. She was pulling the ship out of orbit and setting a course for the asteroid cluster where her fellow Solar Guards were hiding. Royce said, "I thought about locking myself in with him, but I couldn't bear the thought of having to put up with his complaints about my actions all the way to wherever it is we're going."

"You aren't under arrest," she said.

"I'm not? Why not?"

"You're a confidential informant. For months you've been filling me in on the actions of the pirates and helping me plan how best to arrest your old man."

"That's absurd! I never even met you before today."

"A technicality, that's all. Look, everybody and his third cousin seems to have someone on that rock who's been informing to him. Why should I be left out? And furthermore, you helped deliver that rat-assed grind off to me so I could arrest him."

"Do you have to call him that? He is my Daddy, you know. And that means he's going to be your Daddy-in-law, you know."

"Wait up, barf breath. Just when did our engagement happen?'

"Well, it hasn't technically, but, heck, I'll probably be thrown into some hellhole prison soon as we get back to civilization, so we need to take care of all these important details right now."

"What details! What makes you think I'm agreeable to any of this?"

"Well, I can just tell, that's what. Look, sweetie, if you're embarrassed because you can't wear white at the wedding, don't be."

She glared at him. *"What the grind does that mean?"*

"It means I love you just the way you are."

"Look, if you think I'm going to wear any kind of wedding dress other than a white one, you're barking up the wrong mulberry bush," she said, with emotion.

"Fine, then. I just want you to know I'll take you any way you want me to. Not that that sounds like I meant it to."

"You are plumbing new depths of manic insanity here, Royce."

"Which is one of the ways I know we're meant for one another. Have you thought about the song?"

"Song? What song! I haven't thought about any of this."

"What's your favorite song?"

"I don't know any songs."

"Good, then we can play my favorite at the wedding."

"For 'our song?'And what the *bleep* is your favorite?"

Loudly, and with great gusto, he began to sing, "Ninety-nine Bottles of Beer on the Wall…"

The End

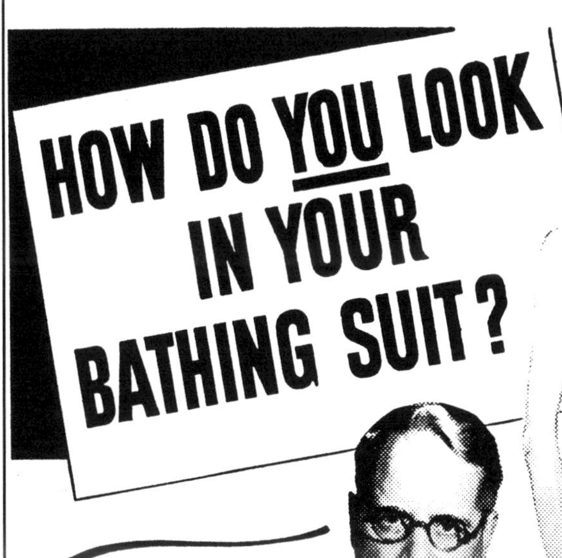

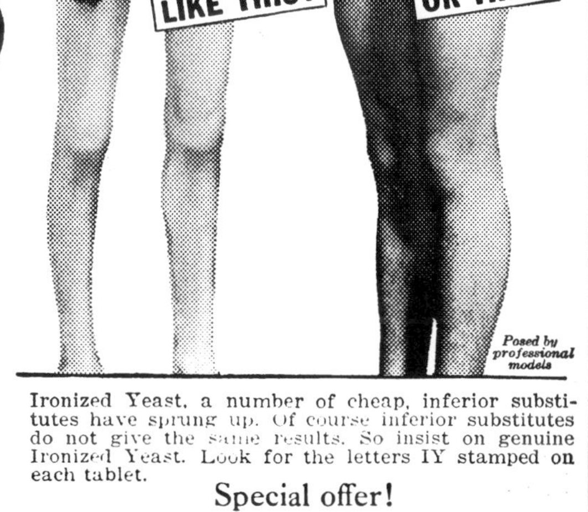

Read how thin, tired-out, nervous, rundown people have gained health and strength—*quick!*

ARE you ashamed to be seen in a bathing suit, because you're too skinny and scrawny-looking? Are you often tired, nervous—unable to eat and sleep properly?

Then here's wonderful news! Thousands of skinny, rundown men and women have gained 10 to 25 pounds, new pep, new popularity—with this scientific vitamin-rich formula, Ironized Yeast.

Why it builds up so quick

Scientists have discovered that countless people are thin and rundown—tired, cranky, washed-out—only because they don't get enough Vitamin B and iron from their daily food. Without enough of these vital substances you may lack appetite and not get the most body-building good out of what you eat.

Now you get these exact missing substances in these marvelous little Ironized Yeast tablets. No wonder, then, that they have helped thousands of people who needed these substances to gain new naturally attractive pounds, new health and pep, new popularity and success—often in just a few weeks!

Make this money-back test

Get Ironized Yeast tablets from your druggist today. If with the first package you don't eat better and FEEL better, with much more strength and pep—if you're not convinced that Ironized Yeast will give you the new pounds, new energy and life you've longed for, the price of this first package promptly refunded.

But just one warning! Due to the success of Ironized Yeast, a number of cheap, inferior substitutes have sprung up. Of course inferior substitutes do not give the same results. So insist on genuine Ironized Yeast. Look for the letters IY stamped on each tablet.

Special offer!

To start thousands building up their health right away, we make this special offer. Purchase a package of Ironized Yeast tablets at once, cut out the seal on the box and mail it to us with a clipping of this paragraph. We will send you a fascinating new book on health, "New Facts About Your Body." Remember, results with the first package—or money refunded. At all druggists. Ironized Yeast Co., Inc., Dept. 506, Atlanta, Ga.

TUNE IN ON THE GOOD WILL HOUR, every Sunday Evening. See your local paper for time and station.

Irvin Echard

Gains 14 lbs. in 5 Weeks

"I was so skinny I didn't want to go out. Finally, I tried IRONIZED YEAST. In five weeks I gained 14 lbs. Now I go out regularly, have good times." Irvin Echard, Barberton, O.

R. Loeffler

Gains 12 lbs., admired now

"Was losing weight and pep. Then I got Ironized Yeast. In 6 weeks I gained 12 lbs. and am full of pep. Everybody admires my physique, too." Ralph Loeffler Arlington, Wash.

Temple Trouble

by **H. Beam Piper**

Miracles to order was a fine way for the paratimers to get mining concessions—but Nature can sometimes pull counter-miracles. And so can men, for that matter....

Originally published in Astounding Science Fiction, April 1951

THROUGH A haze of incense and altar smoke, Yat-Zar looked down from his golden throne at the end of the dusky, many-pillared temple. Yat-Zar was an idol, of gigantic size and extraordinarily good workmanship; he had three eyes, made of turquoises as big as doorknobs, and six arms. In his three right hands, from top to bottom, he held a sword with a flame-shaped blade, a jeweled object of vaguely phallic appearance, and, by the ears, a rabbit. In his left hands were a bronze torch with burnished copper flames, a big goblet, and a pair of scales with an egg in one pan balanced against a skull in the other. He had a long bifurcate beard made of gold wire, feet like a bird's, and other rather startling anatomical features. His throne was set upon a stone plinth about twenty feet high, into the front of which a doorway opened; behind him was a wooden screen, elaborately gilded and painted.

Directly in front of the idol, Ghullam the high priest knelt on a big blue and gold cushion. He wore a gold-fringed robe of dark blue, and a tall conical gold miter, and a bright blue false beard, forked like the idol's golden one: he was intoning a prayer, and holding up, in both hands, for divine inspection and approval, a long curved knife. Behind him, about thirty feel away, stood a square stone altar, around which four of the lesser priests, in light blue robes with less gold fringe and dark-blue false beards, were busy with the preliminaries to the sacrifice. At considerable distance, about halfway down the length of the temple, some two hundred worshipers—a few substantial citizens in gold-fringed tunics, artisans in tunics without gold fringe, soldiers in mail hauberks and plain steel caps, one officer in ornately gilded armor, a number of peasants in nondescript smocks, and women of all classes—

ORIGINAL ASTOUNDING SF ILLUSTRATIONS BY HUBERT ROGERS

were beginning to prostrate themselves on the stone floor.

Ghullam rose to his feet, bowing deeply to Yat-Zar and holding the knife extended in front of him, and backed away toward the altar. As he did, one of the lesser priests reached into a fringed and embroidered sack and pulled out a live rabbit, a big one, obviously of domestic breed, holding it by the ears while one of his fellows took it by the hind legs. A third priest caught up a silver pitcher, while the fourth fanned the altar fire with a sheet-silver fan. As they began chanting antiphonally, Ghullam turned and quickly whipped the edge of his knife across the rabbit's throat. The priest with the pitcher stepped in to catch the blood, and when the rabbit was bled, it was laid on the fire. Ghullam and his four assistants all shouted together, and the congregation shouted in response.

The high priest waited as long as was decently necessary and then, holding the knife in front of him, stepped around the prayer-cushion and went through the door under the idol into the Holy of Holies. A boy in novice's white robes met him and took the knife, carrying it reverently to a fountain for washing. Eight or ten under-priests, sitting at a long table, rose and bowed, then sat down again and resumed their eating and drinking. At another table, a half-dozen upper priests nodded to him in casual greeting.

Crossing the room, Ghullam went to the Triple Veil in front of the House of Yat-Zar, where only the highest of the priesthood might go, and parted the curtains, passing through, until he came to the great gilded door. Here he fumbled under his robe and produced a small object like a mechanical pencil, inserting the pointed end in a tiny hole in the door and pressing on the other end. The door opened, then swung shut behind him, and as it locked itself, the lights came on within. Ghullam removed his miter and his false beard, tossing them aside on a table, then undid his sash and peeled out of his robe. His regalia discarded, he stood for a moment in loose trousers and a soft white shirt, with a pistollike weapon in a shoulder holster under his left arm—no longer Ghullam the high priest of Yat-Zar, but now Stranor Sleth, resident agent on this time-line of the Fourth Level Proto-Aryan Sector for the Transtemporal Mining Corporation. Then he opened a door at the other side of the anteroom and went to the antigrav shaft, stepping over the edge and floating downward.

THERE WERE temples of Yat-Zar on every time-line of the Proto-Aryan Sector, for the worship of Yat-Zar was ancient among the Hulgun people of that area of paratime, but there were only a few which had such installations as this, and all of them were owned and operated by Transtemporal Mining, which had the fissionable ores franchise for this sector. During the ten elapsed centuries since Transtemporal had begun operations on this sector, the process had become standardized. A few First Level paratimers would transpose to a selected time-line and abduct an upper-priest of Yat-Zar, preferably the high priest of the temple at Yoldav or Zurb. He would be drugged and transposed to the First Level, where he would receive hypnotic indoctrination and, while unconscious, have an operation performed on his ears which would enable him to hear sounds well above the normal audible range. He would be able to hear the shrill sonar-cries of bats, for instance, and, more important, he would be able to hear voices when the speaker used a First Level audio-frequency step-up phone. He would also receive a memory-obliteration from the moment of his abduction, and a set of pseudo-memories of a visit to the Heaven of Yat-Zar, on the other side of the sky. Then he would be

---

H. Beam Piper (1904 – 1964) is perhaps best known for his Terro-Human Future History series of stories and the shorter series of "Paratime" alternate history tales. First published in *Astounding Science Fiction* in 1947, Piper became one of that magazine's mainstays during the 1950s, primarily dealing with short stories and novellas. His popular Paratime stories, including *Police Operation* (reprinted in *Startling Stories*, Vol.2 No.2), *Last Enemy*, *Time Crime*, and *Temple Trouble* deals with a law enforcement outfit from a parallel world which has learned how to move between timelines while the Terro-Human saga—which includes the novels *Ullr Uprising*, *Four-Day Planet*, *Junkyard Planet*, and *Space Viking*—is a sprawling account of 6,000 years of mankind's future. Other works include *Crisis in 2140* (co-written with John J. McGuire), *Lone Star Planet* (also with McGuire), and the Paratime novel *Lord Kalvan of Otherwhen*. Mr. Piper's story *Omnilingual* has been reprinted often while being referred to in many subsequent stories dealing with the translation of alien languages. While leaving behind but a relatively small body of work he has nonetheless been a great influence for succeeding generations of science fiction authors.

returned to his own time-line and left on a mountain top far from his temple, where an unknown peasant, leading a donkey, would always find him, return him to the temple, and then vanish inexplicably.

Then the priest would begin hearing voices, usually while serving at the altar. They would warn of future events, which would always come to pass exactly as foretold. Or they might bring tidings of things happening at a distance, the news of which would not arrive by normal means for days or even weeks. Before long, the holy man who had been carried alive to the Heaven of Yat-Zar would acquire a most awesome reputation as a prophet, and would speedily rise to the very top of the priestly hierarchy.

Then he would receive two commandments from Yat-Zar. The first would ordain that all lower priests must travel about from temple to temple, never staying longer than a year at any one place. This would insure a steady influx of newcomers personally unknown to the local upper-priests, and many of them would be First Level paratimers. Then, there would be a second commandment: A house must be built for Yat-Zar, against the rear wall of each temple. Its dimensions were minutely stipulated; its walls were to be of stone, without windows, and there was to be a single door, opening into the Holy of Holies, and before the walls were finished, the door was to be barred from within. A triple veil of brocaded fabric was to be hung in front of this door. Sometimes such innovations met with opposition from the more conservative members of the hierarchy: when they did, the principal objector would be seized with a sudden and violent illness; he would recover if and when he withdrew his objections.

Very shortly after the House of Yat-Zar would be completed, strange noises would be heard from behind the thick walls. Then, after a while, one of the younger priests would announce that he had been commanded in a vision to go behind the veil and knock upon the door. Going behind the curtains, he would use his door-activator to let himself in, and return by paratime-conveyer to the First Level to enjoy a well-earned vacation. When the high priest would follow him behind the veil, after a few hours, and find that he had vanished, it would be announced as a miracle. A week later, an even greater miracle would be announced. The young priest would return from behind the Triple Veil, clad in such raiment as no man had ever seen, and bearing in his hands a strange box. He would announce that Yat-Zar had commanded him to build a new temple in the mountains, at a place to be made known by the voice of the god speaking out of the box.

This time, there would be no doubts and no objections. A procession would set out, headed by the new revelator bearing the box, and when the clicking voice of the god spoke rapidly out of it, the site would be marked and work would begin. No local labor would ever be employed on such temples; the masons and woodworkers would be strangers, come from afar and speaking a strange tongue, and when the temple was completed, they would never be seen to leave it. Men would say that they had been put to death by the priest and buried under the altar to preserve the secrets of the god. And there would always be an idol to preserve the secrets of the god. And there would always be an idol of Yat-Zar, obviously of heavenly origin, since its workmanship was beyond the powers of any local craftsman. The priests of such a temple would be exempt, by divine decree, from the rule of yearly travel.

Nobody, of course, would have the least idea that there was a uranium mine in operation under it, shipping ore to another time-line. The Hulgun people knew nothing about uranium, and neither did they as much as dream that there were other time-lines. The secret of paratime transposition belonged exclusively to the First Level civilization which had discovered it, and it was a secret that was guarded well.

STRANOR SLETH, dropping to the bottom of the antigrav shaft, cast a hasty and instinctive glance to the right, where the freight conveyers were. One was gone, taking its cargo over hundreds of thousands of para-years to the First Level. Another had just returned, empty, and a third was receiving its cargo from the robot mining machines far back under the mountain. Two young men and a girl, in First Level costumes, sat at a bank of instruments and visor-screens, handling the whole operation, and six or seven armed guards, having inspected the newly-

arrived conveyer and finding that it had picked up nothing inimical en route, were relaxing and lighting cigarettes. Three of them, Stranor Sleth noticed, wore the green uniforms of the Paratime Police.

"When did those fellows get in?" he asked the people at the control desk, nodding toward the green-clad newcomers.

"About ten minutes ago, on the passenger conveyer," the girl told him. "The Big Boy's here. Brannad Klav. And a Paratime Police officer. They're in your office."

"Uh huh; I was expecting that," Stranor Sleth nodded. Then he turned down the corridor to the left.

Two men were waiting for him, in his office. One was short and stocky, with an angry, impatient face—Brannad Klav, Transtemporal's vice president in charge of operations. The other was tall and slender with handsome and entirely expressionless features; he wore a Paratime Police officer's uniform, with the blue badge of hereditary nobility on his breast, and carried a sigma-ray needler in a belt holster.

"Were you waiting long, gentlemen?" Stranor Sleth asked. "I was holding Sunset Sacrifice up in the temple."

"No, we just got here," Brannad Klav said. "This is Verkan Vall, Mavrad of Nerros, special assistant to Chief Tortha of the Paratime Police, Stranor Sleth, our resident agent here."

Stranor Sleth touched hands with Verkan Vall.

"I've heard a lot about you, sir," he said. "Everybody working in paratime has, of course. I'm sorry we have a situation here that calls for your presence, but since we have, I'm glad you're here in person. You know what our trouble is, I suppose?"

"In a general way," Verkan Vall replied. "Chief Tortha, and Brannad Klav, have given me the main outline, but I'd like to have you fill in the details."

"Well, I told you everything," Brannad Klav interrupted impatiently. "It's just that Stranor's let this blasted local king, Kurchuk, get out of control. If I—" He stopped short, catching sight of the shoulder holster under Stranor Sleth's left arm. "Were you wearing that needler up in the temple?" he demanded.

"You're blasted right I was!" Stranor Sleth retorted. "And any time I can't arm myself for my own protection on this time-line, you can have my resignation. I'm not getting into the same jam as those people at Zurb."

"Well, never mind about that," Verkan Vall intervened. "Of course Stranor Sleth has a right to arm himself; I wouldn't think of being caught without a weapon on this time-line, myself. Now, Stranor, suppose you tell me what's been happening, here, from the beginning of this trouble."

"It started, really, about five years ago, when Kurchuk, the King of Zurb, married this Chuldun princess, Darith, from the country over beyond the Black Sea, and made her his queen, over the heads of about a dozen daughters of the local nobility, whom he'd married previously. Then he brought in this Chuldun scribe, Labdurg, and made him Overseer of the Kingdom—roughly, prime minister. There was a lot of dissatisfaction about that, and for a while it looked as though he was going to have a revolution on his hands, but he brought in about five thousand Chuldun mercenaries, all archers—these Hulguns can't shoot a bow worth beans—so the dissatisfaction died down, and so did most of the leaders of the disaffected group. The story I get is that this Labdurg arranged the marriage, in the first place. It looks to me as though the Chuldun emperor is intending to take over the Hulgun kingdoms, starting with Zurb.

"Well, these Chulduns all worship a god called Muz-Azin. Muz-Azin is a crocodile with wings like a bat and a lot of knife blades in his tail. He makes this Yat-Zar look downright beautiful. So do his habits. Muz-Azin fancies human sacrifices. The victims are strung up by the ankles on a triangular frame and lashed to death with iron-barbed whips. Nasty sort of a deity, but this is a nasty time-line. The people here get a big kick out of watching these sacrifices. Much better show than our bunny-killing. The victims are usually criminals, or overage or incorrigible slaves, or prisoners of war.

"Of course, when the Chulduns began infiltrating the palace, they brought in their crocodile-god, too, and a flock of priests, and King Kurchuk let them set up a temple in the palace. Naturally, we preached against this heathen idolatry in our temples, but religious bigotry isn't one of the numerous imperfections of this sector. Everybody's deity is as good as anybody else's—indifferentism, I believe, is the theological term. Anyhow, on that basis things went along fairly well, till two years ago, when we had this run of bad luck."

"Bad luck!" Brannad Klav snorted. "That's the standing excuse of every incompetent!"

"Go on, Stranor; what sort of bad luck?" Verkan Vall asked.

"WELL, FIRST we had a drought, beginning in early summer, that burned up most of the grain crop. Then, when that broke, we got heavy rains and hailstorms and floods, and that destroyed what got through the dry spell. When they harvested what little was left, it was obvious there'd be a famine, so we brought in a lot of grain by conveyer and distributed it from the temples—miraculous gift of Yat-Zar, of course. Then the main office on First Level got scared about flooding this time-line with a lot of unaccountable grain and were afraid we'd make the people suspicious, and ordered it stopped.

"Then Kurchuk, and I might add that the kingdom of Zurb was the hardest hit by the famine, ordered his army mobilized and started an invasion of the Jumdun country, south of the Carpathians, to get grain. He got his army chopped up, and only about a quarter of them got back, with no grain. You ask me, I'd say that Labdurg framed it to happen that way. He advised Kurchuk to invade, in the first place, and I mentioned my suspicion that Chombrog, the Chuldun Emperor, is planning to move in on the Hulgun kingdoms. Well, what would be smarter than to get Kurchuk's army smashed in advance?"

"How did the defeat occur?" Verkan Vall asked. "Any suspicion of treachery?"

"Nothing you could put your finger on, except that the Jumduns seemed to have pretty good intelligence about Kurchuk's invasion route and battle plans. It could have been nothing worse than stupid tactics on Kurchuk's part. See, these Hulguns, and particularly the Zurb Hulguns, are spearmen. They fight in a fairly thin line, with heavy-armed infantry in front and light infantry with throwing-spears behind. The nobles fight in light chariots, usually at the center of the line, and that's where they were at this Battle of Jorm. Kurchuk himself was at the center, with his Chuldun archers massed around him.

"The Jumduns use a lot of cavalry, with long swords and lances, and a lot of big chariots with two javelin men and a driver. Well, instead of ramming into Kurchuk's center, where he had his archers, they hit the extreme left and folded it up, and then swung around behind and hit the right from the rear. All the Chuldun archers did was stand fast around the king and shoot anybody who came close to them: they were left pretty much alone. But the Hulgun spearmen were cut to pieces. The battle ended with Kurchuk and his nobles and his archers making a fighting retreat, while the Jumdun cavalry were chasing the spearmen every which way and cutting them down or lancing them as they ran.

"Well, whether it was Labdurg's treachery or Kurchuk's stupidity, in either case, it was natural for the archers to come off easiest and the Hulgun spearmen to pay the butcher's bill. But try and tell these knuckle-heads anything like that! Muz-Azin protected the Chulduns, and Yat-Zar let the Hulguns down, and that was all there was to it. The Zurb temple started losing worshipers, particularly the families of the men who didn't make it back from Jorm.

"If that had been all there'd been to it, though, it still wouldn't have hurt the mining operations, and we could have got by. But what really tore it was when the rabbits started to die." Stranor Sleth picked up a cigar from his desk and bit the end, spitting it out disgustedly. "Tularemia, of course," he said, touching his lighter to the tip. "When that hit, they started going over to Muz-Azin in droves, not only at Zurb but all over the Six Kingdoms. You ought to have seen the house we had for Sunset Sacrifice, this evening! About two hundred, and we used to get two thousand. It used to be all two men could do to lift the offering box at the door, afterward, and all the money we took in tonight I could put in one pocket!" The high priest used language that would have been considered unclerical even among the Hulguns.

* * * * * * * *

VERKAN VALL nodded. Even without the quickie hypno-mech he had taken for this sector, he knew that the rabbit was domesticated among the Proto-Aryan Hulguns and was their chief meat animal. Hulgun rabbits were even a minor import on the First Level, and could be had at all the better restaurants in cities like Dhergabar. He mentioned that.

"That's not the worst of it," Stranor Sleth told him. "See, the rabbit's sacred to Yat-Zar. Not taboo; just sacred. They have to use a specially consecrated knife to kill them—consecrating rabbit knives has always been an item of temple revenue—and they must say a special prayer before eating them. We could have got around the rest of it, even the Battle of Jorm—punishment by Yat-Zar for the sin of apostasy—but Yat-Zar just wouldn't make rabbits sick. Yat-Zar thinks too well of rabbits to do that, and it'd not been any use claiming he would. So there you are."

"Well, I take the attitude that this situation is the result of your incompetence," Brannad Klav began, in a bullyragging tone. "You're not only the high priest of this temple, you're the acknowledged head of the religion in all the Hulgun kingdoms. You should have had more hold on the people than to allow anything like this to happen."

"Hold on the people!" Stranor Sleth fairly howled, appealing to Verkan Vall. "What does he think a religion is, on this sector, anyhow? You think these savages dreamed up that six-armed monstrosity, up there, to express their yearning for higher things, or to symbolize their moral ethos, or as a philosophical escape-hatch from the dilemma of causation? They never even heard of such matters. On this sector, gods are strictly utilitarian. As long as they take care of their worshipers, they get their sacrifices: when they can't put out, they have to get out. How do you suppose these Chulduns, living in the Caucasus Mountains, got the idea of a god like a crocodile, anyhow? Why, they got it from Homran traders, people from down in the Nile Valley. They had a god, once, something basically like a billy goat, but he let them get licked in a couple of battles, so out he went. Why, all the deities on this sector have hyphenated names, because they're combinations of several deities, worshiped in one person. Do you know anything about the history of this sector?" he asked the Paratime Police officer.

"Well, it develops from an alternate probability of what we call the Nilo-Mesopotamian Basic sector-group," Verkan Vall said. "On most Nilo-Mesopotamian sectors, like the Macedonian Empire Sector, or the Alexandrian-Roman or Alexandrian-Punic or Indo-Turanian or Europo-American, there was an Aryan invasion of Eastern Europe and Asia Minor about four thousand elapsed years ago. On this sector, the ancestors of the Aryans came in about fifteen centuries earlier, as neolithic savages, about the time that the Sumerian and Egyptian civilizations were first developing, and overran all southeast Europe, Asia Minor and the Nile Valley. They developed to the bronze-age culture of the civilizations they overthrew, and then, more slowly, to an iron-age culture. About two thousand years ago, they were using hardened steel and building large stone cities, just as they do now. At that time, they reached cultural stasis. But as for their religious beliefs, you've described them quite accurately. A god is only worshiped as long as the people think him powerful enough to aid and protect them; when they lose that confidence, he is discarded and the god of some neighboring people is adopted instead." He turned to Brannad Klav. "Didn't Stranor report this situation to you when it first developed?" he asked. "I know he did; he speaks of receiving shipments of grain by conveyer for temple distribution. Then why didn't you report it to Paratime Police? That's what we have a Paratime Police Force for."

"Well, yes, of course, but I had enough confidence in Stranor Sleth to think that he could handle the situation himself. I didn't know he'd gone slack—"

"Look, I can't make weather, even if my parishioners think I can," Stranor Sleth defended himself. "And I can't make a great military genius out of a blockhead like Kurchuk. And I can't immunize all the rabbits on this time-line against tularemia, even if I'd had any reason to expect a tularemia epidemic, which I hadn't because the disease is unknown on this sector; this is the only outbreak of it anybody's ever heard of on any Proto-Aryan time-line."

"No, but I'll tell you what you could have done," Verkan Vall told him. "When this Kurchuk started to apostatize, you could have gone to him at the head of a procession of priests, all paratimers and all armed with energy-weapons, and pointed out his spiritual duty to him, and if he gave you any back talk, you could have pulled out that needler and rayed him down and then cried, 'Behold the vengeance of Yat-Zar upon the wicked king!' I'll bet any sum at any odds that his successor would have thought twice about going over to Muz-Azin, and none of these other kings would have even thought once about it."

"Ha, that's what I wanted to do!" Stranor Sleth exclaimed. "And who stopped me? I'll give you just one guess."

"Well, it seems there was slackness here, but it wasn't Stranor Sleth who was slack," Verkan Vall commented.

"Well! I must say; I never thought I'd hear an officer of the Paratime Police criticizing me for trying to operate inside the Paratime Transposition Code!" Brannad Klav exclaimed.

VERKAN VALL, sitting on the edge of Stranor Sleth's desk, aimed his cigarette at Brannad Klav like a blaster.

"Now, look," he began. "There is one, and only one, inflexible law regarding outtime activities. The secret of paratime transposition must be kept inviolate, and any activity tending to endanger it is prohibited. That's why we don't allow the transposition of any object of extraterrestrial origin to any time-line on which space travel has not been developed. Such an object may be preserved, and then, after the local population begin exploring the planet from whence it came, there will be dangerous speculations and theories as to how it arrived on Terra at such an early date. I came within inches, literally, of getting myself killed, not long ago, cleaning up the result of a violation of that regulation. For the same reason, we don't allow the export, to outtime natives, of manufactured goods too far in advance of their local culture. That's why, for instance, you people have to hand-finish all those big Yat-Zar idols, to remove traces of machine work. One of those things may be around, a few thousand years from now, when these people develop a mechanical civilization. But as far as raying down this Kurchuk is concerned, these Hulguns are completely nonscientific. They wouldn't have the least idea what happened. They'd believe that Yat-Zar struck him dead, as gods on this plane of culture are supposed to do, and if any of them noticed the needler at all, they'd think it was just a holy amulet of some kind."

"But the law is the law—" Brannad Klav began.

Verkan Vall shook his head. "Brannad, as I understand, you were promoted to your present position on the retirement of Salvan Marth, about ten years ago; up to that time, you were in your company's financial department. You were accustomed to working subject to the First Level Commercial Regulation Code. Now, any law binding upon our people at home, on the First Level, is inflexible. It has to be. We found out, over fifty centuries ago, that laws have to be rigid and without discretionary powers in administration in order that people may be able to predict their effect and plan their activities accordingly. Naturally, you became conditioned to operating in such a climate of legal inflexibility.

"But in paratime, the situation is entirely different. There exist, within the range of the Ghaldron-Hesthor paratemporal-field generator, a number of time-lines of the order of ten to the hundred-thousandth power. In effect, that many different worlds. In the past ten thousand years, we have visited only the tiniest fraction of these, but we have found everything from time-lines inhabited only by subhuman ape-men to Second Level civilizations which are our own equal in every respect but knowledge of paratemporal transposition. We even know of one Second Level civilization which is approaching the discovery of an interstellar hyperspatial drive, something we've never even come close to. And in between are every degree of savagery, barbarism and civilization. Now, it's just not possible to frame any single code of laws applicable to conditions on all of these. The best we can do is prohibit certain flagrantly immoral types of activity, such as slave-trading, introduction of new types of narcotic drugs, or out-and-out piracy and brigandage. If you're in doubt as to the legality of anything you want to do outtime, go to the Judicial Section of the Paratime Commission and get an opinion on it. That's where you made your whole mistake. You didn't find out just how far it was allowable for you to go."

He turned to Stranor Sleth again. "Well, that's the background, then. Now tell me about what happened yesterday at Zurb."

"WELL, A week ago, Kurchuk came out with this decree closing our temple at Zurb and ordering his subjects to perform worship and make money offerings to Muz-Azin. The Zurb temple isn't a mask for a mine: Zurb's too far south for the uranium deposits. It's just a center for propaganda and that sort of thing. But they have a House of Yat-Zar, and a conveyer, and most of the upper-priests are paratimers. Well, our man there, Tammand Drav, alias Khoram, defied the king's order, so Kurchuk sent a company of Chuldun archers to close the temple and arrest the priests. Tammand Drav got all his people who were in the temple at the time into the House of Yat-Zar and transposed them back to the First Level. He had orders" —Stranor Sleth looked meaningly at Brannad Klav— "not to resist with energy-weapons or even ultrasonic paralyzers. And while we're on the subject of letting the local yokels see too much, about fifteen of the under-priests he took to the First Level were Hulgun natives."

"Nothing wrong about that: they'll get memory-obliteration and pseudo-memory treatment," Verkan Vall said. "But he should have been allowed to needle about a dozen of those Chulduns. Teach the beggars to respect Yat-Zar in the future. Now, how about the six priests who were outside the temple at the time? All but one were paratimers. We'll have to find out about them, and get them out of Zurb."

"That'll take some doing," Stranor Sleth said. "And it'll have to be done before sunset tomorrow. They are all in the dungeon of the palace citadel, and Kurchuk is going to give them to the priests of Muz-Azin to be sacrificed tomorrow evening."

"How'd you learn that?" Verkan Vall asked.

"Oh, we have a man in Zurb, not connected with the temple," Stranor Sleth said. "Name's Crannar Jurth; calls himself Kranjur, locally. He has a swordmaker's shop, employs about a dozen native journeymen and apprentices who hammer out the common blades he sells in the open market. Then, he imports a few high-class alloy-steel blades from the First Level, that'll cut through this local low-carbon armor like cheese. Fits them with locally-made hilts and sells them at unbelievable prices to the nobility. He's Swordsmith to the King; picks up all the inside palace dope. Of course, he was among the first to accept the New Gospel and go over to Muz-Azin. He has a secret room under his shop, with his conveyer and a radio.

"What happened was this: These six priests were at a consecration ceremony at a rabbit-ranch outside the city, and they didn't know about the raid on the temple. On their way back, they were surrounded by Chuldun archers and taken prisoner. They had no weapons but their sacrificial knives." He threw another dirty look at Brannad Klav. "So they're due to go up on the triangles at sunset tomorrow."

"We'll have to get them out before then," Verkan Vall stated. "They're our people, and we can't let them down; even the native is under our protection, whether he knows it or not. And in the second place, if those priests are sacrificed to Muz-Azin," he told Brannad Klav, "you can shut down everything on this time-line, pull out or disintegrate your installations, and fill in your mine-tunnels. Yat-Zar will be through on this time-line, and you'll be through along with him. And considering that your fissionables franchise for this sector comes up for renewal next year, your company will be through in this paratime area."

"You believe that would happen?" Brannad Klav asked anxiously.

"I know it will, because I'll put through a recommendation to that effect, if those six men are tortured to death tomorrow," Verkan Vall replied. "And in the fifty years that I've been in the Police Department, I've only heard of five such recommendations being ignored by the commission. You know, Fourth Level Mineral Products Syndicate is after your franchise. Ordinar-

ily, they wouldn't have a chance of getting it, but with this, maybe they will, even without my recommendation. This was all your fault, for ignoring Stranor Sleth's proposal and for denying those men the right to carry energy weapons."

"Well, we were only trying to stay inside the Paratime Code," Brannad Klav pleaded. "If it isn't too late, now, you can count on me for every co-operation." He fiddled with some papers on the desk. "What do you want me to do to help?"

"I'll tell you that in a minute." Verkan Vall walked to the wall and looked at the map, then returned to Stranor Sleth's desk. "How about these dungeons?" he asked. "How are they located, and how can we get in to them?"

"I'm afraid we can't," Stranor Sleth told him. "Not without fighting our way in. They're under the palace citadel, a hundred feet below ground. They're spatially co-existent with the heavy water barriers around one of our company's plutonium piles on the First Level, and below surface on any unoccupied time-line I know of, so we can't transpose in to them. This palace is really a walled city inside a city. Here, I'll show you."

GOING AROUND the desk, he sat down and, after looking in the index-screen, punched a combination on the keyboard. A picture, projected from the microfilm-bank, appeared on the view-screen. It was an air-view of the city of Zurb—taken, the high priest explained, by infrared light from an airboat over the city at night. It showed a city of an entirely pre-mechanical civilization, with narrow streets, lined on either side by low one and two story buildings. Although there would be considerable snow in winter, the roofs were usually flat, probably massive stone slabs supported by pillars within. Even in the poorer sections, this was true except for the very meanest houses and outbuildings, which were thatched. Here and there, some huge pile of masonry would rear itself above its lower neighbors, and, where the streets were wider, occasional groups of large buildings would be surrounded by battlemented walls. Stranor Sleth indicated one of the larger of these.

"Here's the palace," he said. "And here's the temple of Yat-Zar, about half a mile away." He touched a large building, occupying an entire block; between it and the palace was a block-wide park, with lawns and trees on either side of a wide roadway connecting the two.

"Now, here's a detailed view of the palace." He punched another combination; the view of the City was replaced by one, taken from directly overhead, of the walled palace area. "Here's the main gate, in front, at the end of the road from the temple," he pointed out. "Over here, on the left, are the slaves' quarters and the stables and workshops and store houses and so on. Over here, on the other side, are the nobles' quarters. And this," —he indicated a towering structure at the rear of the walled enclosure— "is the citadel and the royal dwelling. Audience hall on this side; harem over here on this side. A wide stone platform, about fifteen feet high, runs completely across the front of the citadel, from the audience hall to the harem. Since this picture was taken, the new temple of Muz-Azin was built right about here." He indicated that it extended out from the audience hall into the central courtyard. "And out here on the platform, they've put up about a dozen of these triangles, about twelve feet high, on which the sacrificial victims are whipped to death."

"Yes. About the only way we could get down to the dungeons would be to make an airdrop onto the citadel roof and fight our way down with needlers and blasters, and I'm not willing to do that as long as there's any other way," Verkan Vall said. "We'd lose men, even with needlers against bows, and there's a chance that some of our equipment might be lost in the melee and fall into outtime hands. You say this sacrifice comes off tomorrow at sunset?"

"That would be about actual sunset plus or minus an hour; these people aren't astronomers, they don't even have good sundials, and it might be a cloudy day," Stranor Sleth said. "There will be a big idol of Muz-Azin on a cart, set about here." He pointed. "After the sacrifice, it is to be dragged down this road, outside, to the temple of Yat-Zar, and set up there. The temple is now occupied by about twenty Chuldun mercenaries and five or six priests of Muz-Azin. They haven't, of course, got into the House of Yat-Zar; the door's of impervium steel, about six inches thick, with a plating of collapsed nickel under the gilding. It would take a couple of hours to cut through it with our best atomic torch; there isn't a tool on this time-line that could even scratch it. And the insides of the walls are lined with the same thing."

"Do you think our people have been tortured, yet?" Verkan Vall asked.

"No." Stranor Sleth was positive. "They'll be fairly well treated, until the sacrifice. The idea's to make them last as long as possible on the triangles; Muz-Azin likes to see a slow killing, and so does the mob of spectators."

"That's good. Now, here's my plan. We won't try to rescue them from the dungeons. Instead, we'll transpose back to the Zurb temple from the First Level, in considerable force—say a hundred or so men—and march on the palace, to force their release. You're in constant radio communication with all the other temples on this time-line, I suppose?"

"Yes, certainly."

"All right. Pass this out to everybody, authority Paratime Police, in my name, acting for Tortha Karf. I want all paratimers who can possibly be spared to transpose to First Level immediately and rendezvous at the First Level terminal of the Zurb temple conveyer as soon as possible. Close down all mining operations, and turn over temple routine to the native under-priests. You can tell them that the upper-priests are retiring to their respective Houses of Yat-Zar to pray for the deliverance of the priests in the hands of King Kurchuk. And everybody is to bring back his priestly regalia to the First Level; that will be needed." He turned to Brannad Klav. "I suppose you keep spare regalia in stock on the First Level?"

"Yes, of course; we keep plenty of everything in stock. Robes, miters, false beards of different shades, everything."

"And these big Yat-Zar idols: they're mass-produced on the First Level? You have one available now? Good. I'll want some alterations made on one. For one thing, I'll want it plated heavily, all over, with collapsed nickel. For another, I'll want it fitted with antigrav units and some sort of propulsion-units, and a loud-speaker, and remote control.

"And, Stranor, you get in touch with this swordmaker, Crannar Jurth, and alert him to co-operate with us. Tell him to start calling Zurb temple on his radio about noon tomorrow, and keep it up till he gets an answer. Or, better, tell him to run his conveyer to his First Level terminal, and bring with him an extra suit of clothes appropriate to the role of journeyman-mechanic. I'll want to talk to him, and furnish him with special equipment. Got all that? Well, carry on with it, and bring your own paratimers, priests and mining operators, back with you as soon as you've taken care of everything. Brannad, you come with me, now. We're returning to

First Level immediately. We have a lot of work to do, so let's get started."

"Anything I can do to help, just call on me for it," Brannad Klav promised earnestly. "And, Stranor, I want to apologize. I'll admit, now, that I ought to have followed your recommendations, when this situation first developed."

BY NOON of the next day, Verkan Vall had at least a hundred men gathered in the big room at the First Level fissionables refinery at Jarnabar, spatially co-existent with the Fourth Level temple of Yat-Zar at Zurb. He was having a little trouble distinguishing between them, for every man wore the fringed blue robe and golden miter of an upper-priest, and had his face masked behind a blue false beard. It was, he admitted to himself, a most ludicrous-looking assemblage; one of the most ludicrous things about it was the fact that it would have inspired only pious awe in a Hulgun of the Fourth Level Proto-Aryan Sector. About half of them were priests from the Transtemporal Mining Corporation's temples; the other half were members of the Paratime Police. All of them wore, in addition to their temple knives, holstered sigma-ray needlers. Most of them carried ultrasonic paralyzers, eighteen-inch batonlike things with bulbous ends. Most of the Paratime Police and a few of the priests also carried either heat-ray pistols or neutron-disruption blasters; Verkan Vall wore one of the latter in a left-hand belt holster.

The Paratime Police were lined up separately for inspection, and Stranor Sleth, Tammand Drav of the Zurb temple, and several other high priests were checking the authenticity of their disguises. A little apart from the others, a Paratime Policeman, in high priest's robes and beard, had a square box slung in front of him; he was fiddling with knobs and buttons on it, practicing. A big idol of Yat-Zar, on antigravity, was floating slowly about the room in obedience to its remote controls, rising and lowering, turning about and pirouetting gracefully.

"Hey, Vall!" he called to his superior. "How's this?"

The idol rose about five feet, turned slowly in a half-circle, moved to the right a little, and then settled slowly toward the floor.

"Fine, fine, Horv," Verkan Vall told him, "but don't set it down on anything, or turn off the antigravity. There's enough collapsed nickel-plating on that thing to sink it a yard in soft ground."

"I don't know what the idea of that was," Brannad Klav, standing beside him, said. "Understand, I'm not criticizing. I haven't any right to, under the circumstances. But it seems to me that armoring that thing in collapsed nickel was an unnecessary precaution."

"Maybe it was," Verkan Vall agreed. "I sincerely hope so. But we can't take any chances. This operation has to be absolutely right. Ready, Tammand? All right; first detail into the conveyer."

He turned and strode toward a big dome of fine metallic mesh, thirty feet high and sixty in diameter, at the other end of the room. Tammand Drav, and his ten paratimer priests, and Brannad Klav, and ten Paratime Police, followed him in. One of the latter slid shut the door and locked it; Verkan Vall went to the control desk, at the center of the dome, and picked up a two-foot globe of the same fine metallic mesh, opening it and making some adjustments inside, then attaching an electric cord and closing it. He laid the globe on the floor near the desk and picked up the hand battery at the other end of the attached cord.

"Not taking any chances at all, are you?" Brannad Klav asked, watching this operation with interest.

"I never do, unnecessarily. There are too many necessary chances that have to be taken, in this work." Verkan Vall pressed the button on the hand battery. The globe on the floor flashed and vanished. "Yesterday, five paratimers were arrested. Any or all of them could have had door-activators with them. Stranor Sleth says they were not tortured, but that is a purely inferential statement. They may have been, and the use of the activator may have been extorted from one of them. So I want a look at the inside of that conveyer-chamber before we transpose into it."

He laid the hand battery, with the loose-dangling wire that had been left behind, on the desk, then lit a cigarette. The others gathered around, smoking and watching, careful to avoid the place from which the globe had vanished. Thirty minutes passed, and then, in a queer iridescence, the globe reappeared. Verkan Vall counted ten seconds and picked it up, taking it to the desk and opening it to remove a small square box. This he slid into a space under the desk and flipped a switch. Instantly, a view-screen lit up and a three-dimensional picture appeared—the interior of a big room a hundred feet square and some seventy in height. There was a big desk and a radio; tables, couches, chairs and an arms-rack full of weapons, and at one end, a remarkably clean sixty-foot circle on the concrete floor, outlined in faintly luminous red.

"How about it?" Verkan Vall asked Tammand Drav. "Anything wrong?"

The Zurb high priest shook his head. "Just as we left it," he said. "Nobody's been inside since we left."

ONE OF the policemen took Verkan Vall's place at the control desk and threw the master switch, after checking the instruments. Immediately, the paratemporal-transposition field went on with a humming sound that mounted to a high scream, then settled to a steady drone. The mesh dome flickered with a cold iridescence and vanished, and they were looking into the interior of a great fissionables refinery plant, operated by paratimers on another First Level time-line. The structural details altered, from time-line to time-line, as they watched. Buildings appeared and vanished. Once, for a few seconds, they were inside a cool, insulated bubble in the midst of molten lead. Tammand Drav jerked a thumb at it, before it vanished.

"That always bothers me," he said. "Bad place for the field to go weak. I'm fussy as an old hen about inspection of the conveyer, on account of that."

"Don't blame you," Verkan Vall agreed. "Probably the cooling system of a breeder-pile."

They passed more swiftly, now, across the Second Level and the Third. Once they were in the midst of a huge land battle, with great tanklike vehicles spouting flame at one another. Another moment was spent in an air bombardment. On any time-line, this section of East Europe was a natural battleground. Once a great procession marched toward them, carrying red banners and huge pictures of a coarse-faced man with a black mustache—Verkan Vall recognized the environment as Fourth Level Europo-American Sector. Finally, as the transposition-rate slowed, they saw a clutter of miserable thatched huts, in the rear of a granite wall of a Fourth Level Hulgun temple of Yat-Zar—a temple not yet infiltrated by Transtemporal Mining Corporation agents. Finally, they were at their destination. The dome around them became visible, and an overhead green light flashed slowly on and off.

Verkan Vall opened the door and stepped outside, his needler drawn. The House of Yat-Zar was just as he had seen it in the picture photographed by the automatic reconnaissance-conveyer. The others crowded outside after him. One of the regular priests pulled off his miter and beard and went to the radio, putting on a headset. Verkan Vall and Tammand Drav snapped on the visiscreen, getting a view of the Holy of Holies outside.

There were six men there, seated at the upper-priests' banquet table, drinking from golden goblets. Five of them wore the black robes with green facings which marked them as priests of Muz-Azin; the sixth was an officer of the Chuldun archers, in gilded mail and helmet.

"Why, those are the sacred vessels of the temple!" Tammand Drav cried, scandalized. Then he laughed in self-ridicule. "I'm beginning to take this stuff seriously, myself; time I put in for a long vacation. I was actually shocked at the sacrilege!"

"Well, let's overtake the infidels in their sins," Verkan Vall said. "Paralyzers will be good enough."

He picked up one of the bulb-headed weapons, and unlocked the door. Tammand Drav and another of the priests of the Zurb temple following and the others crowding behind, they passed out through the veils, and burst into the Holy of Holies. Verkan Vall pointed the bulb of his paralyzer at the six seated men and pressed the button; other paralyzers came into action, and the whole sextet were knocked senseless. The officer rolled from his chair and fell to the floor in a clatter of armor. Two of the priests slumped forward on the table. The others merely sank back in their chairs, dropping their goblets.

"Give each one of them another dose, to make sure," Verkan Vall directed a couple of his own men. "Now, Tammand; any other way into the main temple beside that door?"

"Up those steps," Tammand Drav pointed. "There's a gallery along the side; we can cover the whole room from there."

"Take your men and go up there. I'll take a few through the door. There'll be about twenty archers out there, and we don't want any of them loosing any arrows before we can knock them out. Three minutes be time enough?"

"Easily. Make it two," Tammand Drav said.

HE TOOK his priests up the stairway and vanished into the gallery of the temple. Verkan Vall waited until one minute had passed and then, followed by Brannad Klav and a couple of Paratime Policemen, he went under the plinth and peered out into the temple. Five or six archers, in steel caps and sleeveless leather jackets sewn with steel rings, were gathered around the altar, cooking something in a pot on the fire. Most of the others, like veteran soldiers, were sprawled on the floor, trying to catch a short nap, except half a dozen, who crouched in a circle, playing some game with dice—another almost universal military practice.

The two minutes were up. He aimed his paralyzer at the men around the altar and squeezed the button, swinging it from one to another and knocking them down with a bludgeon of inaudible sound. At the same time, Tammand Drav and his detail were stunning the gamblers. Stepping forward and to one side, Verkan Vall, Brannad Klav and the others took care of the sleepers on the floor. In less than thirty seconds, every Chuldun in the temple was incapacitated.

"All right, make sure none of them come out of it prematurely," Verkan Vall directed. "Get their weapons, and be sure nobody has a knife or anything hidden on him. Who has the syringe and the sleep-drug ampoules?"

Somebody had, it developed, who was still on the First Level, to come up with the second conveyer load. Verkan Vall swore. Something like this always happened, on any operation involving more than half a dozen men.

"Well, some of you stay here: patrol around, and use your paralyzers on anybody who even twitches a muscle." Ultrasonics were nice, effective, humane police weapons, but they were unreliable. The same dose that would keep one man out for an hour would paralyze another for no more than ten or fifteen minutes. "And be sure none of them are playing 'possum."

He went back through the door under the plinth, glancing up at the decorated wooden screen and wondering how much work it would take to move the new Yat-Zar in from the conveyers. The five priests and the archer-captain were still unconscious; one of the policemen was searching them.

"Here's the sort of weapons these priests carry," he said, holding up a short iron mace with a spiked head. "Carry them on their belts." He tossed it on the table, and began searching another knocked-out hierophant. "Like this—*Hey!* Look at this, will you!"

He drew his hand from under the left side of the senseless man's robe and held up a sigma-ray needler. Verkan Vall looked at it and nodded grimly.

"Had it in a regular shoulder holster," the policeman said, handing the weapon across the table. "What do you think?"

"Find anything else funny on him?"

"Wait a minute." The policeman pulled open the robe and began stripping the priest of Muz-Azin; Verkan Vall came around the table to help. There was nothing else of a suspicious nature.

"Could have got it from one of the prisoners, but I don't like the familiar way he's wearing that holster," Verkan Vall said. "Has the conveyer gone back, yet?" When the policeman nodded, he continued: "When it returns, take him to the First Level. I hope they bring up the sleep-drug with the next load. When you get him back, take him to Dhergabar by strato-rocket immediately, and make sure he gets back alive. I want him questioned under narco-hypnosis by a regular Paratime Commission psycho-technician, in the presence of Chief Tortha Karf and some responsible Commission official. This is going to be hot stuff."

Within an hour, the whole force was assembled in the temple. The wooden screen had presented no problem—it slid easily to one side—and the big idol floated on antigravity in the middle of the temple. Verkan Vall was looking anxiously at his watch.

"It's about two hours to sunset," he said, to Stranor Sleth. "But as you pointed out, these Hulguns aren't astronomers, and it's a bit cloudy. I wish Crannar Jurth would call in with something definite."

Another twenty minutes passed. Then the man at the radio came out into the temple.

"O. K.!" he called. "The man at Crannar Jurth's called in. Crannar Jurth contacted him with a midget radio he has up his sleeve; he's in the palace courtyard now. They haven't brought out the victims, yet, but Kurchuk has just been carried out on his throne to that platform in front of the citadel. Big crowd gathering in the inner courtyard; more in the streets outside. Palace gates are wide open."

"That's it!" Verkan Vall cried. "Form up; the parade's starting. Brannad, you and Tammand and Stranor and I in front; about ten men with paralyzers a little behind us. Then Yat-Zar, about ten feet off the ground, and then the others. Forward—*ho-o!*"

THEY EMERGED from the temple and started down the broad roadway toward the palace. There was not much of a crowd, at first. Most of Zurb had flocked to the palace earlier; the lucky ones in the courtyard and the late comers outside. Those whom they did meet stared at them in open-mouthed amazement, and then some, remembering their doubts and blasphemies, began howling for forgiveness. Others—a substantial majority—realizing that it would be upon King Kurchuk that the real weight of Yat-Zar's six hands would fall, took to their heels, trying to put as much distance as possible between them and the palace before the blow fell.

As the procession approached the palace gates, the crowds were thicker, made up of those who had been unable to squeeze themselves inside. The panic was worse, here, too. A good many were trampled and hurt in the rush to escape, and it became necessary to use paralyzers to clear a way. That made it worse: everybody was sure that Yat-Zar was striking sinners dead left and right.

Fortunately, the gates were high enough to let the god through without losing altitude appreciably. Inside, the mob surged back, clearing a way across the courtyard. It was only necessary to paralyze a few here, and the levitated idol and its priestly attendants advanced toward the stone platform, where the king sat on his throne, flanked by court functionaries and black-robed priests of Muz-Azin. In front of this, a rank of Chuldun archers had been drawn up.

"Horv; move Yat-Zar forward about a hundred feet and up about fifty," Verkan Vall directed. "Quickly!"

As the six-armed anthropomorphic idol rose and moved closer toward its saurian rival, Verkan Vall drew his needler, scanning the assemblage around the throne anxiously.

"Where is the wicked King?" a voice thundered—the voice of Stranor Sleth, speaking into a midget radio tuned to the loud-speaker inside the idol. *"Where is the blasphemer and desecrator, Kurchuk?"*

"There's Labdurg, in the red tunic, beside the throne," Tammand Drav whispered. "And that's Ghromdur, the Muz-Azin high priest, beside him."

Verkan Vall nodded, keeping his eyes on the group on the platform. Ghromdur, the high priest of Muz-Azin, was edging backward and reaching under his robe. At the same time, an officer shouted an order, and the Chuldun archers drew arrows from their quivers and fitted them to their bowstrings. Immediately, the ultrasonic paralyzers of the advancing paratimers went into action, and the mercenaries began dropping.

"Lay down your weapons, fools!" the amplified voice boomed at them. *"Lay down your weapons or you shall surely die! Who are you, miserable wretches, to draw bows against Me?"*

At first a few, then all of them, the Chulduns lowered or dropped their weapons and began edging away to the sides. At the center, in front of the throne, most of them had been knocked out. Verkan Vall was still watching the Muz-Azin high priest intently; as Ghromdur raised his arm, there was a flash and a puff of smoke from the front of Yat-Zar—the paint over the collapsed nickel was burned off, but otherwise the idol was undamaged. Verkan Vall swung up his needler and rayed Ghromdur dead; as the man in the green-faced black robes fell, a blaster clattered on the stone platform.

"Is that your puny best, Muz-Azin?" the booming voice demanded. *"Where is your high priest now?"*

"Horv; face Yat-Zar toward Muz-Azin," Verkan Vall said over his shoulder, drawing his blaster with his left hand. Like all First Level people, he was ambidextrous, although, like all paratimers, he habitually concealed the fact while outtime. As the levitated idol swung slowly to look down upon its enemy on the built-up cart, Verkan Vall aimed the blaster and squeezed.

In a spot less than a millimeter in diameter on the crocodile idol's side, a certain number of neutrons in the atomic structure of the stone from which it was carved broke apart, becoming, in effect, atoms of hydrogen. With a flash and a bang, the idol burst and vanished. Yat-Zar gave a dirty laugh and turned his back on the cart, which was now burning fiercely facing King Kurchuk again.

"Get your hands up, all of you!" Verkan Vall shouted, in the First Level language, swinging the stubby muzzle of the blaster and the knob-tipped twin tubes of the needler to cover the group around the throne, "Come forward, before I start blasting!"

LABDURG RAISED his hands and stepped forward. So did two of the priests of Yat-Zar. They were quickly seized by Paratime Policemen who swarmed up onto the platform and disarmed. All three were carrying sigma-ray needlers, and Labdurg had a blaster as well.

King Kurchuk was clinging to the arms of his throne, a badly frightened monarch trying desperately not to show it. He was a big man, heavy-shouldered, black-bearded; under ordinary circumstances he would probably have cut an imposing figure, in his gold-washed mail and his golden crown. Now his face was a dirty gray, and he was biting nervously at his lower lip. The others on the platform were in even worse state. The Hulgun nobles were grouped together, trying to disassociate themselves from both the king and the priests of Muz-Azin. The latter were staring in a daze at the blazing cart from which their idol had just been blasted. And the dozen men who were to have done the actual work of the torture-sacrifice had all dropped their whips and were fairly gibbering in fear.

Yat-Zar, manipulated by the robed paratimer, had taken a position directly above the throne and was lowering slowly. Kurchuk stared up at the massive idol descending toward him, his knuckles white as he clung to the arms of his throne. He managed to hold out until he could feel the weight of the idol pressing on his head. Then, with a scream, he hurled himself from the throne and rolled forward almost to the edge of the platform. Yat-Zar moved to one side, swung slightly and knocked the throne toppling, and then settled down on the platform. To Kurchuk, who was rising cautiously on his hands and knees, the big idol seemed to be looking at him in contempt.

"Where are my holy priests, Kurchuk?" Stranor Sleth demanded in to his sleeve-hidden radio. *"Let them be brought before me, alive and unharmed, or it shall be better for you had you never been born!"*

The six priests of Yat-Zar, it seemed, were already being brought onto the platform by one of Kurchuk's nobles. This noble, whose name was Yorzuk, knew a miracle when he saw one, and believed in being on the side of the god with the heaviest artillery. As soon as he had seen Yat-Zar coming through the gate without visible means of support, he had hastened to the dungeons with half a dozen of his personal retainers and ordered the release of the six captives. He was now escorting them onto the platform, assuring them that he had always been a faithful servant of Yat-Zar and had been deeply grieved at his sovereign's apostasy.

"Hear my word, Kurchuk," Stranor Sleth continued through the loud-speaker in the idol. *"You have sinned most vilely against me, and were I a cruel god, your fate would be such as no man has ever before suffered. But I am a merciful god; behold, you may gain forgiveness in my sight. For thirty days, you shall neither eat meat nor drink wine, nor shall you wear gold nor fine raiment, and each day shall you go to my temple and beseech me for my forgiveness. And on the thirty-first day, you shall set out, barefoot and clad in the garb of a slave, and journey to my temple that is in the mountains over above Yoldav, and there will I forgive you, af-*

ter you have made sacrifice to me. I, Yat-Zar, have spoken!"

The king started to rise, babbling thanks.

"Rise not before me until I have forgiven you!" Yat-Zar thundered. *"Creep out of my sight upon your belly, wretch!"*

THE PROCESSION back to the temple was made quietly and sedately along an empty roadway. Yat-Zar seemed to be in a kindly humor; the people of Zurb had no intention of giving him any reason to change his mood. The priests of Muz-Azin and their torturers had been flung into the dungeon. Yorzuk, appointed regent for the duration of Kurchuk's penance, had taken control and was employing Hulgun spearmen and hastily-converted Chuldun archers to restore order and, incidentally, purge a few of his personal enemies and political rivals. The priests, with the three prisoners who had been found carrying First Level weapons among them and Yat-Zar floating triumphantly in front, entered the temple. A few of the devout, who sought admission after them, were told that elaborate and secret rites were being held to cleanse the profaned altar, and sent away.

Verkan Vall and Brannad Klav and Stranor Sleth were in the conveyer chamber, with the Paratime Policemen and the extra priests; along with them were the three prisoners. Verkan Vall pulled off his false beard and turned to face these. He could see that they all recognized him.

"Now," he began, "you people are in a bad jam. You've violated the Paratime Transposition Code, the Commercial Regulation Code, and the First Level Criminal Code, all together. If you know what's good for you, you'll start talking."

"I'm not saying anything till I have legal advice," the man who had been using the local alias of Labdurg replied. "And if you're through searching me, I'd like to have my cigarettes and lighter back."

"Smoke one of mine, for a change," Verkan Vall told him. "I don't know what's in yours beside tobacco." He offered his case and held a light for the prisoner before lighting his own cigarette. "I'm going to be sure you get back to the First Level alive."

The former Overseer of the Kingdom of Zurb shrugged. "I'm still not talking," he said.

"Well, we can get it all out of you by narco-hypnosis, anyhow," Verkan Vall told him. "Besides, we got that man of yours who was here at the temple when we came in. He's being given a full treatment, as a presumed outtime native found in possession of First Level weapons. If you talk now it'll go easier with you."

The prisoner dropped the cigarette on the floor and tramped it out.

"Anything you cops get out of me, you'll have to get the hard way," he said. "I have friends on the First Level who'll take care of me."

"I doubt that. They'll have their hands full taking care of themselves, after this gets out." Verkan Vall turned to the two in the black robes. "Either of you want to say anything?" When they shook their heads, he nodded to a group of his policemen; they were hustled into the conveyer. "Take them to the First Level terminal and hold them till I come in. I'll be along with the next conveyer load."

THE CONVEYER flashed and vanished. Brannad Klav stared for a moment at the circle of concrete floor from whence it had disappeared. Then he turned to Verkan Vall.

"I still can't believe it," he said. "Why, those fellows were First Level paratimers. So was that priest, Ghromdur: the one you rayed."

"Yes, of course. They worked for your rivals, the Fourth Level Mineral Products Syndicate; the outfit that was trying to get your Proto-Aryan Sector fissionables franchise away from you. They operate on this sector already; have the petroleum franchise for the Chuldun country, east of the Caspian Sea. They export to some of these internal-combustion-engine sectors, like Europo-American. You know, most of the wars they've been fighting, lately, on the Europo-American Sector have been, at least in part, motivated by rivalry for oil fields. But now that the Europo-Americans have begun to release nuclear energy, fissionables have become more important than oil. In less than a century, it's predicted that atomic energy will replace all other forms of power. Mineral Products Syndicate wanted to get a good source of supply for uranium, and your Proto-Aryan Sector franchise was worth grabbing.

"I had considered something like this as a possibility when Stranor, here, mentioned that tularemia was normally unknown in Eurasia on this sector. That epidemic must have been started by imported germs. And I knew that Mineral Products has agents at the court of the Chuldun emperor, Chombrog: they have to, to protect their oil wells on his eastern frontiers. I spent most of last night checking up on some stuff by video-transcription from the Paratime Commission's microfilm library at Dhergabar. I found out, for one thing, that while there is a King Kurchuk of Zurb on every time-line for a hundred para-years on either side of this one, this is the only time-line on which he married a Princess Darith of Chuldun, and it's the only time-line on which there is any trace of a Chuldun scribe named Labdurg.

"That's why I went to all the trouble of having that Yat-Zar plated with collapsed nickel. If there were disguised paratimers among the Muz-Azin party at Kurchuk's court, I expected one of them to try to blast our idol when we brought it into the palace. I was watching Ghromdur and Labdurg in particular; as soon as Ghromdur used his blaster, I needled him. After that, it was easy."

"Was that why you insisted on sending that automatic viewer on ahead?"

"Yes. There was a chance that they might have planted a bomb in the House of Yat-Zar, here. I knew they'd either do that or let the place entirely alone. I suppose they were so confident of getting away with this that they didn't want to damage the conveyer or the conveyer chamber. They expected to use them, themselves, after they took over your company's franchise."

"Well, what's going to be done about it by the Commission?" Brannad Klav wanted to know.

"Plenty. The syndicate will probably lose their paratime license; any of its officials who had guilty knowledge of this will be dealt with according to law. You know, this was a pretty nasty business."

* * * * * * * * *

"YOU'RE TELLING me!" Stranor Sleth exclaimed. "Did you get a look at those whips they were going to use on our people? Pointed iron barbs a quarter-inch long braided into them, all over the lash-ends!"

"Yes. Any punitive action you're thinking about taking on these priests of Muz-Azin—the natives, I mean—will be ignored on the First Level. And that reminds me: you'd better work out a line of policy, pretty soon."

"Well, as for the priests and the torturers, I think I'll tell Yorzuk to have them sold to the Bhunguns, to the east. They're always in the market for galley slaves," Stranor Sleth said. He turned to Brannad Klav. "And I'll want six gold crowns made up, as soon as possible. Strictly Hulgun design, with Yat-Zar religious symbolism, very rich and ornate, all slightly different. When I give Kurchuk absolution, I'll crown him at the altar in the name of Yat-Zar. Then I'll invite in the other five Hulgun kings, lecture them on their religious duties, make them confess their secret doubts, forgive them, and crown them, too. From then on, they can all style themselves as ruling by the will of Yat-Zar."

"And from then on, you'll have all of them eating out of your hand," Verkan Vall concluded. "You know, this will probably go down in Hulgun history as the Reformation of Ghullam the Holy. I've always wondered whether the theory of the divine right of kings was invented by the kings, to establish their authority over the people, or by the priests, to establish their authority over the kings. It works about as well one way as the other."

"What I can't understand is this," Brannad Klav said. "It was entirely because of my respect for the Paratime Code that I kept Stranor Sleth from using Fourth Level weapons and other techniques to control these people with a show of apparent miraculous powers. But this Fourth Level Mineral Products Syndicate was operating in violation of the Paratime Code by invading our franchise area. Why didn't they fake up a supernatural reign of terror to intimidate these natives?"

"Ha, exactly because they *were* operating illegally," Verkan Vall replied. "Suppose they had started using needlers and blasters and antigravity and nuclear-energy around here. The natives would have thought it was the power of Muz-Azin, of course, but what would you have thought? You'd have known, as soon as they tried it, that First Level paratimers were working against you, and you'd have laid the facts before the Commission, and this time-line would have been flooded with Paratime Police. They had to conceal their operations not only from the natives, as you do, but also from us. So they didn't dare make public use of First Level techniques.

"Of course, when we came marching into the palace with that idol on antigravity, they knew, at once, what was happening. I have an idea that they only tried to blast that idol to create a diversion which would permit them to escape—if they could have got out of the palace, they'd have made their way, in disguise, to the nearest Mineral Products Syndicate conveyer and transposed out of here. I realized that they could best delay us by blasting our idol, and that's why I had it plated with collapsed nickel. I think that where they made their mistake was in allowing Kurchuk to have those priests arrested, and insisting on sacrificing them to Muz-Azin. If it hadn't been for that, the Paratime Police wouldn't have been brought into this, at all.

"Well, Stranor, you'll want to get back to your temple, and Brannad and I want to get back to the First Level. I'm supposed to take my wife to a banquet in Dhergabar, tonight, and with the fastest strato-rocket, I'll just barely make it."

As Told to John Casey and Jack Nemo

The city of Tokyo was doomed to destruction from the gargantuan beast... that is, until love—or was it lust?—inspired a novel solution!!

I, Harou Murami, never dared dream to be the savior of my nation. As an engineer in the ultra-conservative, Tokyo-based Nakatomi Corporation my days, my lot, my duty in life was to complete my assignments in an orderly, exacting, and above all timely fashion. My nights were taken up with many purely personal scientific experiments and an unrequited love for the beautiful Ama Hotto.

She was fair of skin, dark of hair, long of leg and blessed with optical pools of the purest almond. As Special Assistant of Public Relations at Nakatomi, her days—and nights—were consumed with war hero, deep sea diver, matinee idol, and Vice President of Public Relations (not to mention Special Underwater Projects Manager), Teichou Kyoutendouchi.

While I could conceive of no greater nor demanding glory; just such a magnificent triumph awaited me on that monumentally horrific day that devastation greeted the City of Tokyo.

Every building spared the decades-old ravages of Mr. B* was demolished by the one-hundred-meter horror of Yajuu.

While our glorious Army, Navy and Air Forces fought with skill, devotion and honor all was in vain. In but a matter of hours all districts of our great and beloved metropolis lay in ruin, while the monster retreated to rest at the bottom of Tokyo Bay.

Beyond the military police barricade lining the shore, the wizened, wise and eminent zoologist Dr. Nanto Dare (Ph.D. in GERM**) was desperate for a humane solution. His brilliant and beautiful daughter, the forlorn Nanisama Dare pled silently with her comely, opal-hued eyes for any and all of the Sons of Nippon to provide an answer to the city's salvation.

Fearing a return of Yajuu, the military prepared to destroy the beast in the Bay with an untested "Secret Weapon"—wielded by none other than Teichou. Realizing that something as puny as the "Secret Weapon" being held in the vainglorious (but honorable hands of Teichou Kyoutendouchi) would risk Ama Hotto and all Tokyo with *total* destruction, I leaped across the barricade and through the corridor of military police. Inspiration had seized my body as well as my mind. Before a Sumo-sized sergeant wres-

*Japanese nickname for the American Boeing B-29 Superfortress.

**GERM—Gigantic Enraged Rampaging and/or Radioactive Monster.

(With The Honorable Assistance of the Army, Navy and Air Force of Japan)

Illustration by William Carney

tled me to the ground, I seized the wizened zoologist and quickly outlined my plan.

"Yes!" he cried in what became a continuous mantra, nodding his head in stately agreement. Quickly calling over the honorable commanders of the armed forces, Dr. Dare was able to relate my plan for the defense of the city.

Preparations were made in orderly haste. The Navy was able to airlift in the equipment I needed, so—with the sound of the Army's caterpillar tracks echoing the Navy helicopter rotors—the combined honorable armed services began to implement Phase One. I, myself, supervised the final placement of the "New Secret Weapon". This was no puny, untried device wielded by the honorable hands of Teichou Kyoutendouchi. This weapon—*my* weapon—required the lifting power of six Navy *Raiden* helicopters.

Barely had the preparations been completed when with a deafening roar, Yajuu emerged anew from rubble-choked Tokyo Bay. Now the Air Force was committed to vex and goad the monster into my carefully chosen field of battle.

Slowly the behemoth came into view. Any fears I had of failure were soon dismissed. My initial estimates of Yajuu's height, mass and stride were indeed correct.

Out of range of the dragon's fire, I shouted "Banzai!" as the beast entered my trap.

*The author is mistaken and must be referring to the 440-ton sisal rope curtain the helped conceal the construction of the 263-meter battleship *Yamoto*.

Down went the ponderous right foot, carrying with it the combined mass of two *Mogami*-class heavy cruisers. Down through the massive tatami mat.* The same mat that once had covered and camouflaged the nine-hundred-foot super battleship, *Yamoto*. The same mat that required six Raiden helicopters to hoist into position served one last duty of honor for the Yamoto nation.

The duty of fiendishly covering a ten-meter pit.

A hole no deeper than the foundation and basement of the Nakatomi Plaza.

With a sickening crack, the monster's right femur and tibia were pulverized. An impotent and futile blast of fire upward into the sky was the monster's last act of defiance. With its leg shattered it was helpless, unable to struggle upright, doomed by its own incalculable weight.**

I knew the battle was won.

"Banzai!!" I shouted again. This time accompanied by tens of thousands of countrymen and women. Little did I care if the beast died from blood loss, shock or starvation. Little did I care or heed the mutterings of "Howinda*hell*—" from the pompous lips of American reporter, William 'Doc' Murray.

I cared only for the lusty, appreciative stares of the two women, Ama and Nanisama.

Ah, Duty.....

**Again the author is mistaken and must be referring to the very calculable <u>mass</u> of two *Mogami*-class heavy cruisers.

The End

Footnotes courtesy of Jack Nemo

John Casey has jumped out of perfectly good airplanes, worked as a lifeguard, gone head to head with a barracuda and was vice-president of a dot com before it went dot under. Currently the creator and co-writer of the new series *Two Shades of Soul*.

Jack Nemo has worked every other retail job there is or as he calls it "The Nightmares at Christmas," been a busboy, Wawa Deli "boy" and worked two years four months and three days in a County Jail. Currently the co-writer of the new series *Two Shades of Soul*.

SAVE THE LAST BULLET:
A Review of Dark Adventure Radio Theatre

by Chris Carney

BACK IN 2005, I had the good fortune to receive an amazing gift for Christmas, a copy of the recently released film adaptation of H.P. Lovecraft's *The Call of Cthulhu*. There may be some of you readers out there who may not be aware of this particular gem. Perhaps you've been living in a wilderness shack in Montana, driven there into self-imposed exile by fears of terrorism, anthrax, and Glenn Beck. Perhaps your flight back from the international space station got delayed because… well, you had to come back on a Russian rocket, and you know how that goes. Perhaps you just don't hang out with the right sort of people. Whatever. For the unwashed out there, The Call of Cthulhu is an utterly faithful adaptation of one of Lovecraft's best tales told in just the way that Lovecraft himself might have seen it: as a silent movie. It was produced by the fans at the H.P. Lovecraft Historical Society (HPLHS, for short.)

I'm not here to heap whatever considerable praise I can throw at this splendid feature. Suffice to say that the effort is stupendous. Everything works and the attention to detail by HPLHS is outstanding. It's certainly the best film adaptation of any Lovecraft story to date. (*Re-Animator* may be entertaining enough, due primarily to

Jeffrey Coombs, and *From Beyond* isn't horrible, but I can't stomach *Die, Monster, Die*—a C-grade effort to adapt *The Colour Out of Space*. And as a dues-paying member of The Wesley Crushers, let's not even mention that piece of crap *The Curse* starring Wil Wheaton!)

No, my faithful droogies. I'm here to provide you with my views (however acerbic or uninformed as they may be) on another venture of the H.P. Lovecraft Historical Society, one which works just as splendidly as their silent-film adaptation. How can one follow-up on a period-accurate silent film adaptation of *The Call of Cthulhu*, you may ask? By tackling other Lovecraft stories in the form of 1930s radio dramas!

Capitalizing upon their success with TCOC, the fan boys (and girls) at HPLHS moved into audio format and started their line of "radio" adaptations. Hosted by Chester Langfield (voiced always by Noah Wagner) and "sponsored" by Fleur de-Lys Cigarettes, Dark Adventure Radio Theatre presents dramatizations of four of Lovecraft's tales. The first release in 2006 is one of Lovecraft's best stories, *At the Mountains of Madness*. I won't bore you with the plot details because I'm sure you all know it by now…expedition from Miskatonic University travels to the Antarctic, finds city of the Old Ones, it's not quite deserted, blah blah blah. You've all read it by now. (What's that? You're holding a copy of *Startling Stories* in your grubby mitts and haven't read *At the Mountains of Madness*?! Then, put this issue down and back slowly away from the table. You've got some homework to do.)

In any case, the folks at HPLHS give us yet another winner. The result is not a mere reading of the story, as you would expect from an audio-book. No, this is a true radio dramatization with characters, dramatic music, sound effects, and even the obligatory 1930s cigarette ad. The liner notes provide some interesting information and back story on the tale itself, but the execution of the adaptation is the real reason to buy this. Imagine being 13 years old again; you're curled up on the floor beneath your family's RCA Victor. Roosevelt just finished one of his famous firesides, and your dad reaches over to dial in the next program, one that will convince you there is more to fear than fear itself. If I'd been a kid back then, this is the kind of radio program I would have listened to. Screw Ralphie and his obsession with Little Orphan Annie.

If I have only one problem with this adaptation, it's a relatively minor one. In their attempt to replicate the sound of radio transmissions from the Antarctic expedition, the producers go just a little overboard with the sound effects. I'm sure it sounds authentic enough, but it makes it just a tad difficult to hear what's being said by the characters. Other than that, it's a faithful adaptation. They don't make up characters or events that aren't in the original story. In

fact, much of the narration and dialogue are Lovecraft's own words and descriptions.

It seems that their dramatization of *At the Mountains of Madness* was such a rousing success that fans began clamoring for more. (I heard there were even riots in Paris, but that could have been over something else entirely, like some uncouth politico threatening to take away their weekly government benefits of camembert and Grenache Blanc.) So, for their next endeavor, Dark Adventure Radio Theatre turned their sights on one of Lovecraft's true masterpieces, *The Dunwich Horror.*

Again, I won't bother you with the plot because you should have this story practically memorized by now. If not, all I can suggest is chasing a ball across I-95 in Baltimore during the morning rush or some other equally gruesome means of suicide. Our tale is again hosted by Chester Langfield and ably narrated by co-producer Sean Branney (he gets all the good roles.) This time around, the producers really step up their game with an increasing cast size doing multiple voices, just as you would expect in an authentic radio adaptation. This effort really expands on previous efforts, relying as much on dialogue as it does narration. Again, I have only one quibble, and that's the effect of Wilbur Whateley's voice. Somehow, it doesn't sound the way I think it should, but then I'm not really sure what the devilish half-breeded mutant should sound like. Overall, though, the results are stunning, and it's one I never get tired of hearing.

Their next installment is possibly their most ambitious because it's one of Lovecraft's most cerebral (pun intended) and abstruse stories. The 2008 release of *The Shadow Out of Time* carries on the tradition set by its predecessors, but somehow this one falls a little flat for me. I don't think it's any fault of the producers. They do an admirable job of translating and adapting the story, but it's one of Lovecraft's stories that I have a hard time putting my arms around. Frankly, I've always found it to be a bit of a yawner, so it's difficult for me to really enjoy this adaptation. Still, the producers do their best to dramatize a story that doesn't really lend itself to adaptation. They don't really muck about with the plot and ruin it in any way, but they do have to add some elements to successfully dramatize the story. In this case, they find it necessary to add a character, a ship's doctor to whom the narrator can tell his story. Without this, the story probably would have become a mere book-on-tape. It's not bad, by any means, but it is my least favorite of the series.

However, when I heard that Dark Adventure Radio Theatre's fourth installment would be *The Shadow Over Innsmouth*, I nearly burst out of my Docker's. I couldn't wait to get my hands on this puppy! Any fan of old Howard Phillips will tell you this is one of his best, and the gang at HPLHS don't let us down. This is a tale that was begging for a radio dramatization. I'd be really hard-pressed to say whether it's better than Dunwich, but it's probably the one I listen to most. Barry Lynch turns in one of the great eccentric vocal performances as Zadok Allen, and given his central role in the story, you get to hear a lot of him. When he starts raving, it really sets your hair on end, and the surprising cliff-hanger style ending is absolutely perfect! It left me maddeningly wondering what really happened.

So far, I've only provided a gloss-over of the quality of these productions, touching only upon the adaptations themselves. What I haven't talked about yet are the special bonuses that come with each CD, and it's here that the folks at HPLHS really shine. Every one comes with extras and props specific to the story.

At The Mountains of Madness, for example, comes with a "vintage" newspaper clipping about the expedition from *The Arkham Advertiser*, copies of photographs taken of the ruined city by the expedition, and even a page of sketches and notes ripped from Danforth's notebook. *The Dunwich Horror* gives us another clipping from *The Advertiser* about the Whateley family, a vintage map of Dunwich (complete with a note from the librarian,) a page from young Wilbur's inexact copy of the dreaded Necronomicon, and a page from his diary. *The Shadow Out of Time* comes with a page torn from the "original" Unausssprechlicen Kulten (including annotations), yet another clipping from *The Advertiser*, part of an article about Peaslee and his dreams, and the telegram he receives from his son on an authentic Marconigram. If anything, they saved the best for last with *The Shadow Over Innsmouth*. The goodies here include a used matchbook from the Gilman House hotel, a postcard from the Newburyport Historical Society, a clipping from the *New York Evening Graphic* describing the raid on Innsmouth (note the Calvin Coolidge lovechild story on the reverse side) and the map drawn for the main character by the clerk at the First National Chain which is, believe it or not, scratch-n-sniff! (Yes, Virginia. There really is something fishy in Innsmouth.)

These bonuses are so detailed and so lovingly crafted that one can't help but appreciate the effort it took to produce them. The creators call themselves the H.P. Lovecraft Historical Society for a reason. These are true fans and connoisseurs of the Old Man of Providence, and it shows in their work. Their adaptations are utterly faithful, both to the letter and the spirit of the stories, and their work on these bonuses is unparalleled.

The dramatizations are available individually on the producer's website (www.cthulhulives.org) along with numerous other goodies. However, I recommend buying the entire set because it comes packaged in a handsome display case which, appropriately enough, is made to look like an old-time radio.

I can only hope that the group will continue to produce more of these wonderful radio dramatizations because there are other Lovecraft tales that are ripe for adaptation. *The Rats in the Walls, The Colour Out of Space* and *The Haunter of the Dark* are just three that immediately spring to mind. (Sean and the rest of the folks at HPLHS, are you reading this? Hint hint.) And be on the lookout for the group's next production, another film adaptation of *The Whisperer in Darkness*, which is currently in post-production and due out (hopefully) next year.

And remember to "save the last bullet for yourself." (Cue dramatic musical coda.)

SF On Television In The 1970's

by Rob Morganbesser

AS THE 1970's began televised science fiction—before *Logan's Run* and *Star Wars* revitalized the genre (how many people remember that *Logan's Run* was a huge hit for MGM? Everything got overshadowed by the *Star Wars* steamroller)—was a vast wasteland. Most of the shows were bad, completely bad. Many took what was a fine concept and diluted it into toilet water.

How many of us remember that the *Six Million Dollar Man* (based on the excellent novel "Cyborg", by Martin Caidin), was an adult-themed show wherein Steve Austin was a spy, a kind of bionic James Bond? Or that Gerry Anderson's *Space:1999* was supposed to be the second season of *UFO*? *The Six Million Dollar Man*, which quickly devolved into a kid-friendly show, was one of the best shows of the 70's, head and shoulders above the dross that followed it. So let's take a look at Science Fiction Television from the good to the bad (which, tragically, outnumbers the good by quite a large margin).

The Good: There are a few; *The Six Million Dollar Man, The Bionic Woman, UFO, The Incredible Hulk*. I note that three of these (the bionic shows and *The Incredible Hulk*) employed Kenneth Johnson, who later went on to make the first *V* mini-series the excellent show it was. Johnson overcame the budgetary limitations of TV with excellent writing (aping the original run of *Doctor Who* over in England, which had some of the best writing in SF—but then again British TV has always had less money to spend, and so had to depend on their writing) and acting. Lee Majors may not have won any Emmy's but a generation of kids grew up with him as their hero as he went from adventure to adventure. Originally, the show started as part of a rotating Saturday night show, playing every three weeks. Before becoming a weekly, there were three (the original pilot, called *Cyborg: The Six Million Dollar Man*) ninety minute episodes. The second, called "Wine, Woman and War" starred David McCallum, Britt Ekland and Eric Braeden (star of *The Rat Patrol* and *Escape From the Planet of The Apes*) and dealt with arms dealing. Not only was it adult-themed, it had a very catchy theme song! *SMDM*'s spin off, *The Bionic Woman* (a spectacular failure in the 2000's, thanks to forgetting that it's the bionics people tuned in for, not conspiracy theories), was a bit gentler, but again, under the guidance of Kenneth Johnson, had some very good episodes.

Johnson's *The Incredible Hulk*, while lacking in budget (the Hulk never faced any of his comic foes), made up for it again in the writing. Lead Bill Bixby played a fine version of the tormented Bruce Banner, although in this his name was David. And all his aliases used those two letters. Body-builder Lou Ferrigno made for a fierce, if cheap looking Hulk and had enough muscle to make his strength believable. *Hulk* was one of the longest running superhero shows to be on TV and is fondly remembered.

UFO was another adult-themed SF show. In it, SHADO (Supreme Headquarters Alien Defense Organization) had the business of defending Earth from aliens who, as might be expected, are not coming to conquer the Earth but instead to kidnap people and harvest their organs. This raised an excellent question—were these aliens, or were they humans from the future? Featuring some excellent SFX by Derek Meddings (a trademark of all Gerry Anderson's shows) and some fine episodes, *UFO* really deserved a second season.

Wonder Woman, starring Lynda Carter (who made for an excellent Amazonian Princess) was better in its first season, set in WW2 when she was fighting the Axis, especially Nazis. Carter filled out the costume well and could throw a mean punch. While the stories were somewhat simplistic, *WW* certainly did honor the character and remained faithful to her origin and her supporting cast from the comics. A fun show that also suffered from budgetary problems. But that first season is certainly worth watching.

Now we come to the **BAD**. And most of these aren't just BAD, they're terrible. The sad part, as will be seen, is that many of these had a great idea behind them, only the writers or producers didn't know what to do with them.

Battlestar Galactica was at one time, hour for hour, the most expensive show on TV. It had a fine premise; that of an alien race driving humanity to the brink of extinction. Unfortunately, creator Glen Larson (the Irwin Allen of the 70's and early 80's) took what could have been a great show and distilled it from what should have been a fine liquor to tap water. The genocide of humanity core was forgotten once Jane Seymour was killed off on the planet of Kobol, and the show degenerated into ripping off old movie plots. "The Gun on Ice Planet Zero" was *The Guns of Navarone* and another episode was basically *High Noon*. The acting got worse and the expensive special effects were 90 percent recycled from the pilot. The show simply got worse as it went on. It spawned a completely wretched sequel, *Galactica 1980*, which won't be discussed here. The recent re-imagining of the show on the SciFi Channel was so much better than this that they cannot be compared.

Buck Rogers In The 25th Century, another brainstorm (or perhaps brain-fart?) from Larson again had a fine idea behind it. A post-holocaust Earth (the 'Yellow Peril' menace of the original strip was wisely dumped), rebuilding and united, has reached the stars. The evil Draconian empire, led by Princess Ardalla (a very lovely Pamela Hensley) and Killer Kane threatens earth. Lasting for two seasons, the first had Buck on Earth, beating back its enemies, while the second turned the show into a second rate *Star Trek*, with Buck and crew off into space in a ship called The Searcher (they were looking for lost Earth colonies). The second season was about on par with the first which is to say, turn your mind off because there's nothing challenging about it.

The Fantastic Journey. A family gets lost in the Bermuda Triangle which, it turns out, is a pathway to alternate dimensions. Once again, every single SF cliché is used. The smart-ass kid, a cowardly adult, the stalwart hero (who is from the 22nd century, so the paths traverse time as well as dimensions). Basically this was *Lost in Space* without a spaceship. The stories were dumb and the series didn't last long.

The Starlost was created by Harlan Ellison who had his name ripped from it as fast as he could. Again, the idea behind this was brilliant—Earth's sun is going to supernova, destroying everything as far as the orbit of Mars. Earth builds a gigantic Ark to evacuate the planet. A disaster strikes and the command crew is killed, leaving the ship on a collision course with disaster. An albeit not original but potentially great idea that was produced terribly! The SFX are trash (but Canadian TV, which produced the show, had the same problem as the British—no money). And the writing was even worse. Each of the domes on the Ark hold a different culture—an idea that's patently ridiculous. If Earth can get together and build an Ark that would save humanity, why would one culture be virtually Amish (where the three heroes are from), another primitives and a third full of gigantic bees? It is amazing that there are so many other great SF shows not on DVD yet, but this turkey has been released.

Space:1999 had it all. Gerry Anderson's production team, a decent budget, and a novel idea (Earth being blasted out of orbit due to a chain reaction among nuclear waste stored there). So the topics of survival and possible evacuation to another Earth-like world are common concerns. The problem is—the show was as dull as watching paint dry! There also wasn't any 'science' to the science fiction. Black holes are traversed, the moon goes at FTL speeds and in one episode ships called Hawks, a military version of the Eagle (one of the great spaceship designs of all time) attack Moonbase Alpha, using SONIC weapons in space! The second season was more exciting and a bit more colorful, but it was also twenty times dumber, falling back on using their new resident alien, Maya—who was a shape shifter—to escape from predicaments. While there were a few episodes worth watching, the show itself has to be considered a failure. (One has to wonder what Ron Moore, the genius behind *Star Trek: Deep Space Nine* and the reimagined *Battlestar Galactica* could do with this show).

Logan's Run, based on the 1976 movie of the same name (which itself was based on the classic SF novel by William F. Nolan and George Clayton Johnson), was afflicted with the same problems as the previous shows. 1) it had a very low budget and; 2) the writing stunk. Really this is too bad, since it had an engaging pair, Gregory Harrison and Heather Menzies (the love interest from *SSSsssss*) as Logan and Jessica, but the idea behind it—continuing the movie with the pair running from Francis—who is now working, not for the Thinker, the great computer that ran the domed city, but the council of Old Men who actually do run it. If Francis catches them, he will be granted long life and a seat on the Council. Logan and Jessica also make friends with a humaniform android, but the stories are really stupid, bordering on the inane. This was just a loser from the very beginning. Oddly enough, this is also available on DVD.

So, this is just a sampling of some of the mostly terrible shows that networks foisted on an unsuspecting public in the 1970's. Science Fiction was still an oddity then, with people asking "How can you watch that trash?" or "How can you read that trash?" But better times were ahead, if mostly for movies than TV. A film was coming along that would bring SF back into the positive limelight in a good way. An enormous event that would put SF back on the map and keep it there, leading the way for good, and even great, Science Fiction movies and TV series. A turning point for the most imaginative of all genres was about to come and it would bear a simple name:

STAR WARS.

World's Greatest Collection Of Strange & Secret Photographs

NOW you can travel round the world with the most daring adventurers. You can see with your own eyes, the weirdest peoples on earth. You witness the strangest customs of the red, white, brown, black and yellow races. You attend their startling rites, their mysterious practices. They are all assembled for you in these five great volumes of the SECRET MUSEUM OF MANKIND.

600 LARGE PAGES

Here is the World's Greatest Collection of Strange and Secret Photographs. Here are Exotic Photos from Europe, Harem Photos from Africa, Torture Photos, Female Photos, Marriage Photos from Asia, Oceania, and America, and hundreds of others. There are almost 600 LARGE PAGES OF PHOTOGRAPHS, each page 62 square inches!

1,000 REVEALING PHOTOS

You see actual courtship practiced in every quarter of the world. You see magic and mystery in queer lands where the foot of a white man has rarely trod. You see Oriental modes of marriage and female slavery in China, Japan, India, etc. Through the close-up of the camera you witness the exotic habits of every continent and female customs in America, Europe, etc. You are bewildered by ONE THOUSAND LARGE PHOTOGRAPHS, including 130 full-page photos, and thrilled by the hundreds of short stories that describe them.

Contents of 5-Volume Set
VOLUME 1
The Secret Album of Africa
VOLUME 2
The Secret Album of Europe
VOLUME 3
The Secret Album of Asia
VOLUME 4
The Secret Album of America
VOLUME 5
The Secret Album of Oceania

5 PICTURE-PACKED VOLUMES

Specimen Photos
Dress & Undress Round the World
Various Secret Societies
Civilized Love vs. Savage
Strange Crimes, Criminals
Flagellation and Slavery
Omens, Totems & Taboos
Mysterious Customs
Female Slave Hunters
1,000 Strange & Secret Photos

The SECRET MUSEUM OF MANKIND consists of five picture-packed volumes (solidly bound together for convenient reading). Dip into any one of these volumes, and as you turn its daring pages, you find it difficult to tear yourself away. Here, in story and uncensored photo, is the WORLD'S GREATEST COLLECTION OF STRANGE AND SECRET PHOTOGRAPHS, containing everything from Female Beauty Round the World to the most Mysterious Cults and Customs. These hundreds and hundreds of large pages will give you days and nights of thrilling instruction.

SEND NO MONEY

Simply sign & mail the coupon. Remember, each of the 5 Volumes is 9½ inches high, and, opened, over a foot wide! Remember also that this 5-Volume Set formerly sold for $10. And it is bound in expensive "life-time" cloth. Don't put this off. Fill out the coupon, drop it in the next mail, and receive this huge work at once.

FORMERLY ~~$10~~
NOW ONLY
$1.98
FOR THE COMPLETE
5 VOLUME SET
ALL FIVE VOLUMES BOUND TOGETHER
THE SECRET MUSEUM OF MANKIND

METRO PUBLICATIONS, 70 5th Ave., Dept. 405, New York
Send me "The Secret Museum of Mankind" (5 great volumes bound together). I will pay postman $1.98, plus postage on arrival. If not delighted, I will return book in 5 days for full refund of $1.98.

Name ....
Address ....
City .... State ....
☐ CHECK HERE if you are enclosing $1.98, thus saving mailing costs. Same Money-Back Guarantee.
Canadian orders $2.50 in advance

DAGON'S DISCIPLES
CHRIS AND WILLIAM CARNEY
A WILD CAT BOOKS PUBLICATION

A WILDCAT BOOKS PUBLICATION

AN EPIC FANTASY

by the Author of The KESRICK Series and THE ETERNAL WARRIOR

UNDER THE SUNS OF ANTARES

Made in the USA
Charleston, SC
10 January 2012